INTO THE LIGHT

Untwisted Book Three

Alice Raine

Published by Accent Press Ltd

ISBN 9781783753918

Copyright © Alice Raine 2014

The right of Alice Raine to be identified as the author
of this work has been asserted by her in accordance
with the Copyright, Designs and Patents Act 1988.

Published by Accent Press Ltd – 2014

'We can easily forgive a child who is afraid of the dark; the real tragedy of life is when men are afraid of the light.'

Plato

Chapter One - Stella

It was just before lunch on Monday. I was at my desk staring vacantly at my laptop and pretending to work, but really I was being completely and utterly unproductive as my mind went over and over the events of the last two days. Talk about a busy and heart-wrenchingly stressful weekend. I literally had no idea where my relationship with Nathan stood now, and a huge sigh puffed out of my cheeks at the hopeless mess I'd gotten myself into. I felt the start of a migraine every time I replayed the insensitive and callous way that Nathan had thrown me out of his apartment on Saturday night after the arrival of his brother. Shaking my head in exasperation I began to chew on a much-abused fingernail. I understood that family was important, and it was clear that Nathan's brother had had a crisis of some sort, but still, a little civility on my exit wouldn't have gone amiss.

Groaning in frustration at the futility of my thoughts I rubbed my eyes to clear my mind, but only succeeded in intensifying my headache and shifting it to my eye sockets. Now I had white dots dancing in my vision to accompany the throb in my temples. How marvellous, I thought dryly. Heaving out another huge sigh I gave up on trying to ease the ache and instead slumped back in my chair giving up all pretence of work.

My fingers instinctively rose to the necklace that Nathan had given me, and I began tangling the diamond threads gently around my fingers like a very expensive set of worry beads as I thought about him and all his complexities. Being asked to leave Nathan's so abruptly had left me with a lot of unanswered questions about my relationship with him, questions I still hadn't been brave enough to fully analyse because regardless of how used I'd felt on Saturday, I couldn't deny the fact that I still wanted him. In our admittedly unconventional time together as dominant and submissive, he'd sparked some kind of visceral response in me and I just couldn't get enough of him.

Leaving my necklace alone for fear of snapping it, I began twirling my thumb ring anxiously instead as I thought of the last time I had spent with him. It hadn't exactly been the smoothest of weekends, I thought with a grimace. After being called in to work last Saturday I'd ending up in the office when I should have been spending the day with Nathan, then he unceremoniously chucked me out later that night when Nicholas had unexpectedly arrived. It meant I'd only seen Nathan briefly on Friday and Saturday nights. As a result I was now feeling emotional, pathetically vulnerable, and cranky, not to mention annoyingly horny.

Meeting his brother had been pretty unconventional too, I thought as I blew some wayward hairs out of my face. No polite family drinks and introductions for us, no, Nicholas Jackson had let himself into Nathan's apartment and then seemingly had some sort of mental breakdown right there in the hallway. Quite frankly he'd seemed more than a little unhinged as he'd ranted about 'losing it' and 'losing her', whatever the hell that meant.

As a consequence of my shitty weekend I was now exhausted from the near-constant debate in my head about whether or not I should finish with Nathan. I was in far too deeply now, feeling things for him that were well outside the boundaries of our ridiculous contract, so I knew that either option would ultimately be painful for me. I'd also made the uncomfortable discovery that two evenings of sex with Nathan just weren't enough for me; apparently I needed an entire weekend to get my fill so that I could survive a full week without him. A sordid little realisation that merely added to my foul mood this morning.

The familiar voices and footsteps of two of my managers floated in the air as they approached my office discussing which restaurant to go to for lunch, so I quickly scrabbled myself upright, stared vacantly at my laptop screen, and then cringed at my own earlier thoughts. '*Survive a full week without him?*' Christ, I sounded like an alcoholic or something. I rolled my eyes, I had turned into a frigging Nathan-a-holic, and as much as I might try to deny it to myself, I was in desperate need of a fix.

A sudden and shrill ringing broke me from my depressing thoughts, and after a second I dazedly realised it was my mobile phone ringing and vibrating its way across the shiny surface of my desk. Mobiles weren't permitted in the office, but in my exhausted daze this morning I'd forgotten to silence the bloody thing. Snatching it up I glared at the screen as if it had rung on purpose to get me into trouble, but not recognising the number I frowned, walking away from the main office to answer it. Flicking open my phone once I had reached the safety of the corridor I rammed it next to my ear, 'What?' I snapped, flinching as I realised how moody I sounded and praying it wasn't my mother, or an important client.

'Stella, hi!' My eyes widened as I recognised the male voice on the other end of the line and I immediately felt some of the tension dissipate from my body as a huge grin spread across my face. This was certainly a very well timed, very welcomed interruption to my earlier self-inflicted misery.

'Simon? Oh my God, Simon!' I shrieked as I practically jumped on the spot, but when I noticed several colleagues further down the corridor had stopped and turned to look at me in surprise I bit my tongue to calm myself down. I was on the phone in an office corridor, not screaming out an Abba classic in a hushed library, for heaven's sake, so I really didn't know what their problem was, but I lowered my voice, then gave them an apologetic shrug and turned to face the window with a smirk. I might have been feeling pretty grumpy after my disastrous weekend with Nathan, but hearing Simon's voice was just amazing and so unexpected that I couldn't seem to calm the jittery excitement coursing through my veins.

'When did you get back?'

'This morning. I've only got four days leave but I was hoping you might be free to meet for a drink tonight?' he asked expectantly, in that lovely rich baritone of his.

There was no hesitation from me, 'Yes! Yes! Just tell me where and when and I'll be there!' I exclaimed excitedly, deciding that Simon's visit gave me the perfect opportunity to further delay making any decisions about my relationship with Nathan. *If our weekly contracted shag sessions could even be called a relationship*, I thought with a self-derisive snort.

Hanging up, I went back to work with a new energy, and my thoughts of Nathan were temporarily forgotten – not that you could ever really 'forget' someone as enigmatic at Nathaniel Jackson – but at least my mind was on more constructive things now, and my depressingly dull and empty Monday evening looked like it would be far more interesting. I couldn't wipe the grin off my face; a full evening with Simon, I couldn't wait. Glancing down at my rather drab office clothes I scrunched up my nose. With the swanky venue he had chosen I was definitely going to need to go home and change before I headed out. Deciding to skip lunch so I could leave work an hour early I dug in my desk for a cereal bar and then munched on it as I hummed happily to myself, ridiculously glad that Simon had chosen today of all days to call me.

Twirling in front of the mirror in my hallway I dismissed

my current outfit with a scowl. This trouser suit made me look like Lady Gaga on steroids. Huffing out an impatient breath I strode back into my bedroom and peeled off the purple material, depositing it on the floor. It was just as well that I'd left work early, because I'd been trying on outfits for my night with Simon for the past 40 minutes and was still undecided. My bedroom now looked like a complete bombsite; there was a vast array of underwear, skirts, trousers, and dresses littering every available surface and my poor wardrobe was looking decidedly bare. Spotting a dress on a hanger towards the back, I grinned; my old favourite - it would be perfect for tonight – providing it still fit me, that was.

Carefully removing it from the hanger and slipping it over my head I was relieved to find that not only did the dress still fit, but luckily it looked pretty amazing on me too. Phew. Crisis averted, outfit chosen.

As I gazed at my reflection in the mirror my mind flitted to Nathan. Would he like my outfit? Pausing in my preparations a frown settled on my brows, and my fingers once again sought out the collar around my neck. His collar. It matched the dress beautifully. I'd worn it every single day since he gave it to me, as per our agreement. Sighing, I fingered the delicate stones gently; they were my ever-present link to him, but after the way our weekend ended I wasn't sure if I should be wearing it anymore. Chewing on my lower lip a little sadly I left the necklace in place for now, I would decide later if it should stay or go, and then padded to the bathroom to apply my make-up.

My heels click-clacked loudly on the spotless black and white tiles as I made my way self-consciously past the top-hatted doorman and started across the sumptuous foyer of Claridge's Hotel. Yes, that's right, I was in Mayfair, attempting to act as if I were perfectly at home in the surroundings of one of the most exclusive hotels in London, if not the world. Everything, and everyone around me seemed to be effortlessly elegant and stylish, but I felt nervous, clumsy and out of place in the formidable surroundings – especially with my high heels rudely disturbing the peace – and was immensely glad when I finally reached the door to the bar without having fallen over or embarrassed myself.

Approximately sixteen seconds after I entered the smaller, slightly less imposing bar, simply titled 'Claridge's Bar', I found myself wrapped up in two strong arms and being swung around several times by a huge hunk of man, causing me to yelp excitedly as I clung on to Simon for dear life. Gosh, he felt taller than I remembered and if anything his biceps were even bigger. Life with the Royal Navy obviously suited Simon down to the ground.

The surroundings of the wine bar blurred in front of my vision until finally Simon stopped swinging me and I could re-align my focus. Wow, this place was *am-az-ing*, my internal design radar couldn't help but be hugely impressed. Done out with soft beige walls, the floors were a pale wood, and smart red leather stools lined the long bar that ran the length of the room. The bar even had a marble fireplace standing proudly at one end, but instead of an open fire it was lit with several pillar candles and had great plumes of white flowers lining its mantle. All in all this place was gorgeous. I had never ventured into Claridge's before; it was just a tad out of my usual price range, but it was typical of Simon to book somewhere ridiculously pricey when he was visiting.

Depositing me on slightly wobbly legs Simon grinned at me boyishly, landed a sloppy kiss on my lips, then winked before slipping an arm around my waist and steering me towards a group of people I instantly recognised as his close friends. Even though I only saw them when I was with Simon they still welcomed me with broad grins, hugs, and air kisses to my cheeks before depositing a glass of champagne into my hand with relish.

Posh champagne in Claridge's hotel, brilliant. It really doesn't get much better than this, does it?

'Simon, it's so good to see you.' I beamed up at him happily, causing Simon to drape his arm around my shoulder and pull me close for another affectionate squeeze. It had to have been at least nine months since I'd last seen him and I sighed contentedly as I snuggled against him, ridiculously pleased to be with him again. I knew he loved the Navy, and I knew he had his reasons for signing up, but there wasn't a day that went by that I didn't miss him.

'Likewise, Stella. You look great by the way,' he said with a grin as he leaned away to check out my outfit. Smiling back I felt myself relax, the forty minutes trying to plan what outfit was suitable for such an upmarket hotel clearly hadn't been wasted. The old favourite that I'd finally settled on was a pale gold cocktail dress and matching high heels. Apparently I had chosen well.

My shared grin with Simon was broken when Jessica, one of Simon's friends, leant forwards and furiously tapped my arm to catch my attention. 'Oh my God, Stella, don't look now but there's an unbelievably handsome man staring at you!' she whispered frantically, her eyes wide with excitement as she glanced over my shoulder to somewhere behind me.

I'm a naturally inquisitive person, always have been, so when someone says 'don't look now' it just makes me practically itch with curiosity and want to look even more. So I did, swivelling my neck to see across the bar before my stomach plummeted sickeningly to my boots when I saw Nathan at the bar looking over towards us. Nathan was *here*? Suddenly I couldn't breathe properly; my chest felt as if I had a band around it and my heart had sped up so rapidly that it now pumped furiously in my ears as I stared at him. Standing next to Nathan was his brother Nicholas, who had bags under his eyes and still looked decidedly rough. Obviously whatever the 'personal situation' was, it still hadn't been resolved, but Nicholas wasn't the focus of my gaze, Nathan was – or to be more precise, the deathly glower that Nathaniel Jackson, my bad-boy bed buddy was sending my way.

Bloody hell. Swallowing loudly I registered with trepidation that he looked immensely pissed off, so much so that I felt myself taking a small step backwards, which was ridiculous seeing as he was a good ten metres away from me. I felt a prickle on the back of my neck as a nervous sweat broke out, but no matter how hard I tried I couldn't seem to tear my gaze away from the depths of his piercing blue eyes.

This was certainly unexpected – not to mention terrifying. I'd never seen him outside of our allotted dates, how the hell was I supposed to act? Especially given the uncomfortable way that last weekend had ended. With my eyes still glued to his I found myself twisting my thumb ring frantically as a frown settled on my own brows – I certainly wasn't calling him Sir in here, that was for sure. And on top of that, what the hell was he doing here? Although actually, as I thought about it I realised it made perfect sense; the posh interior of Claridge's bloody hotel was probably just like a local pub for someone as rich as Nathan. Before I had a chance to disengage Simon's arm from my shoulder and give Nathan an attempt at a 'hello' wave, Jessica had leant forward and gripped my arm again.

'Oh my God, Stella, I think he's going to come over!' Jessica gushed excitedly, 'Do you know him? Is he single?' The slightly squeaky tone of her voice told me that Jessica was interested in Nathan, probably more than interested in him – but then what straight woman wouldn't be? He was sexiness personified, with a heavy handed dash of broody and intense thrown into the mix for good measure. Instead of feeling jealous at Jessica's possible interest though, all I could think about was how the hell I was going to explain this all to Nathan before he combusted on the spot.

'Uhhh …' The rest of my explanation was lost as I busied myself shrugging guiltily out of Simon's arm before looking over my shoulder again where I saw Nathan still at the bar, but now talking heatedly to Nicholas, his knuckles blanched white with tension and his brows as low as I'd ever seen them, practically hiding his top eyelids. A loud, nervous swallow escaped my throat when I caught the look in Nathan's eye as he turned towards me – *murderous*. Crikey, he clearly wasn't bothered about eye contact tonight because he was full on glaring at me with a fearsome glint in his icy blue eyes – which was enough to make my legs weaken below me. Biting my lip anxiously I vaguely registered that my body's instant response to him was partly from concern, but also from intense arousal, because boy, did Nathan look hot when he was bristling with dominance like this; it was simultaneously hitting me in all the right places and making me feel decidedly needy.

Managing a limp, watery smile I was about to go across and try to explain to him when I watched in horror as Nathan muttered one final thing to Nicholas, before swiftly stepping away from the bar and striding purposefully towards me with his usual easy gait. Gulping loudly I couldn't help but notice that Nathan had gone for his knock 'em dead corporate image; light grey three piece suit, white shirt, and a burgundy tie. He looked utterly stunning. Masculine, powerful, and controlled. He drew almost every female eye in the place with his elegant grace, and a few of the men too, but his eyes never left mine as he glided towards me with his frown still well and truly in place.

Oh bloody hell. In other circumstances I would have been thrilled by his eye contact and undiluted focus, but not tonight, because he really looked positively freaking furious. My palms suddenly felt clammy from the nervous energy bouncing around my system and I was twirling my thumb ring so fast I was surprised it wasn't giving me a burn.

By the time he reached my side I think it would be fair to say that my heart was well and truly in my mouth – no doubt along with several more of my internal organs if my inability to swallow was anything to go by. I fully expected him to scream at me, or demand an explanation about who Simon was, or perhaps just start a fight with him, but he did none of these. Instead Nathan simply stopped, loosened off his neck with an audible click, then grabbed my hand in a painfully hard hold and began dragging me towards the exit.

'Hey, what the fuck?' Within seconds Simon was barrelling towards us with an equally thunderous look on his face, but I desperately wanted to keep him out of this; Simon might be in the Navy, but Nathan was still bigger and stronger and if his laboured, speedy breathing was anything to go by, way, way, *way* more pissed off.

'It's OK,' I stuttered, throwing Simon my attempt at a reassuring smile and as I was dragged backwards I raised my hand to indicate that I was definitely fine. The next second Simon had disappeared from view as I was bundled into the corridor outside the bar and then shoved into what appeared to be a large cleaning cupboard.

Sucking in a shaky breath so I could explain who Simon was and why he had his arm around me, I turned towards Nathan only to let out a high-pitched squeak as he gripped my shoulders and spun me back around. Forcing me face first against the wall my poor breasts were squashed flat like pancakes, but I managed to turn my head so my cheek was pressed to the cool surface. The air was practically knocked from my lungs as Nathan pounced on me, his hands roaming possessively across my body whilst his lips delved through my hair to find the collar at my neck. I'd opted to keep it on in the end, somehow taking it off just hadn't felt right, and now that I'd had this chance meeting with Nathan I was rather glad that I had.

Blimey. I had not expected this. As I regained my breath in my trapped position I realised there was no questioning or shouting like I'd expected, in fact there were no words at all. Nathan was simply swamping me with his hot, hard body and given his strength there was very little I could do about it. Luckily I was rather enjoying the abrupt attention and shamelessly found myself moaning from the pleasure as he began to feverishly lick and kiss the skin around my necklace. Nathan's free hand pushed up the wall in front of my body and paid rough attention to my breasts through the fabric of my dress, pulling and pinching at my nipples until my head fell back and I groaned again.

Before we'd barely even got started I felt Nathan tugging my dress up around my waist with one hand before thrusting a finger straight inside my panties to see if I was wet or not. As embarrassing as it was to acknowledge, after his rather arousing dominant manhandling of me, I knew I definitely would be. 'Green?' he demanded harshly next to my ear, his breath hot and damp against my skin. *Green*, one of our shared safe words and his way of asking if I was okay to continue. As surprising as this all was, there was no way I wanted him to stop, so I managed a silent nod in response as I clung to the wall. No sooner had I nodded he pushed a finger deeply inside me and I gasped at the sudden intrusion of his probing digit as it circled ruthlessly in my heat. Nathan merely grunted his apparent satisfaction of my readiness, and then with no further warning or foreplay tugged my panties to the side and wasted no time in unzipping himself and thrusting inside me ferociously. *Fucking hell!* From then on there was very little interaction from me because the tempo he set was ridiculous, his hips like a piston as he thrust in and out of me furiously with the occasional hard grind thrown in for good measure to drive me crazy!

It was literally all I could do to cling to the white wooden wall and keep myself upright. My climax began to build absurdly fast and from the feel of Nathan expanding within me, so did his. Then just as I was about to explode, Nathan dug his teeth into my neck and sucked furiously whilst thrusting out his final three strokes causing both of us to detonate with truly violent releases that had me thrashing around in my trapped position and Nathan growling indecipherable words into my ear. Holy shit. That had probably taken about two minutes from start to finish – talk about a quickie.

I clung to the wall, my panting breaths making the wood sticky under my cheek, but in my current state I barely noticed. That had been completely unexpected, and totally amazing, but I cringed as I realised that the entire hotel may well have heard my screams of pleasure. God, I was probably going to be thrown out of one of London's top hotels for an orgasmic noise violation, how mortifying would that be?

It could only have been a second or two after his climax when Nathan abruptly pulled out of me, making me wince at the sudden empty feeling left behind. He didn't clean me off with a hanky like usual either, so I was left feeling quite sticky and uncomfortable. By the time I had managed to catch my breath, right my clothes, and turn to him I found him already zipping up his trousers and looking immaculate. With every hair on his head in place and barely a flush to his cheeks. How the hell did he manage that? Huffing out an irritable breath I shook my head, I no doubt looked so thoroughly well fucked that no amount of primping in front of a mirror would sort it out, but in mere milliseconds he looked back to his usual drop dead gorgeous self.

Closing the gap between us Nathan was suddenly right within my personal space, glaring down at me whilst a muscle erratically twitched on the corner of his tight jaw. 'Who the hell was that fucker with his arm round you?' he demanded in a gritty tone, with such an ominous look on his face that it sent chills flooding through my bloodstream and made me shiver.

Just as the sheer drama of the moment was about to overwhelm my system it hit me, that hadn't just been a normal shag for Nathan ... he had been claiming his territory – *me*. He hadn't been set on pleasuring me until I begged him like usual, he'd simply taken what he'd wanted. Although deep down I had to acknowledge that regardless of how mad, angry, or upset he was, I knew Nathan would definitely have stopped if I'd said 'red'.

My hazy left over arousal quickly evaporated as anger flared in my system. How dare he behave this way! God, if I hadn't enjoyed it quite as much I might even feel a bit violated by that performance, and now I think back to the way he sucked my neck I bet he'd given me a frigging love bite too!

My eyes widened with my rising anger, 'You don't say one word to me as you fuck me up against a wall like a whore, and *then* you ask questions?' I screamed, I was livid, no, I was way beyond livid. He actually looked a little shocked by my outburst, perhaps he'd been expecting to see guilt or remorse on my features. Well, he'd been sorely mistaken, I had nothing to feel guilty about. What a fucking nerve! As if I hadn't already been feeling a little vulnerable about our situation after being chucked out of Nathan's apartment in the middle of the night ... well now I just felt down right used.

Nathan's right hand lifted as if reaching for me, but I batted it away furiously with my knuckles making a loud slapping sound, 'How fucking dare you?' I screeched in a

13

furious whisper, on the verge of losing it completely in a bloody broom cupboard. Suddenly it became crystal clear to me that my emotions where this man were concerned were strung way too tightly at that moment, and I knew I needed to get away from him before I said or did something that I might regret later. 'Go to hell, Nathan.' I spat, before stalking from the cupboard and doing my best to hastily straighten my appearance. I ran my hands through my erratic hair and smoothed my dress again. Crap, I wished there was a mirror so I could check my neck, but the achy feeling just below my ear left me with little doubt that I must have a hickey, so I pulled my hair around my neck as best I could and then walked as calmly as possible back towards Simon and his friends.

'Everything OK?' Simon asked me curiously, slipping his arm across my shoulders again as I got to his side and averted my eyes. No doubt all his friends were staring at me and wondering why I'd just been literally dragged from the room by a large, fuming, blond-haired Adonis.

Tensing in his grasp I was hideously aware that I quite possibly smelled like sex now, and just to exacerbate my unease I became hyperaware of the stickiness between my legs. I should have gone to the toilets before returning so I could have cleaned up a bit more, but I'd been so flustered I hadn't thought to. God, this was uncomfortable.

'Yeah, sorry about that.' I smiled tightly. Simon seemed to be weighing up if he should probe further, but before he had a chance I saw his eyes dart over my shoulder and narrow and I just knew Nathan was there. Actually I didn't need Simon's glance to tell me this, my skin had already tingled in anticipation of Nathan's closeness like it always did. A huge sigh filled my lungs and escaped between tight lips. God I could so do without this right now, my stupidly over possessive dominant was no doubt about to make a huge scene in the middle of the bar. And not just any bar, but Claridges Bar, of all places. Closing my eyes briefly I tried to reign in my bubbling anger before turning towards him.

'Stella.' Nathan said in a tight clipped tone with a nod. He tugged unnecessarily on his already perfect shirt cuffs to straighten them before slipping his hands in his trouser pockets, and then stood before me with a wide, confident stance. For some reason, the way he was standing made me instinctively want to look at his groin, but I somehow avoided the urge and raised my eyes to his face. Nathan might have been addressing me, but I didn't miss the fact that his eyes were firmly glued to Simon and the arm that was thrown around my shoulders. I sighed heavily. Clearly he wasn't about to leave this then. I so was fucking mad I wanted to scream at him and beat out my anger on his chest, but I was desperate not to make a fuss in front of Simon and his friends so reluctantly I turned and gave him a tight nod.

'Hi ... Nathan.' Gosh, even with my anger it felt weird saying his name out loud. Since we'd started our relationship I barely ever used his given name, normally I found it easier to just avoid using any direct title for him, except for 'Sir' in the bedroom of course.

Tilting his head Nathan angled his furious blue eyes on me and then looked pointedly at Simon again until I realised through the foggy haze of anger and the remnants of my orgasm that he was waiting for an introduction.

'Nathan, this is Simon.' I said coldly, with a wave of my hand, '... *my brother.'* I added tightly, emphasising it slowly and clearly and wanting to make sure Nathan and all of his stupid possessiveness fully understood that he had totally misread things, and that the situation was completely innocent.

Feeling Simon's arm shift slightly across my shoulders I knew he must sense my tension so tried to lighten the air slightly by returning the introduction.

'Simon, this is Nathan, a ... umm ... *friend of mine.'* I

15

finished awkwardly with a small grimace, our relationship could hardly be described as friendship could it? Especially after what had just occurred in the cupboard, but what else was I supposed to say? *'Simon, this is Nathan, the man who ties me up and shags me on the weekends and who just fucked me senseless in a cupboard like a cheap kerbside whore?'* I clenched my teeth until they hurt – that would hardly go down well with my already overprotective brother. No, I might be mad with Nathan, but I in no way wanted to cause a huge fight to break out.

The look on Nathan's face when I said Simon was my brother actually made me feel much better about recent events because he looked well and truly mortified with himself, remorse pouring from his features as his eyes widened and his mouth opened and closed silently several times like a goldfish. In fact I don't think I've ever seen quite as much expression come from Nathan, apart from on Saturday when he was caring for his brother, that is. He was usually so shuttered when I was around him that reading his expressions was difficult, but I was also fairly certain that I saw a flash of relief cross his face too. Now that was interesting. Not that it made up for the way he had just treated me in the cupboard.

'Simon, it's nice to meet you,' Nathan murmured, extending his hand for a shake, 'I'm sorry to keep stealing your sister, but would you please excuse us again for a second? I just need to speak briefly with Stella again.' I was seriously tempted to stamp my foot and refuse, but that would just end up creating more awkwardness for me to explain to Simon later, so with a well disguised sigh I allowed Nathan to take my hand in his and lead me into the hotel lobby and over to a quiet corner.

My stark realisations in the cupboard about how emotionally attached I was becoming to Nathan had left me feeling particularly uneasy, not to mention tetchy, so I stubbornly kept my body tense and my head dipped, if he wanted to speak he could work for it, I wasn't about to initiate anything.

After an age of silence I finally relented and looked up to find Nathan leaning over and contemplating me with such fierce intensity that I shivered and found myself wrapping my arms protectively around my chest. To be honest, knowing Nathan's dominant ways I suspect he'd deliberately been waiting me out and forcing me to make the first move, and as usual I'd done exactly what he bloody wanted.

'You'd do well to memorise the next ten seconds, Stella, because I don't apologise often.' He growled menacingly, leaning in close to my ear. 'I'm sorry for the way I treated you, I was wrong in my assumption.' I waited for more, but he stood back, crossed his arms, and was silent again. Was that it? He made it sound like I should be grateful for his apology! I scoffed out a breath and looked up at him in astonishment, the cheeky sod! Although for a man as power crazy as Nathan I had to admit that this was probably quite a major relinquishment of his usual control.

I gazed up at him speechless. He was now avoiding eye contact again, but I knew that wasn't from guilt, that was just normal for Nathan, but what did he really expect me to say?

'I don't know what to say, Nathan.' I muttered sourly, carefully keeping my voice low because of the hushed lobby we were stood in, 'You treated me like some kind of tart you'd pick up in a bar for a quick fuck.' I frowned at the unpleasant thought and lowered my gaze.

As quick as a flash, one of Nathan's hands flew to my chin and gripped it with his finger and thumb as he glared down at me. 'I do not consider you a quick fuck, Stella, or a cheap tart. Don't be so dramatic.' His jaw was tense and I could tell he was chewing endlessly on the inside of his lower lip, but apart from his heated comment he remained

17

silent and I had the feeling that no more apologies would be falling from Nathan's tongue in the near future.

Dramatic? If anyone had been overly dramatic tonight it was Nathan and his virtual caveman impression earlier. 'And what the hell is this about?' I demanded in a whisper, pulling back my hair and glancing in the mirror behind me to see just what the damage was. Frigging hell, I'd been right, a bright red love bite glowed happily just below my left ear. Just great, I looked like an over grown hormonal teenager. The skin was reddened almost to the point of turning purple in places and I could faintly see the imprints of his teeth around the edge. Unbelievable.

'You are mine.' he stated simply with a trace of a shrug.

As ridiculous as it was, those three words thrilled me, not to mention put my mind slightly more at ease about our situation, but regardless of that I wasn't going to let him off the hook that easily. 'That's it? *You are mine?*' I hissed, my eyes widening as I did my best attempt at copying his stupidly possessive tone. 'That's supposed to make up for me having a great big hickey on my neck? It's going to last for weeks Nathan! *Weeks*!' My voice rose several notches on my last word and I had to work hard to tamp down my rising hysteria so I didn't draw attention to us.

In response his eyes darkened and a small smirk curled his upper lip, as he completely ignored my flustered state, 'Then men will know that you are taken, won't they?' he added, reaching out a hand and curiously inspecting my humongous hickey with his thumb and looking quite pleased with himself. Oh my God, if I was reading his expression correctly then I think he was actually considering repeating it when this one faded. Not a chance in hell!

His thumb moved from the sore spot on my neck to trace down and across the necklace he had given me and I heard a hum of approval rumble in his throat. This was crazy, after a sleepless night spent thinking that he was through with me I had now been branded by him, and was left dazed and trying to work out exactly what Nathan's possessiveness meant, if anything, but before I could come to any conclusions he interrupted my thoughts, 'Just imagine if it had been the other way round, Stella.' he murmured, 'If you had seen me with another woman, what would you have done?'

I tried to imagine this scenario and unfortunately was immediately inundated with visions of Nathan and various different beauties hanging adoringly from his arm with sickly sweet smiles on their plastic faces, and tiny dresses on their equally fake boobs. Ugh, it was far too easy to picture. Clearly with his looks and bedroom skills Nathan hadn't been short on partners in his past, but I had to say the images left me with a tight knot in my stomach and a distinctly bad taste in my mouth.

'Fine, I get it, but I wouldn't just have dragged you off and claim-fucked you, I would have spoken to you and asked what was going on.' I muttered moodily. Not mentioning that I would probably also have slapped the woman around the face, kicked Nathan in the nuts, and then stormed off.

'Claim-fucked?' he raised an eyebrow in apparent amusement, but I swear to God if he smiled I would punch him. 'You're certainly swearing a lot this evening, Stella.' Nathan chastised me calmly. My eyes widened at his frustrating coolness. *You think?* I fucking wonder why? I stood staring at him in open-mouthed disbelief as he continued.

'I see your reasoning, but for me words mean very little. Actions are clearer.' That sounded a bit strange, but kind of made sense of what I'd already noticed about Nathan in our time together; he wasn't a big talker and physical contact and sex *did* seem to be his way of communicating with me. Shaking my head I ran a

19

trembling hand over my face to try and clear my head. God, I had a lot to try and process after tonight.

'I'll see you Friday?' he questioned briskly, in a tone that was more statement than request, but once again I thought that maybe, just maybe, there was a hint of concern in his tone, which brought my eyes to his in curiosity.

Considering all the dominance and fierceness that I knew he kept trapped inside him, Nathan actually looked rather childlike as he stood there chewing on his lip and gazing at me expectantly with his huge blue eyes averted just below my gaze as usual. Sighing heavily I was at a loss for what to do. He hadn't harmed me in any way this evening – actually if I'm honest I'd enjoyed the way he'd emphatically taken me in the cupboard, and stupidly there was a little part of me that was thrilled that Nathan had felt possessive enough to want to mark me as his, but still his behaviour had been pretty extreme. On the other hand what else could I do? I definitely still wanted to keep our arrangement going and I'd already got an apology from him, which by all accounts didn't happen very often, so really it came down to a simple choice; stay with him, or to tell him that because of his irrational behaviour both tonight and last Saturday, that it was over between us.

I let out one final huffed breath to show that he'd really over-stepped the line tonight before finally conceding to him, yet again, 'Yes. I'll see you Friday.' I said softly. Nodding his approval with what sounded distinctly like a sigh of relief, Nathan then grabbed my hand and, without waiting to see if I was following, dragged me back off in the direction of the bar. God, with all this drama my brother was going to be firing questions at me later, I just knew it.

To my horror, instead of just escorting me back to the bar Nathan soothed and massaged my hand with gentle swirls of his thumb as he walked me right up to Simon and smiled broadly as if absolutely nothing unusual had occurred this evening. *Un-frigging-believable.*

Finally letting go of my hand I could feel the skin tingling with remnants of his touch and tucked it back at my side to hide the pathetic trembling he had caused. 'Sorry about that, Simon, here she is, safe and sound.' Nathan said popping me back at my brother's side, but I couldn't help but scoff at how Nathan had suddenly turned into this light hearted man – talk about changeable!

'I didn't realise Stella had a brother.' he commented mildly whilst raising an eyebrow at me almost accusingly. Shrugging slightly I flushed. Seeing as all Nathan and I did together was sexy stuff, family trees hadn't exactly come up in conversation.

'So where did you say you two met?' Simon asked me with an amused smirk, making me baulk. I hadn't said where we'd met because I'd been deliberately avoiding talking about him! Glaring at Simon I saw his eyes dancing, could he tell how nervous I was? He bloody could as well, he was laughing at me, the git.

'Ummm …' I was lost for words and quite frankly finding this whole evening rather overwhelming. I could tell the truth – *we met at a sex club where I asked Nathan to be my dominant partner and introduce me to the joys of being a willing sexual submissive.* Nooo, perhaps not, God, seeing Nathan outside his apartment had clearly scrambled my brain if that was the best I could come up with, but I literally couldn't think straight enough to come up with anything better.

'We met through work.' Nathan supplied calmly and I flashed him an appreciative glance, my shoulders relaxing marginally. Seeing my look he gave me a tiny lopsided smile in return. It had been almost undetectable, but wow, a real genuine smile from Nathan … and it was directed at me. That definitely got committed to my memory as a first time occurrence.

'So, Simon, do you live locally?' Nathan enquired lightly, accepting the bottle of expensive Spanish beer that my brother handed him from the table.

'I have a small apartment in London but I'm an officer in the Royal Navy so I'm mostly based down south or out at sea.' Simon explained before taking a swig of his own beer and considering Nathan over the top of his bottle. I could almost hear the cogs turning in my brother's head as he continued to study Nathan thoughtfully and I chewed on my lip nervously, knowing that it would be a bloody miracle if I managed to avoid an inquisition from Simon later.

'Wow, very impressive, I imagine it's a job that never gets dull.' I stood back to observe this new side of Nathan as he chatted easily with my brother – gone was the dark, brooding man I was used to, instead he was relaxed, laid-back, and conversational. It was quite an eye-opener. Not to mention attractive … *very* attractive.

'Well, it was a bit of a surprise seeing Stella here so I thought I'd pop over and say hello, but I should get back to my brother so I'll leave you to it.' Nathan said with a nod. Words that I translated to *'I just wanted to drag my submissive off into a cupboard and fuck some sense into her to make sure she wasn't messing around with another bloke on the side.'*

Raising an ironic eyebrow to let Nathan know I knew exactly what he'd been thinking I was completely taken aback when he leaned in and placed a hand on my waist, caressing my hip with the briefest of touches.

'You look very beautiful tonight, Stella.' he murmured next to my ear before gently kissing me on the cheek. 'I'll see you soon.' he promised softly in what I can only describe as his 'panty-soaking sex voice', leaving me rather flushed and overcome as he sauntered away. Wow, he'd never been that affectionate with me before.

Turning back to the group of Simon's friends I

22

immediately flushed as I saw their inquisitive glances – especially from the females – and gave them a weak smile and shrug as if nothing out of the ordinary had just occurred. Awkwardly trying to avoid eye contact so I didn't have to answer any Nathan related questions, I realised that as well as being about as red as a post box, I was also missing Nathan's closeness already. Stupid girl. Rolling my eyes at my own utter ridiculousness I reached forwards for my glass of champagne and then took a long and very unladylike swig of the cool, bubbly liquid to try and calm my shaky composure.

Unfortunately even with my lips around a glass of crisp deliciousness I couldn't fail to see the questioning way that Simon was looking at me. No, not looking, *staring* would be more accurate.

'So he's just a friend from work then, Stella?' Simon whispered, thankfully leaning in so no-one else could hear.

'Yep.' I replied, a bit too curtly, wincing as I realised how guilty my overly speedy reply made me look.

'Come on sis, I've never seen you get flustered before, let alone over a guy, but God, Stella, you flushed redder than a beacon when he came over!' Damn my cheeks, I knew it! Although if anything, Simon pointing it out only made my flush deepen to the point where my cheeks felt like they were on fire.

'And where did you two disappear off to in such a hurry?' he asked with narrowed eyes, continuing his scrutiny. Knowing that my inquisitive brother wouldn't let up until he had got to the bottom of the matter I sighed and lifted my glass to my lips again. Perhaps if I drank for long enough my brother would lose interest, but no, after my overly long sip of champagne I found Simon still intently looking at me, waiting patiently for my reply.

I would be completely plastered and flat on my back soon if I didn't ease up on the champagne, so reluctantly I lowered my glass, and my eyes too. 'It's complicated,

Simon.' I muttered in way of cryptic explanation. But boy, was it the truth! Nathaniel Jackson was complication personified!

'Complicated as in you used to see him but broke up? Or complicated as in you haven't quite got down and dirty yet but you both want to?' he enquired with a sly grin and a nudge of his shoulder.

'Simon!' I exclaimed flushing yet again. I rolled my eyes. Complicated as in he's a stupidly possessive, but completely closed-off, mystery to me that I'm getting more attached to by the day but can never really have. I groaned out loud at my minds frank appraisal of my hopeless situation, but luckily Simon misread my groan for embarrassment.

'Sorry, Royal Navy, remember, we boys tend to get straight to the point.' Simon explained with an unapologetic shrug. 'The chemistry between you two was obvious, Stella.' he pointed out bluntly. Hmm, I'm sure it was; my skin seemed to come alive in buzzing tingles whenever Nathan was nearby and my breathing always hitched just a little too. Regardless of his oddities, there was no denying that Nathan and I did indeed have chemistry – explosive chemistry, in fact. I wouldn't be lying if I said we were dynamite in bed together. I certainly thought so anyway.

Shrugging, I sighed again. Would Simon think less of me if he knew I was simply sleeping with Nathan but not officially in a couple? 'Let's just say I'm too busy for a relationship but that I know Nathan fairly well, all right?'

A smile tweaked on Simon's lips which quickly bloomed into a broad grin accompanied by a hearty chuckle, 'Well, well, my little sister's got herself a rich fuck buddy, who'd have thought it!'

Even though he had hit the nail right on the head I cringed at my brother's crudeness before rolling my eyes and pouring myself another glass of champagne, all the while deliberately avoiding eye contact with Simon.

'Hey,' Simon said in a gentler tone nudging me until I reluctantly looked up, 'Don't look embarrassed, Stella, we've all been there, just make sure he treats you right otherwise he'll have me to answer to, OK?'

Relaxing, I smiled at my brother's words. If Simon knew how Nathan treated me – bondage, spanking, and rough sex in cupboards – he'd go ballistic. A sneaky grin split my face; what would probably shock my brother even more was just how much I enjoyed it.

Although I was loving the chance to catch up with Simon I kept finding myself casually turning around every five minutes or so to see if Nathan was still in attendance. He was, and every time I looked he caught my eye and smiled smugly. Bugger, I hadn't wanted him to see me looking! Especially as I was still pretending to be a little bit annoyed with him for his earlier behaviour. Mind you, the fact that he always seemed to be looking in my direction when I glanced across was secretly rather pleasing, and my heart accelerated as I considered the possibility that he might feel the same magnetic pull between us that I did.

It had to have been at least three hours since Nathan's little freak out in the cupboard and in that time I'd downed the best part of a bottle of champagne on my own, if not more, and was now feeling rather relaxed and content. Also known as: tipsy.

Being in the same room as Nathan but not being *with* Nathan wasn't helping me slow my drinking either. I had those nervous trembles in my tummy that you get when you are out and make eye contact with someone you fancy like mad, add to that the free flowing champagne and it was all making me feel rather giddy.

Feeling my handbag vibrate under my arm I dug in amongst the random debris of lipsticks and chewing gum and retrieved my phone, which was flashing up a new message. Opening it up my heartbeat suddenly shot through the roof as I scanned the words on the screen and almost choked on my mouthful of champagne.

From: Nathaniel Jackson

Sent: 21:34pm

From your repeated glances I take it you want me again just as much as I want you. Meet me in the ladies' toilets in 4 minutes. Don't make me wait.

My eyebrows skyrocketed towards my hairline. He wanted me again? Although truth be told I could easily go another round, but I wasn't going to make it that easy for him, not after his earlier behaviour. I was more than a little tipsy now and I decided to take advantage of the additional liquid courage to type out a cheeky reply.

From: Stella Marsden

Sent: 21:34pm

I'm still not speaking to you after your appalling behaviour earlier.

Let's see what he makes of that! I glanced over at him with as serious an expression on my face as I could muster, which meant that I was half frowning and half grinning, but immediately saw the look of scorn he threw me. As he read my text his eyebrow rose so impressively high it almost touched his hair and I couldn't help but giggle. Oops, clearly he wasn't impressed. I watched as his thumb rapidly moved across the screen of his phone and then a message arrived in my hand almost immediately.

From: Nathaniel Jackson

Sent: 21:35pm

You are making me mad again, Stella. I apologised and you accepted it.

Yikes, making him mad again? When did I make him mad first time around? By being here with my brother? How frigging unreasonable was that! But before I could consider this another text pinged onto my screen.

From: Nathaniel Jackson

Sent: 21:35pm
I'll call it apology sex if it makes you feel better?

Now it was my turn for my eyebrows to rise significantly. Apology sex? I quite liked the idea of that! Plus it almost sounded like he was trying to compromise which was good, also he hadn't referred to it as a 'fuck' so maybe he really did mean it would be apologetic. My stupidly muddled champagne brain just couldn't help itself this evening though, and I typed out another quick reply and pressed send before I could rethink it.

From: Stella Marsden
Sent: 21:36

Apology sex does sound quite appealing, but toilet sex? That's a little low-class, Sir, plus it's hardly hygienic is it?

Knowing how obsessed he was with cleanliness, particularly his hands, an image of him meticulously scrubbing his fingers, then bending me over and taking me sprung to my mind, making me smirk into my glass. Rolling my lips together I tried to supress my growing grin as I imagined how frustrated he must be getting at my disobedience. Once again a reply pinged to my phone almost immediately and I grinned – playing games with Nathan was actually quite fun.

From: Nathaniel Jackson
Sent: 21:36pm

Luckily this swanky hotel more than makes up for my lack of class and also has immaculate toilets.

Was I brave enough to do something as daring as have sex in a public toilet? I flushed at the thought and a thumping settled low between my legs as if my body was shouting 'yes!' at me. Well I'd already done it in a cupboard tonight, so a toilet was hardly worse than that, was it? I was distracted from my contemplation as my phone buzzed in my hand yet again causing me to look down.

From: Nathaniel Jackson

A small squeak slipped from my lips, but luckily fate was on my side because at the exact same moment someone dropped a glass, causing a small commotion in the bar as the panicked barman ran to sort it out. I smirked at his rushed sweeping, suspecting that people don't usually make a mess in somewhere as swanky as Claridge's.

They probably don't usually have sex in the toilets either, I thought in embarrassment as I slipped from my stool and placed my glass down. I knew that no matter how nervous the thought of sneaking into the toilets for an intimate liaison was, it wasn't anywhere near as bad as the things Nathan would do to me on Friday night if I ignored his request – his *demand* – and made him mad. *Again.*

Besides, now my earlier anger had subsided, seeing Nathan here looking so dashing and relaxed had made me ridiculously horny, even after the cupboard session, and I'd be lying to myself if I said that some relief wouldn't be welcome right now. Replaying my own thoughts I cringed – I was turning into a kinky sex-obsessed freakster like Nathan!

I needed to play this right; telling the gathered group that I was going to the toilet would inevitably end up with one of Simon's female friends trying to accompany me in the typical girly way that women do, so instead I frowned down at my phone which was still clamped in my hand.

'I've just had an urgent message from the office, I need to call them back. I'll just nip outside, won't be long.' Much to my relief no-one batted an eyelid as I left, or questioned why the office would be texting me at gone nine at night, before I hastily headed to the toilets by the entrance.

Seeing a small plastic triangle outside the ladies toilets that stated 'Closed for Cleaning' I hesitated briefly before mustering my courage, sidestepping the sign and entering the toilets as stealthily as I could. The door had barely closed before I found myself pressed up against it by firm hands on my shoulders and being kissed furiously by Nathan as if his life depended on it, his tongue thrusting and circling with mine in mere seconds, forcing me to open my lips and give in to his demands. Groaning my approval my hands instantly found their way to his shoulders, pulling him even closer so our bodies were fused together, one hand gripping his soft hair as Nathan so often did to mine and the other practically clawing at the skin of his neck.

When he finally pulled back I tried desperately to catch my jerky breathing. 'So is this my second apology of the night then?' I asked jokily between pants, but in response my shoulders were gripped and I was shifted across the room and folded forwards over the sink unit with Nathan pressing himself firmly against my back.

Raising my eyes to the mirror in front of me I could see our reflection and it was quite possibly the hottest thing I've ever witnessed – me panting, submissive, and flushed as Nathan stood breathing heavily, studying me intently and dominating me completely by pressing my body down so I couldn't move an inch. As usual he was avoiding eye contact, but the frown line on his forehead told me that he had taken enough of my playful teasing for one night.

'Don't fucking push me, Stella.' he warned in a low and deadly tone, grinding his hips sharply against my bum as one hand gripped my hair tightly to keep me still. I probably should have been a little scared by his apparent aggression, but I knew this was just how Nathan was; intense and formidable, and his behaviour merely upped my arousal tenfold and sent a new flood of arousal rushing to my panties and no doubt soaking them. Christ, the effect this man had on me was just inexplicable. I might have to start carrying a spare pair of knickers in my handbag in case of any chance encounters with him in future.

Suddenly pulling me upright, Nathan led me to a chaise longue in the corner of the swanky bathroom and wasted no time in laying me down and following suit so that I was caged in by his body. Even in my heightened state of arousal my champagne-filled brain couldn't help but giggle at the plushness of our surroundings. 'I have to say this isn't quite the toilet sex I had first imagined.' I mumbled though a smile against his lips as I caught a glance of a chandelier on the ceiling above us.

Leaning back Nathan examined every part of my face intently, avoiding my eyes of course, then drew in several ragged breaths through his nose before scooping me up without a word. Kicking his way into a cubicle he lowered me down his hard body and pressed my back up against the wall. 'Is this better? More down and dirty? I wouldn't want to disappoint you.' he breathed against my neck, apparently teasing me.

'Ummm ... yes ... this is more what I imagined.' I giggled, high on the mix of champagne and Nathan currently in my system. Without further preamble Nathan had my skirt hoisted up and his trousers open before drawing his hips back and thrusting into me so hard the toilet roll holder sprung off the wall, causing me to cry out far too loudly.

Jeez, talk about a speedy start! 'Wrap your legs around me.' he ordered, and I immediately did, causing our connection to be even deeper and even more delicious. I groaned against his neck, burying my face in his warm skin, *holy hell,* Nathan was really going for it tonight – each thrust in was a hard, precise strike to my G-spot making stars appear in front of my eyes, and each retraction was pure unadulterated pleasure as he rubbed his shaft over my clit. Jeez, with these skilled movements I wouldn't last much longer.

'You never disappoint, Sir.' I panted in between his

hard thrusts. Nathan gave a grunt that I took as appreciation for my comment, but then speech became impossible as Nathan increased his tempo even further so that the entire cubicle was rattling and shaking with his movements.

And that was it ... one more savage thrust from Nathan's skilful hips and I was suddenly shattering into a spiralling climax that had shot up on me far quicker than expected. I couldn't help the surprised scream of pleasure that flew from my mouth, but thankfully I was still lucid enough to silence it by burying my face in Nathan's damp neck as I rode out my orgasm in his arms.

Nathan hadn't come yet, but stilled his movements and stood allowing me to recover, cradling me against his body and stroking my hair as his raging hard on still throbbed and twitched inside me.

'Sorry ... that one sort of took me by surprise.' I murmured apologetically. Nathan didn't verbally reply, but he placed one short kiss on my neck which I took as acceptance. Then supporting my weight by sliding his hands under my bum Nathan gently slid out of me and exited the cubicle with me still wrapped around him panting.

Placing me on the sink unit his hands twisted in my hair, pulling me forwards where he kissed me deeply and thoroughly and much more sensually than before, lapping his tongue against mine, sucking my lower lip into his mouth, and gently nibbling on the already swollen flesh as he took his time exploring. Hmmm, he was such a good kisser. Perhaps this part was the 'apology' sex he'd been taking about.

Finally lifting his head he dropped his gaze, 'Turn around' he instructed me in a low and promising tone, 'I want to take you from behind while you watch in the mirror.' Crikey, again? But even as tired – and frankly well used – as I now was, I still followed his instructions immediately and turned to face the large, illuminated mirrors. A gentle hand between my shoulder blades told me he expected me to lay forwards, so I did, my chest pressing against the cool marble and my arms spread either side of me. Once he was happy with my position Nathan's eyes flicked to mine in the mirror for a split second and then after flipping my dress up over my back he gave me a sharp, ringing slap on my right buttock, pushed my thong to the side, and plunged into me again.

I gasped at the slap, then closed my eyes in pleasure at his swift entry. It was all so overwhelming that I tipped my head down to rest my forehead on the cool marble of the sink unit, but I had only been there a second before suddenly feeling Nathan's grip on my hips tighten. 'No. Open your eyes, watch as I take you, Stella. Watch as I claim you and make you come again,' he demanded. Which seeing as I wasn't allowed to look him in the eye was a bit of an odd comment really – not that I voiced this out loud. Instead I peeled my eyes open, tipped my neck up, and watched as his powerful body repeatedly thrust into me and retreated at a steady but firm rate. He looked so sexy still half dressed in his impeccable suit jacket, shirt and tie as his hands gripped my hips and yanked me backwards to allow him maximum depth. God, it was so erotic to watch this beautiful, neurotic man controlling both me and his powerful body as he had his way with me.

Fuck, this was good. The tilted angle of my hips over the sink edge meant that his hot length was rubbing against my front wall with every single mind-numbing thrust, charging me straight towards yet another orgasm, not to mention the idea that he was apparently 'claiming me' – which had me far more excited than it ever really should. Apparently noting my oncoming climax Nathan gripped my hips harder, 'You will wait for me Stella, control it, don't you dare come until I say.' His words were ground out between clenched teeth, an expression that I was mirroring myself as I desperately tried to follow his demand, but it was becoming too much, his contact was too perfect, hitting me in just the right spot with every thrust. 'Oh God … Sir … I don't think I can hold on …'

Deviously I used the last of my energy to squeeze my inner muscles around him as tight as possible, hoping to finish him off, and, thank God, it worked. Nathan let out a low bark of approval before thrusting in deep and grinding a hard circle once, 'Now,' he growled, before he exploded his climax inside of me. It couldn't have come at a better time, and as he ground himself down against me I clamped around him in ecstasy, milking every last drop from him as I screamed my release into my own forearm to dull the sound.

My body was awash with sensations but somehow also seemed numb from that fierce coupling. I was aware of the cold marble beneath me, the heavy weight of Nathan collapsed on my back and his hot panted breaths in my hair, but everything else was fuzzy and unfocused.

Holy fuck, that had been intense. If that was apology sex then maybe I needed to catch Nathan doing things wrong more often.

Chapter Two - Nathan

The relationship between myself and Stella was certainly keeping me on my toes as I had first predicted, and wasn't that just the understatement of the fucking year? I had no idea where I was with her; one minute I was in control, the next minute I was completely freaking out and dragging her into a cupboard in Claridges. 'Claim-fucking' her, as Stella had so accurately termed it. Regardless of my loss of control that night, I still couldn't help the smirk that curved my lips as I replayed our illicit trysts in my head again. My hands tightened on the steering wheel as I recalled just how receptive she'd been to my furious advances. The woman was fucking perfection.

Pulling into a parking space I switched off the car and remained in my seat as I took several deep cleansing breaths to clear my head and rid me of the arousal that was lingering after my daydreams of Stella.

Calm and stable again I climbed from my car, locked the door, and then paused to run a hand across my hair to smooth it down before I walked the last part of my journey whilst continuing my pondering. My time together with Stella was undoubtedly satisfying my sexual needs, there was no doubt about that. Stella was an almost exact match for my tastes in the bedroom, but I had definitely underestimated the power of the physical draw between the two of us. In fact there was such a spark that as soon as Stella arrived on Friday nights I had trouble keeping my hands off of her. That thought made me smirk again. I might have trouble keeping my hands to myself, but Stella didn't seem to object in the slightest.

As well as this, in her own way Stella was somehow moulding our time together into something different to the usual relationships I had experienced with my previous submissives. Somehow we had slipped into an easier companionship than I was used to; Stella was still compliant, subservient, and obedient as I expected, averting her eyes at all times and following my instructions to the letter, but on occasions she would completely surprise me with sweet gestures like bringing me a coffee when I hadn't asked for it, or preparing a snack for herself and making a portion for me too, which she either delivered to me with a shy, sexy smile or left wrapped in the fridge for me to find later.

It was a strange, perplexing balance we had come to. Stella always referred to me as Sir when we were in the bedroom, or if I was in a particularly bad mood, but she rarely used it outside of these times, something I thought would have annoyed me, but for some reason didn't. When we'd agreed our contract I'd thought the 'Sir' issue might be a deal-breaker for me, but truthfully I didn't mind as much as I thought I would, but I put my leniency down to the fact that Stella satisfied my needs so well in every other way that I would allow her this little indulgence.

No matter how off-kilter or unbalanced Stella might have me I would never show it though, which was one of the reasons for today's little excursion. It was always good to keep Stella on her toes, show her who was boss, I decided with a dark smile as I strode towards the offices of Markis Interiors – otherwise known as Stella's office. It was the Wednesday morning following our interlude at the bar in Claridges, so only two days since I'd last seen her, but I couldn't avoid one simple fact: I wanted to see her again, perhaps even have a sneaky mid-week tryst to slake the lust I could feel bubbling away in my veins. Stubbornly I was avoiding thinking about the reasons behind my new and unfamiliar need for Stella, and instead breaking all my own rules by indulging it and surprising her with a visit. A cruel smirk curled my lip at this thought – seeing as I'd never set foot in the Markis offices before today it should be a really bloody big surprise for her.

Just before I entered her building my phone vibrated in my pocket. Digging into my jacket I pulled it out, and as I glanced at the screen I scowled when I saw Gregory's number flashing up at me. Talk about shitty timing. 'Greg, give me some fucking good news.' I demanded as I strode in a tight circle on the pavement, silently praying that he'd found whoever it was that was sneaking my company's financial data out to my main competitor and allowing them to undercut my bids and steal business away from me.

'I'm afraid not, Nathan. I've run background checks on all staff members with office access and they've all come up clean. Is there anyone else you want me to check? Family members? Or is there anyone at your personal residence with access to your home office? A girlfriend? A cleaner?'

Both, I thought, then scowled at my slip of labelling Stella as a girlfriend. What the fuck had gotten into me lately? Shaking that off I frowned at the idea of Stella going behind my back. She would never do that, it was ridiculous, and I couldn't imagine Miranda my unassuming, 56-year-old cleaner doing anything like that either. 'Both, but I trust them explicitly, and it's not a family member. I only have my brother and there's no way he would do this to me.'

'OK, Nathan, whatever you say. I'll run some deeper checks then, see what I can dredge up.' Gregory heavily sighed.

Snapping my phone shut I shoved it violently into my pocket before cursing viciously under my breath. This issue with my business was starting to become a real fucking problem now. Spinning around in aggravation I let out a further growl of annoyance that drew the attention of several passers-by on the pavement, but they soon scampered away when I threw them by best snarled glare.

Shaking my head I cleared the rising anger that was threatening to engulf me and did a quick, much-needed countdown in my head, *5, 4, 3, 2, 1, 0.* Then, taking a deep breath in through my nose I calmed myself and looked up at the impressive glass frontage of the Markis building. My visit to Stella couldn't have been better timed; I needed a distraction and right now and I couldn't think of any better distraction than five foot seven inches of toned, blonde, fuckable woman.

Stella

Stifling an enormous yawn with the back of my hand, I pushed through the glass doors to my offices as I returned from yet another dull meeting. I was exhausted, my feet hurt from these stupidly high heels, and my diary this week was just chock-a-block with hideously boring meetings. Trying to balance my hectic schedule with my brother being in town had just about tipped the scale on my exhaustion levels; I'd been out Monday and Tuesday evenings with Simon, both late nights, and now I was seriously struggling to stay awake. Caffeine was the only thing getting me through the days, but my last coffee had been over 2 hours ago and was seriously wearing off now.

It was crazy really, my job used to be everything to me, literally my entire world had revolved around the office, and I'd found it anything but boring, but recently it had taken a back seat, what with Simon's visit and not to mention since starting my relationship with Nathan – if you could call it that – I'd increasingly found myself distracted, but certainly a good deal more sexed and less stressed, which was a positive, I thought with a small giggle.

Thinking of Nathan, which I did frequently and far more often than was healthy, I smiled indulgently to myself. My concerns about him wanting to finish things with me had been soothed by his actions and possessive statements in Claridge's on Monday night. He might be completely mercurial and an expert at driving me totally nuts, but I was drawn to him like a magnet and regardless of his recent slip ups I just couldn't stay away. My smile turned to a grin as a cheeky idea came to my mind that I simply couldn't resist.

We never communicated between our weekend sessions, so this was a serious breach of the norm, but I just couldn't help myself. Perhaps it was my exhaustion making me act impulsively, but I grabbed my phone, typed out a quick text to Nathan, and pressed send before I could change my mind.

From: Stella Marsden
Time: 13:08
Due to your love bite I've had to wear my hair down to work for the last two days. I've had 17 compliments on my new hair style. All from men. Thanks, Sir xx

It was so naughty, not to mention way too casual. No doubt he would probably go berserk, but I just couldn't help the grin that spread across my face as I popped my phone back into my bag. It was a total load of rubbish of course. Natalie, my assistant, had mentioned my change in hair style and one or two of my other colleagues had made passing comments, but certainly not seventeen, and certainly not all men. Ah well, it'd keep Nathan on his toes and a little white lie here and there couldn't do any harm could it?

As I got to the end of my corridor I was surprised to see Natalie's desk empty, but then seconds later she dashed from the direction of the conference room and practically knocked down the water machine and a potted plant in her rush to get to me. My eyes widened; blimey, my usually ultra-cool and calm assistant was barrelling towards me wobbling precariously on her 'too-high-high-heels' in her haste and looked decidedly flushed.

'Oh my God, Stella, thank God you're back!' Her red face and high tone was anything but cool and calm, what the heck was wrong? 'We have an important visitor and he wants a tour of the offices. I've put him in the conference room for now.'

Puffing out my cheeks I groaned out a sigh, 'Oh God, it's not the Mayor again is it?' I grimaced as I thought back to a couple of years ago when the Mayor of London had appeared in the office unannounced and randomly begun handing out free doughnuts and coffee. It had all been a bit strange really, but had conveniently – and suspiciously – happened just a few days before mayoral elections were due. I doubted he'd ever be back, we ate his doughnuts, but we didn't vote for him.

Natalie joined me and together we continued down the corridor until we reached the door to my office, 'No, someone much more exciting.' Natalie gushed as I dropped off my handbag and briefcase on my desk, desperately wishing I could just kick off my high heels and crawl under the desk to sleep. 'Nathaniel Jackson, you know, as in *the* Nathaniel Jackson, our biggest client.'

Luckily I had already put my briefcase down otherwise there was no doubt I would have dropped it as Natalie spoke. *Holy frigging shit!* Nathan was here? Why? Why the hell was he *here*? Because of the text I just sent? Suddenly my knees felt rather weak, and my office felt oppressively hot. Fanning myself with my hand I wiped gingerly at the film of sweat that had instantaneously formed on the back of my neck before looking back to Natalie and trying to school my features into a non-panicked expression.

Completely oblivious to my sudden palpitating shock and approaching mental breakdown, she continued, 'He runs such a huge important company that I'd always assumed he'd be old, you know? But my God, Stella! He's young! And he's so hot! You won't believe it!'

My lip twitched. Actually I would believe it. He's smoking hot not to mention absolutely killer in the sack. And here at my office. *Fuuuucccck!* Trying to swallow down the sudden urge to throw up the lunch I'd eaten in my last meeting I tried to make my face blank as I feigned

41

disinterest and turned to Natalie with a tight smile.

'Really? He's hot, huh? Well, it's better than the Mayor, I suppose.' I murmured as an attempted joke, but with my current nerves the humour was slightly lacking from my strained tone.

'Totally. I Googled him when I was waiting for you, he's obviously pretty secretive because there wasn't much on him except for the fact that he's totally loaded, thirty-one years old, and probably single because he's never really pictured out with the same partner twice.'

Why hadn't I thought to Google him? I wondered with a wry smile, perhaps I could try that tonight and see what else I could discover about him. Then a shudder ran though me, actually, on second thoughts no, Natalie's statement of *'he's never pictured with the same partner twice'* made me change my mind as my stomach twisted uncomfortably. I didn't want to turn into some jealous little bimbo trawling the Internet and looking at pictures of Nathan with a horde of different women on his arm as I cried into a glass of wine and a tub of ice-cream.

Desperate to distract myself from *those* images, and mindful that I shouldn't keep Nathan waiting any longer I smoothed down my teal silk blouse and thanked the gods that I had opted for my best black skirt and heels today. At least I looked professional and presentable … and possibly slightly sexy too. Crikey, my tiredness was a thing of the past, I was wide awake now and more than slightly terrified. Who needed caffeine when you had Nathaniel Jackson and his surprise visits around?

Nodding to embolden myself I headed from my office towards the conference room standing as tall and confidently as I could and leaving an uncharacteristically flustered Natalie behind me faffing with her hair.

I entered the conference room and closed the door behind me before even daring to look at Nathan. When I did I swallowed loudly, too loudly, before licking my lips nervously as my eyes ran over his appearance. He was wearing a navy three piece suit, navy shirt, and burgundy tie and looked absolutely frigging stunning. Breathing became far harder than it should be, until my flustered state had me almost on the verge of panting. We stood in silence for an absolute age, me avoiding eye contact, trying not to wheeze and wiping the sweat from my palms guiltily, and Nathan standing coolly with his hands tucked in his trouser pockets and his legs slightly spread with an unreadable expression on his face under his lowered brows. Blimey, Nathan looked so unbelievably hot when he was brooding like this that I was tempted to throw myself on the conference table there and then and offer myself to him.

Just when I was wondering if Nathan was going to speak at all I suddenly saw him start to stalk towards me and my belly flip flopped at the determination in his steps.

'I like your hair.' he murmured, but considering the text I'd just sent him the irony of the comment wasn't lost on me. Stopping in front of me Nathan reached up to flick my long hair back over my shoulders and exposed my love bite and necklace. A small growl of appreciation rumbled in his chest as he traced his fingers first across the chain, before landing on the ridiculously red bite on my neck with the tips of his fingers. As usual his touch sparked tingles of delight across my skin and I only just held back a fevered moan of pleasure. Well, at least I think I held it back.

'So which of these seventeen men do I need to kill first?' Nathan questioned softly in a suspiciously deadly tone as his fingers continued to caress my neck with small, warm swirls of his thumb. Oh God! I should never have sent that bloody text, there was going to be a massacre in my office and it was all going to be my fault.

'None of them ... I was only joking,' I murmured sheepishly as I turned my head to give him greater access

43

to the red circle on my skin that claimed me as his.

'Ah, I see. Lying to me, Miss Marsden? I think perhaps there should be consequences for such actions,' he murmured. Consequences? Like punishments? My thumb ring was being twirled at the speed of light by this point and I swallowed loudly, shamefully acknowledging that I definitely hadn't managed to suppress my moan of arousal that time, because Nathan's mouth twitched as he finally smoothed my hair back into place and lowered his hand to his side.

'So ... do you, er ... do you want a ... er ... a tour?' Jeez, I was stuttering like a complete gibbering fool, but my tongue felt so thick in my mouth I could barely speak.

'Of the office? Or of you?' Nathan murmured salaciously, inching himself closer to me so that he was well within my personal space where I could smell his delicious scent and instantly wanted to bury my face in his neck. 'Because I'm already rather well acquainted with your body, but I certainly wouldn't turn down a re-cap.' Wow, how did he get me so hot with just a few words? My entire body felt shaky and there was no ignoring the fact that I was now damp between my legs and panting. But there was no way I was risking a liaison in the conference room ... was I? *No* ... for one thing I was at work so it was totally unprofessional, but the main deciding factor was the fact that the blinds in the conference room had been taken down for cleaning yesterday so it would be like performing in a fish bowl. Damn the stupidly efficient cleaners.

Desperately needing to recover my usual control and momentum I turned and opened the door holding it wide for him. 'A tour of the office.' I replied curtly with a raised eyebrow as I tried to hold back a smile at how light hearted and teasing he seemed to be today.

Stepping past me Nathan ran his hand across my hip in the briefest of touches that could have been interpreted as accidental if viewed by an outsider, but I knew full well had been every bit intentional as he stepped into the corridor, 'Spoilsport,' he murmured as he passed me.

Keeping a professional demeanour whilst showing Nathan around the offices was almost impossible. Firstly, he kept 'accidentally' brushing against me, perhaps a small touch of his fingers to my elbow as he questioned me about something, or a brief passing of his hand across the side of my breast as he stepped aside to let me proceed through a door before him. It was utterly infuriating, but simultaneously the most arousing thing ever and after twenty minutes was making my already wobbly legs even more jellified and my pulse spike wildly with every contact. Secondly, every frigging female worker in the Markis Office had suddenly become insistent on speaking to me whilst flashing flirtatious glances and annoyingly pathetic giggles at Nathan, who just politely smiled back and then smirked at me once they left. It was very obvious that he was well aware the effect he had on the female species, and he clearly loved my barely reigned in jealously as I stood clenching my teeth and trying not to bitch slap each and every one of my colleagues who dared approach him.

After a tortuously slow half an hour the tour was finally done and we were heading back to the blessed sanctuary of my office. Nathan had been the perfect guest – apart from his teasing – smiling at the appropriate moments and appearing interested as I spoke, but I couldn't help but wonder exactly *why* he was here today. Finally I got to rest my shaky legs and as I took a seat behind my desk I was just about to ask him the purpose of his visit when one of my co-workers Robert came in looking flustered. Nathan sat himself on the couch in my office patiently and listened to me dealing with an urgent emergency with one of *his* buildings, well, as 'urgent' as interior design issues can get – a missing shipment of expensive Italian tiles – and then sat back watching me intently with his eyes narrowed.

'Very professional, Miss Marsden. I'm impressed,' he murmured once Robert had left. Then he rested one elbow on the end of the sofa and began rubbing his index finger casually across his top lip. My eyes zeroed in on the movement. Back and forth. Back and forth. In less than two seconds I found myself almost hypnotised by one frigging finger. God this man was just sexiness personified, I thought as I drew in a ragged breath.

'You should work for me,' he pondered, still rubbing his damn lip. But his statement finally broke my trance. *What?* Work for him? No thank you, as much as I loved him dominating me on the weekends I didn't fancy it happening every single day in the office too. I liked my own space, not to mention that I had worked damn hard to get my position at Markis and had no intention of giving up to become Nathan's personal sex assistant.

'You are our biggest client, Nathan, so I basically do work for you.' I replied sweetly, rather pleased with how calm I sounded when under my skin my heart was rampaging from my restless arousal.

He nodded slowly and made a humming noise in the back of his throat. 'Take off your panties.' He suddenly requested out of the blue in a complete change of conversation.

What? 'No!' My eyes flew open in shock at his unbelievable request. 'I'm at work!'

Standing up, Nathan locked my door with a flick of his wrist, pulled the cords of my blinds to angle them so no one could see in and then closed the distance between us, rotated my chair away from the desk, and squatted down in front of me. Without saying a single word he leant forwards, placed his warm hand on my knee and slid it straight up my skirt, pushing my panties to the side before gently rubbing a knuckle across my soft, sensitive skin.

I was utterly stunned. Christ, talk about swift work! All

my earlier hesitations about no sex in the office quickly left my mind as Nathan's skilled fingers set to work and in seconds I was so wet I started to worry about soaking my chair and staining my skirt.

'If you were in my office I could do this whenever I pleased,' he murmured seductively. That was indeed a persuasive argument and if Nathan kept up his ministrations much longer I may just give in to his crazy demand, but as I lay my head back and sluttishly opened my legs a little wider for him we were interrupted by a shrill and annoying ring which made me try to close my legs in shock.

Frowning, Nathan planted his hands firmly on my thighs and opened them again before he continued with his fondle whilst digging in his inside jacket pocket with his free hand. Removing his phone he glanced at the screen and his scowl deepened. 'Damn it, it's a meeting reminder.' Nathan glanced up at me, 'It's an important one too, I've got to go, I'll have to finish this later.' he murmured with a smirk as I gasped in disappointment at the thought of being left so aroused and needy for an entire afternoon.

'Can I see you tonight?' he asked suddenly, snapping me out of my delicious pre-orgasm fog in an instant. As much as his question thrilled me, I couldn't help my eyebrows rising at his request. Nathan and I had never discussed extending our agreed times together beyond the weekends and as much as I wanted to agree, I'd left work early the last two nights to see my brother and so now had tonnes of tasks still to get done today.

Reluctantly I shook my head, hating myself as I did so. 'I'd love to … but I've still got loads of overtime to catch up on.' I was clinging to the arms of my chair by this point, my insides melting and my legs writhing uncontrollably against Nathan's hand and its skilled work as he took me closer and closer to the peak I so desperately craved.

'That's a shame,' Nathan murmured, still lightly running his fingers around between my legs and driving me wild with his gentle swirls and flicks and pinches. 'Seeing you in charge today has been quite a turn on, I was thinking we could have done a little switch.' With his fingers doing their thing I was pretty much past speech by now, but I managed to frown. *Switch*? What the hell was that?

'Switching is where we change roles, I thought maybe you could be in charge for a night. Well, just a small part of a night.' He clarified firmly, apparently reluctant to relinquish too much control over to me. 'But if you're busy then that's just too bad.' Change roles? I wasn't entirely sure how I felt about that, I loved the way Nathan was in charge in the bedroom. But he'd actually looked quite disappointed when I'd refused, giving me that wide-eyed little boy look that I'd seen briefly at Claridge's on Monday. Before I could think too much about it Nathan's phone beeped again and on a curse he slipped two more fingers inside my panties and with no warning whatsoever ripped them clean from my body with a loud tearing sound that seemed to echo around my office and shunted me forwards on my seat by several inches.

What the fuck!? I kid you not, he literally pulled my knickers so hard that they had split at the back and he was now stood upright holding the destroyed material in his hand and looking rather pleased with himself.

My mouth was hanging open in stunned silence, I had absolutely no clue how to respond to that move.

'They were my favourite knickers,' I protested weakly. They weren't my favourite knickers, but they were a pretty pair and I needed Nathan to understand that he couldn't just go around shredding my pants whenever he felt like it, otherwise it might become a regular occurrence for him.

He shrugged. 'I'll get you some new ones, but seeing as

you wouldn't take them off and now you're refusing to see me tonight I thought I'd take something to keep me company until I see you on Friday.' Then with a smirk he folded my ruined panties into some semblance of a triangle and tucked them into the top front pocket of his suit jacket so they stuck out just like a handkerchief. An aquamarine, lacy handkerchief. Even in my shock I couldn't help a small gurgle of laughter at how funny they looked. Patting them, Nathan grinned wickedly at me as he turned for the door. 'I'll keep them here for my meeting and think of you and your tempting little body.'

Then, with no more words, not even a goodbye, he was gone, leaving no evidence of his visit except my exposed arse and a waft of his gorgeous scent hanging in the air. I still didn't know if it was aftershave or shower gel that I liked so much, but whichever it was I would happily have my office smelling of it on a daily basis. Picking up a client folder I wafted my heated face and blew the errant hair from my eyes. Crikey, that had been a crazy hour, that was for sure. And now I was sat in my office unable to focus on anything other than my huge state of arousal, my heavy breathing, and my very knickerless bottom.

Chapter Three - Stella

This may well go down as my stupidest idea ever. Chewing on my lip and nervously spinning my thumb ring I briefly considered forgetting it and making a run for home, but unfortunately just then I heard a key in the front door and knew that my time to escape had well and truly passed. With a loud swallow I tried to bolster my failing confidence, here we go then.

Adjusting my teeny tiny blouse – one I'd accidentally shrunk in the wash months ago – I checked my cleavage in the wall mirror one more time. Pronounced and perky, with plenty of flesh on display, it was quite impressive tonight, if I do say so myself. Although if I'm being honest that probably had a lot to do with the magic balcony bra I was wearing and not a lot to do with my actual breasts.

Once I was happy that my boobs would have the desired effect I took a seat on the large leather office chair and began to wait. Crikey, my heart was beating so fast I actually felt light headed. Lifting a hand to smooth my hair I realised my hands were also shaking uncontrollably. I was a complete mess. How I expected to carry off my plan in this state I had no idea. Shaking my head I lowered my trembling fingers and gripped the book on the desk to distract me. There really was no two ways about it – this had definitely been a bad idea.

Just then I heard footsteps in the hall and then the next second Nathan was standing in the door to his home office staring at me sitting in *his* office chair. After today's run in at the Markis office I'd had second thoughts about the 'switch' thing and decided to make use of my spare key to come to his house early and surprise him, but the thunderous look of annoyance on his face was drastically making me re-think my choice.

'Stella? What the hell are you doing in my office?' He demanded in a gritty tone. He sounded particularly angry and clearly not pleased to see me which was rather disappointing, but after a deep breath I summoned my inner confidence and decided to stick to my original plan and plough on regardless. This might backfire completely and leave me looking like a total idiot, but I'd spent all afternoon rehearsing it and getting ready so I may as well give it a try.

Straightening my back I tried to think like I did at work. I was a powerful career woman and I needed to act like one now, so arching my eyebrow I narrowed my eyes in disdain and sat back in the chair behind Nathan's desk trying to look like I owned the place.

'Your office?' I asked incredulously, remarkably proud that my voice sounded as calm, aloof and professional as it did, especially seeing as my heart was rampaging in my chest like a herd of wild buffalo. 'I think you're getting a little above yourself Mr Jackson, this is *my* company and *my* office.' God I was good. Nathan's expression was absolutely priceless, his mouth was practically hanging open as he tried to comprehend what the hell was going on. '… and whilst we're on the subject of our working environment I expect you to call me Ms Marsden when you're in *my* office, do you understand?' With a dramatic flick of my hand I removed the glasses I had been wearing to give the effect of professionalism and placed them on the desk, and then proceeded to unclip and shake out my long, loose hair like I was in a shampoo advert so it fell in waves across my shoulders.

Blinking several times Nathan still stood frozen in the doorway apparently at a complete loss for what to say or do, but judging from the twitching muscle in his jaw he looked like his brain might be about to short circuit at any moment. Slamming down the book I had been holding in my other hand – my props were almost as impressive as my acting – I stood up and leaned forwards on the desk giving him a great view of my cleavage whilst flashing him my best attempt at a menacing look. 'I said, *do you understand*?'

There was a lengthy pause where I began to panic, but finally Nathan's face quirked to the side as recognition flashed in his eyes, his bewildered expression clearing as he finally realised what I was doing. I have to say, he was a lot slower on the uptake than I'd expected, so I gave an almost imperceptible nod and then watched as Nathan's eyes lit with excitement.

'Mr Jackson, I asked you a question, do *not* keep me waiting for an answer,' I stated firmly. God this was fun! Just then I noticed the aquamarine lace of my ripped panties still sticking out from his suit pocket and nearly ruined my acting by bursting into a grin – he'd kept them there all day! On show for all and sundry to see!

'Yes I understand, I apologise for not using your correct title, Ms Marsden,' Nathan finally replied in a low, contrite tone. Oh goody, he was getting straight into his role and apparently quite keen to join in with the fun.

'Good, come in and close the door.' With deliberate slowness I walked around to the front of the desk so Nathan would get a complete look at my 'office' outfit. Not that I would ever be seen dead at work in these clothes; beneath my incredibly skimpy skirt – an old netball skirt of mine which made it both short and floaty – I was wearing stockings and suspenders and I had made sure the bottom of the suspender belt was clearly visible alongside the exposed flesh at the top of my thighs. I was also wearing a pair of killer six-inch heels and the whole outfit was topped off with my flimsy shrunken blouse, pushed-up tits, and my hair curled and flowing loose. I

53

wasn't big into ego, but even I knew that I looked like an image from most guys' office porn fantasies tonight.

Propping my bum on the front of the desk I crossed my arms under my breasts, forcing my bosom to almost burst from my low cut shirt and glared at him. Nathan's obvious appreciation of my outfit was clear in his blazing eyes and I allowed myself a second of internal celebration. Licking his lips Nathan's gaze travelled the full length of me twice, and I watched in amusement as he shoved his hands in his pockets, shifted on the spot, and awkwardly adjusted his groin area which seemed to be expanding by the second.

Yes! My plan was working! As much as I loved Nathan dominating me, the realisation that I also had power over him was quite a thrill and I couldn't help a small smile breaking on my lips.

'Would you like to explain why you're late?' I demanded after quickly clearing my throat and realising that with my little daydream I'd paused the whole role play thing for a bit too long.

Smiling to myself I saw that Nathan actually looked like he might burst a blood vessel as he continued to stare at my exposed cleavage and thighs, but after another few moments he gathered his wits, rolled off his shoulders, and answered me. 'I got stuck in a meeting, Ms Marsden.' he answered softly, linking his hands in front of himself.

My eyebrows rose as I noticed this action with interest; linked hands was the pose that signalled my submission. Was that why he was doing it? Was he submitting to me? Giving himself over to the game? Strangely the idea excited me more than I had expected it to.

'I don't tolerate lateness, Mr Jackson.' I snapped, throwing his own words of a few weeks ago back at him before teasing him by slowly uncrossing and re-crossing my legs just like the scene in *Fatal Attraction*. This simple action caused Nathan to noticeably redden and his eyes to widen even further. Gosh, this really was rather good fun!

'I'm sorry, Ms Marsden.' Nathan murmured contritely. It suddenly struck me that his eyes were firmly fixed on mine now, how odd, it seemed that this little role play had made him forget all about his dislike for eye contact. Perhaps it was because he was playing a role and not being himself? Whatever the cause, I liked it. Nathan's eyes were piercingly blue and a glance from him always made my insides tremble in a delicious way. Right now my insides were like a big bowl of squirmy, aroused deliciousness.

'Apart from my timekeeping, can I ask why I'm here, Ms Marsden?' Nathan asked, astonishing me completely. Bugger, I hadn't thought this far ahead. When I'd planned this little surprise for Nathan I'd only considered his reaction to me pretending to be his boss ... after that I'd just kind of assumed that we'd have sex. Preferably on his desk, and hopefully after he'd done something dramatic like sweep the contents off with his forearm and thrown me across it in a fit of passion.

Noticing that he was still staring at me awaiting my reply I winced. Oh God, I was going to have to think on my feet and make something up quickly, 'I wanted to discuss your inadequacies,' I said, saying the first thing that sprung to my mind. Well, that was the type of thing a boss would call you into their office to discuss wasn't it?

'My inadequacies?' Nathan's voice dipped and his eyes narrowed significantly as I watched a muscle flick to life in his jaw line. Uh-oh, this was control freak Nathaniel Jackson I was dealing with – perhaps pretending that he had inadequacies hadn't been the best option. His face was hardening by the second and his body tensing as the control of the situation quickly shifted over to him. I wasn't willing to give in so easily though, and quickly did my best to dig myself out of the hole that I was on the verge of falling into.

'Yes, Mr Jackson, it's come to my notice that your stamp-licking skills are atrocious.' I tried to sound haughty and keep a straight face as I spoke, but stamp licking? Where the hell had I conjured that up from? Oh well, I'd said it now, please let something light-hearted and ridiculous like 'stamp licking' soothe his impending bad mood.

Thankfully I saw the tension leave his body as Nathan's shoulders relaxed and he nearly, *very nearly*, smiled. 'My stamp-licking skills ... I see.' Nathan took a step towards me, his blue eyes still intently focused on mine, but stopped just a few feet in front of me.

'Have I done anything else wrong, Ms Marsden?' Nathan asked, his tone lower and sending a delicious shiver down my spine that was making role playing more and more difficult by the second. In fact it was currently difficult enough just leaning on the desk without sliding off into a molten pool of arousal at his feet.

'Umm ...' I was getting quite hot under the collar now, my very small, shrunken collar. His looks alone were enough to get me frantically turned on, but as if sensing my struggle for what to say next Nathan stepped in to assist me in prolonging our role play.

'I should probably admit that I broke your stapler last week.' A small smile was tugging at the corner of his mouth now, clearly Nathan was loving every minute of this little fantasy. 'Oh yes, and I killed the pot plant in the staffroom.' he admitted with a solemn nod of his head. 'Your favourite one.'

Sucking in a cleansing breath I found my voice again. 'Well Mr Jackson, these indiscretions simply can't go unnoticed, you will have to be dealt with.' I stated clearly, suddenly becoming incredibly uncomfortable with the idea of actually punishing him. I quite liked it when he had spanked me in the past, but spanking him? I didn't think I could do it, it just wouldn't feel right.

'I understand, Ms Marsden, once again I apologise, is there perhaps something I can do to make it up to you?' he added salaciously, his eyes dancing. Ah, maybe Nathan had picked up on my hesitancy with the whole punishment thing and was happy to take on a different type of punishment for me.

'Oh Mr Jackson, I can think of several things.' I replied as I pushed myself further back on the desk so I was actually sat on it with my legs dangling over the side.

Smiling darkly Nathan stepped forwards and leant in to kiss me, but feeling ridiculously brave and slightly power-crazy I placed a firm hand on his chest to stop him. 'I don't think so, Mr Jackson. You made me wait so I think you owe me a little pleasure to make up for your lateness.' Oh my God, did I really just say that?

The look of absolute shock on Nathan's face told me I did. Yes! I was getting to pay him back for the torturous night several weeks ago when he'd made me wait and wait for my orgasm because I'd been late arriving at his apartment. Jeez, the rush of adrenaline from the power of this situation was actually making me dizzy, not to mention unbelievably horny.

The look of utter astonishment on Nathan's face had held and almost caused a bubble of insane laughter to escape from my throat, but thankfully I swallowed it down and raised a stern eyebrow at him just like my witch of a head teacher used to do in high school.

After blinking in shock at my apparent transformation into some power-crazy dominatrix, Nathan straightened his back and linked his hands again, 'Of course, Ms Marsden, what would you suggest I do?'

'Hmmm, why don't we start by practising your stamp-licking skills?' I suggested helpfully, improvising wildly as I did so. A confused look settled on Nathan's features so I shrugged casually, 'Unfortunately, I don't have stamps handy ... I wonder what else you could lick?' I felt quite ridiculous being as blatantly sexual as this, but luckily I was with Nathan who happened to be one of the world's kinkiest men and who clearly didn't mind my little tease at all.

A pleased humming sound resonated from the back of his throat and seemed to travel directly to my groin, making me shiver with delicious anticipation and squirm on the surface of the desk. 'Why don't you let me worry about that?' Nathan suggested, placing his hands on my thighs and slowly sliding them up under the hem of my skirt until it was bunched around my waist. Nathan's eyes lowered to my groin, then he gasped and looked up with a wicked glint in his eye that made me suddenly remember that I'd gone commando to add some extra excitement to the afternoon's proceedings. Well, he'd ripped my panties off and left me knickerless and horny in the office all afternoon, so I had merely decided to maintain the trend.

A smile played on my lips and I almost laughed as the thought crossed my mind that I was acting quite a lot like an extra in a cheesy porn film.

'Oh Ms Marsden it appears you forgot your underwear today.' Nathan observed gruffly, his eyes dancing as he stared up my raised skirt with obvious appreciation. No doubt able to see all my freshly shaved lady bits and the abundant wetness that I could now feel gathered there.

'Did I? How neglectful of me,' I gasped breathlessly, before reaching forwards and running my hand over the lacy material of my ruined panties still sticking out from Nathan's suit pocket. 'It seems I must have lost them somewhere along the way,' I murmured as Nathan's knuckles gently brushed against the dampness of my clit, making me suck in a sharp breath and briefly close my eyes as pleasure washed over me.

Dropping to his knees in front of me Nathan hooked his hands under my knees and suddenly pulled me forwards so my thighs were on either side of his head. 'So ... do you suggest I lick the stamps like this?' he enquired grittily, running his tongue slowly around my clitoris and making me arch my back and let out a moan like a wanton hussy. 'Or perhaps like this?' he asked tracing the entire length of my moist slit with a good, long, hard lick. Crikey, after spending the afternoon preparing for this little scene I'd been so on edge with arousal that I very nearly came at the second swipe of his tongue.

'Oh God, Nathan, both … please …' I rasped, clutching at the edge of the desk for support. Between my legs I felt Nathan's warm breath as he chuckled against me, but I was too absorbed in what he was doing to try and maintain the role play any more or chastise him for laughing at me. Gone were thoughts of office manager Ms Marsden, all that had now been firmly replaced with focusing on Nathan and his superb sexing skills.

As predicted, after the anticipation that had been building in me all afternoon at the prospect of surprising Nathan with my role play I barely lasted any time at all before my body gave in and prepared to climax violently. Sensing my imminent release Nathan laved his tongue more firmly against my clit before thrusting two fingers deep inside of me. Stars exploded before my eyes as my insides clenched in orgasm causing my legs to clamp around Nathan's head shamelessly as he continued to suck and lick at my sensitive flesh and ease me down from my climax before I collapsed back on the desk moaning wantonly.

'Well, Ms Marsden, it appears you can be quite the authoritarian when you want,' Nathan commented mildly as he removed his fingers and wiped them clean on my skirt. Leaning over me he placed a hand on either side of my head, a sexy smile lingering on his lips as he dropped down to place a lingering kiss on my lips.

I kissed him back lazily, my tongue meeting his as they twirled together leisurely, the taste of my arousal obvious on his lips, but I didn't care. 'Huuummm,' was all I could manage in reply. At this point I was almost beyond speech anyway. 'I've obviously learned well from you. Now I think you should take me to bed so we can do something about your pleasure Mr Jackson.' I murmured with a lazy grin, reaching down to cup his sizeable erection. He felt so hot and hard against my hand as he pulsed and twitched in my palm that it was a wonder he hadn't burst through the zipper of his trousers. He had *definitely* enjoyed himself then.

'Oh Ms Marsden I was hoping you might say that.' he said scooping me up in his arms as he turned to head for the bedroom, 'I think I'll take back control now, but your outfit is staying.' he added, running one hand appreciatively across the top of my suspenders with a low growl.

Chapter Four - Nathan

Thoughts of Stella now occupied my mind far more than I'd have liked. It was a daily occurrence, hourly if I was being really honest with myself, and the really disturbing thing was that it wasn't just the sex I was thinking about any more. It was her. Her sweet mannerisms, the way she so desperately tried to avoid eye contact with me when I could see how much she wanted to look at me, even the way her cheeks flushed with embarrassment about a hundred times a day.

Snorting out a frustrated breath I shifted uncomfortably in my seat, well aware that no matter how hard I tried, I couldn't get to grips with my tumultuous emotions where that woman was concerned. Why I was allowing myself to become pussy-whipped was beyond me, but ever since the night Nicholas had turned up out of the blue I'd seemingly developed a mixed-up version of guilt and affection for the first time in my life, and now I couldn't get them out of my system.

After her little 'switch' scene I had spent the remainder of the week pondering why Stella had really been in my office on Wednesday evening. It had been a surprise to me at first, which had then turned out to be a very pleasant and rather naughty roleplay surprise, followed by several hours of very enjoyable sex, but now my mind kept flicking back to my conversation with Gregory about an insider leak. Chewing on the inside of my lip I leant forwards and braced my elbows on my knees, steepling my fingers in front of my face as I considered it – surely Stella wasn't leaking information on me, was she? Frowning I rubbed a palm across my forehead, trying to soothe out the tension gathering there. Had I caught her snooping and she'd simply made up the roleplay idea to cover her tracks? I highly doubted it, her smoking hot 'naughty secretary' outfit that night certainly suggested she'd planned the switch all along, but with my business in trouble I needed to find out for certain. The problem was I wasn't sure how to go about it.

Just as I heard Stella's key in the door as she arrived for our weekend together I finished devising a plan which should work rather nicely. Nodding my head in satisfaction I sat back in my armchair and watched with pleasure as she performed her usual Friday night routine of walking in, hanging up her jacket, and placing down her briefcase before standing in her ready position. Her posture was perfect; upright spine, shoulders tucked back confidently, but face averted and submissive just how I liked it. Mmm … it was a very pleasant sight indeed. Perhaps instead of wasting my time on ridiculous daydreams about her smiles I should commit this image to mind for future fantasies.

'Good evening, Stella.' I murmured from my seat by the fireplace.

'Good evening, Sir,' she replied softly, as I watched the first of no doubt many blushes alight upon her cheeks.

'I think I'm going to have a night off tonight,' I added casually as Stella stood waiting for me to approach her.

My twisted mind found this all rather amusing, I could practically see the cogs in her brain spinning, and at this current moment her facial expression was so easy to read as she frowned deeply, clearly thinking *'Night off? As in no sex?'* I nearly laughed out loud, I wasn't really planning a night off – of course I wasn't, that would be absurd, but I could understand her confusion, usually on a Friday night when she arrived I had pounced on her within minutes after enduring a week of no sex.

'Oh,' Stella murmured, I heard disappointment in her tone and felt rather smug at just how much she apparently needed me, or perhaps just wanted me, 'OK, Sir.' Stella began to turn towards her bedroom when I finally let a dark laugh escape from my throat.

'Where do you think you're going?' I demanded softly in a tone so carnal it seemed to make goose pimples rush to the skin of Stella's arms in great swathes. Turning to face me I could see the confusion in her features and very nearly laughed again. I was a cruel fucker, but she was such fun to tease.

'Well you said you were having a night off so I thought I'd head to my room,' she murmured. I smiled briefly, it wasn't like we ever sat and exchanged small talk or shared an evening in front of the television so I could see her logic, but that wasn't quite how I wanted to play this tonight.

Rubbing my fingers back and forth across the soft leather of my arm chair I tilted my head before continuing, 'I said *I* was having a night off, not you. I'd like you to do a little show for me, Stella,' I informed her from under hooded eyes. I felt my groin begin to tighten at just the thought of what I planned on making her do.

Stella visibly blanched, all the blood draining from her pretty face as she digested my words and began fidgeting on the spot, flicking her thumb ring and chewing on her lower lip. I knew she hated dancing, and from the look of horror on her face she was obviously expecting me to demand a strip tease or lap dance of some sort. Actually a lap dance wasn't a bad idea. Christ, Stella would look sexy as fuck swaying and gyrating in front of me. Swallowing hard I adjusted myself again and decided to store that little pleasure for next time.

'Umm ... what exactly did you have in mind?' she asked hesitantly, worrying her bottom lip between her teeth again until it visibly reddened. She looked so nervous and sexy all at once that I just wanted to pull that lip from within her teeth and bite it myself.

'*Sir,*' I reminded her crisply, keen to get the balance of our relationship back on course after my annoyingly errant thoughts and emotions of the past few days.

Flushing, she flinched, correcting herself. 'Sorry ... what would you like me to do, *Sir*?' I watched as she also remembered to link her hands in front of herself to show her submission. My nostrils flared as I drew in a deep satisfied breath – no matter how many times I saw Stella standing like that it still looked so fucking perfect.

'I want to watch you make yourself come.' I heard her gasp in surprise at my brisk instruction, and couldn't help but smile, oh yes, I would enjoy this very much. 'Take off your clothes.' I caught sight of Stella's uncertain expression as I stood up and shifted the armchair so it was now in front of the sofa. Turning back to her I propped myself on the arm of the chair and was just about to chastise her for not starting her task when she caught my eye, gave a shy smile, and then lifted her hands to the collar of her blouse.

My eyebrows rose – the little minx, she had been waiting for my full attention before starting, well I never. Perhaps she was keener on performing a strip tease than I had first thought; she might look like the perfectly shy submissive, but I had to say I found Stella's inner confidence incredibly attractive. Folding my arms I got comfortable as a dark smile spread on my lips at this sudden turn of events.

Running her finger tips along the collar of her blouse she brushed them against her neck several times and let out a small moan of pleasure which instantly had my cock twitching.

Bringing her fingers slowly back around to the front of her neck Stella's eyes fluttered shut as she traced gentle circles on the exposed skin of her collar bones with a soft sigh. Christ, the sexy little noises she was making were so incredible that I was ready to explode already and she hadn't even removed any clothing!

Gradually Stella's fingers began to trail teasingly up and down the strip of pearl buttons on her blouse until finally she paused at the top one and flicked it open. Much to my appreciation, she performed the same ritual for each button; her right hand would flutter down the join in her blouse until it teasingly brushed the waistline of her skirt, then it would make the return journey back up and pop another button out.

By the time Stella had the top three buttons undone I was squirming on the arm of the chair with a full blown hard-on tenting my trousers, and no doubt a flush of desire reddening my cheeks. This woman, *my woman,* was so fucking hot it nearly undid me.

As the fourth button was opened my eyes became fixed on the flash of cream-coloured lace bra that I could see, and then thankfully buttons five and six ended my torture as Stella finally parted her shirt and delicately shrugged it from her shoulders so it slid down her arms and pooled at her feet.

My breath caught in my throat and I almost gurgled with need. The bra I had glimpsed earlier was even more stunning than I'd hoped; thin lace cups swirled with a fine patterns of flowers and transparent enough in their delicacy to allow me to see the hardened peaks of Stella's rosy pink nipples below. *Fuck me.*

How I held myself back from dragging her to me and covering every inch of her skin with hot kisses was a miracle, but I did, and over the course of the next two minutes Stella shed her skirt, shoes, and stockings until she was stood before me in just her glorious matching underwear.

It would seem that Stella was getting just as impatient and horny as me, because she was a little quicker with the removal of her bra and knickers; only pausing briefly to tease me with some gentle touches to her swollen nipples before slipping the bra off and tossing it in my direction. Her knickers quickly followed suit after a teasing bottom wiggle and then finally Stella stood before me naked.

I needed to calm the fuck down or I was either going to come in my boxer shorts or last about as long a virgin on his first time, so I took a second to stalk around her and appreciate her feminine curves. She was trembling slightly which I took as a good sign, and the quiver in her lightly freckled neck fascinated me so much that I leant in and placed an open mouthed kiss there. Noticing that she was still chewing her lower lip I tutted and reached up to tug it from between her teeth, then leaning in I sucked it into my mouth and gave it a nip with my own teeth. 'No chewing on that soft lip of yours, Stella. That's my job,' I reminded her, before indicating for her to sit on the armchair as I took a position on the sofa directly opposite her. I was now sat almost within touching distance of Stella's soft, pale skin and had a fabulous view of her beautiful body.

'Spread your legs.' Christ, suddenly my voice was high and shaky like a fucking pre-pubescent teenager. Swallowing I cleared my throat, desperately hoping for something a little more manly next time. 'Pretend I'm not here, touch yourself Stella, make yourself come.' I ordered, thankfully in a voice much more my usual dominant tone.

Initially hesitant, I quickly became rather proud of Stella as she got into the swing of things and began by rolling and tweaking her nipples until they were stiff peaks, nearly making me dribble with my need to reach out and touch them. It was a good start, many submissives would have gone straight for their clit when given the instruction I'd issued, but not my Stella, no, she started off the show with a good slow fondle of her lovely breasts. After a few moments Stella's left hand remained on her breast fondling and tugging at her reddened nipple, whilst her right hand began to trail down her body. Gently skimming across her stomach in a teasing trail she finally lowered her hand through the strip of curls at the apex of her thighs and made it to her clitoris where she began to stroke in a circle with the pad of her index finger. Letting out a soft gasp Stella bit her lip, shifted her hips slightly and then repeated the movement with more pressure, closing her eyes as her pleasure increased. Holy shit, she'd barely started and my cock was already trying to burst from my trousers.

The moment that Stella pushed a finger inside of herself and I heard how wet she was, I very nearly pounced on her and satisfied the throbbing need in my dick, but somehow, using every last shred of my self-control, I managed to refrain and watch as she withdrew the finger that was now shiny with her arousal. My eyes widened and I licked my lips greedily, desperate for a taste of her. Fuck me, this was so sexy. Rubbing her moisture around her clit Stella then proceeded to push two fingers deeper within herself and began thrusting them in and out at a faster rate. The heel of her hand was pressing against her clit and as a flush spread across her cheeks I could see she wasn't going to last much longer.

My cock visibly twitched and jumped under the material of my trousers as I watched Stella climax, softly moaning to herself and throwing her head to the side as her hand slowed its movements bringing herself down from the orgasm.

Fuck. Blood was pumping down to my cock so hard I almost felt myself getting dizzy and I had to clear my throat several times before I attempted speech. 'I might be having a night off, but watching you come like that has got me really hard, I wonder if perhaps you might be able to remedy this situation for me?' I asked, indicating to the solid erection that was jutting out under the fabric of my trousers like a frigging mountain. I wasn't certain, but from the feel of it, my cock was the thickest and hardest that it had ever been in my entire life.

'I'm sure that can be arranged, Mr Jackson.' Stella murmured, easing herself forwards on the armchair and then dropping to her knees between my legs where she began to unzip my trousers.

'Would Sir like to find his release using my hand, mouth, or body?' Stella asked huskily, knowing full well that a bit of dirty talk did it for me. She was right it did, and in response my cock jerked wildly in her palm causing a small smile to break on her lips. Yeah, she knew exactly what effect she had on me. The strange thing was, it was only recently that I'd started to acknowledge it too without being terrified by my own similar response to her.

A low growl escaped my throat at her words, 'Fuck, Stella, you surprise me sometimes.' I said with a shake of my head, 'To answer your very naughty question, I think to start with I'll go with option two. Now be a good girl and put my cock in between your lovely lips.' I muttered, swiftly pushing my trousers and boxers the rest of the way down so they bunched around my ankles.

Stella wasted no time in complying with my demand and very soon I found my cock cocooned in the velvety warmth of her amazingly talented mouth. Fuck, that was good. Using the technique that she knew I liked best Stella teased the tip of me for a while with her tongue whilst using her hand on the base of my erection, then gradually built up the depth and speed of her mouth until we were both moaning and writhing around feverishly. Almost overcome with desire I forced myself to open my eyes and watch her as she enthusiastically licked and sucked me closer to climax, and then noticed Stella's free hand drop between her legs and press against her clit again. Well, well, the greedy little minx.

Once again I was amazed by just how aroused Stella

got by servicing me, that surely wasn't the behaviour of a woman who was going behind my back and stealing company figures to help my opposition? Suddenly breaking her contact she looked up at me with wide desperate eyes, 'Nathan, please, I'm throbbing, I need you inside me *now*,' she begged me in a ragged voice. *Need*, not want, my ego rather liked the sound of that. But enough of that, it was time to put my plan into action, so obliging her I kicked off my trousers, scooped her off the floor, and collapsed us both onto the sofa. Then, as I loomed over her panting body I paused with my cock at her entrance – planning on using a little persuasive sexing just to make sure she wasn't the leak in my company.

It was at this point I realised that this was hardly my most well-devised plan. I was practically splitting at the seams with the need to come, so pausing now was fucking killing me, but I just about managed it, knowing that in just a few short seconds I would be buried in Stella's moist centre with her wrapped around me like a glove. Providing she gave me the right answer of course.

Christ, what would I do if she was the leak? I wasn't sure I could give her up now. That really didn't bear thinking about, so I pushed it aside for now and simply asked what I needed to know. 'Was Wednesday the first time you've been in my office alone, Stella?' I asked, rubbing the tip of my cock up and down her sopping slit provocatively, making her mewl softly below me and buck her hips in desperation as she attempted to guide me in.

'Ahhh ... what?' she asked, sounding genuinely baffled and apparently wondering why I was suddenly initiating a talk in the middle of sex. Giving her no warning I thrust myself deeply into her in one swift lunge and then held myself there pinning her to the sofa, 'Answer me,' I requested through gritted teeth, God she felt so perfect wrapped around me that I almost shot my load instantly.

'Oh God ... Yes. Yes it was the first time.'

'Have you ever been through my things, looked at my paperwork?' I demanded with my next sharp thrust.

'No ... no ... of course not ...' Her nails were digging into my shoulders by now and she was panting erratically, obviously enjoying herself, but even so she gripped me tightly to stop my movements and pushed her head back with a questioning look in her eyes.

'Nathan, stop ... stop ... why are you asking this? I don't understand?' The complete look of confusion on her on her face was all I needed to see. I might not make eye contact with people regularly, but I was as sharply business minded as they came and I knew an innocent person when I saw one. Stella wasn't lying, she was genuinely confused by my questioning. She wasn't the leak.

Thank fuck for that. The relief that surged through me was so all consuming that I had to briefly rest my forehead against hers to recover from it. 'Nothing,' I murmured, reassured and then ready to finish off what I'd started as I sunk slowly into her willing flesh again and placed several light kisses around her lips. Nah, fuck that, I couldn't go slow, not now, not with so much build up, so with one foot planted against the end of the sofa and the other jammed on the back cushion I began to pound myself into Stella, releasing all my pent up aggression and relief in one go and exploding in such a violent climax that it immediately set Stella off on her own orgasm too. Jesus, talk about explosive coupling.

Afterwards as I went to move away Stella held my biceps to stop me. 'Why did you want to know if I've been in your office?' she asked, a frown settling on her brows.

Sighing I pulled out of her and rolled over, tugging her with me and debating if I should tell her or not. I definitely was turning soft in the head, because the next second I found myself spilling the whole story before I'd even realised I was talking. 'I've lost a few big bids on new contracts recently, it's probably someone in my company leaking the information they need.' I saw Stella's frown deepen and felt her body tense as she realised why I'd been questioning her, 'My security guy told me I needed to check everyone at home who has access to my office.' Stella's mouth opened to speak, but in her obviously affronted state she didn't seem to know what to say, 'I had to check, but I know now that it wasn't you,' I said simply, cutting off her protests to quell any upset she might be feeling.

Wanting to move away from the topic of my work before Stella could get angry with my accusation I went for a distraction, 'I quite liked you calling me Mr Jackson.' I observed as Stella shifted on top of me and rested her head on my chest, apparently taking my hint and leaving my work issues aside for now. My hand began lazily trailing through the soft lengths of her hair and over her back, making my softening cock begin to consider the tempting possibility of initiating another round.

'Yeah? Well don't get used to it, I can barely manage to say Sir when I'm supposed to.' She mumbled against my chest. I smiled at this, it was true, she was appalling at using my title, not that I really seemed to mind lately.

'Actually I quite liked it when you called me Nathan too,' I added quietly, just as surprised at my own admission as Stella looked to hear it as her head popped up and she looked at me. 'I've hardly ever heard you say my name. I … I liked it.' Fucking hell, I needed to shut the hell up right now.

'Maybe I could use it more often? Instead of Sir?' she asked softly.

I paused, almost wanting to say yes, but somehow completely unable to. 'No,' I snapped, not elaborating on my answer, because quite simply, I couldn't. My semi-erection went soft immediately as my mood abruptly darkened. Suddenly realising my position on the sofa with her cocooned in my arms I grimaced. What the fuck was I doing being so snuggly with her? I was stroking her hair like a total sap, for God's sake. Feeling her tense at my sudden mood change I rolled Stella off me, stood up, gathered my clothes, and left the room without another word or glance in her direction.

Fuck, *I* didn't even understand what was happening inside of me, so being able to vocalise it to Stella just wasn't going to happen.

Slamming my bedroom door I threw my clothes on the bed and headed straight for the bathroom where I stepped into the shower, flicking the taps so it pounded me with icy cold water. After shocking my system for a minute or two I adjusted to a warmer temperature and as the water ran over my skin I let my mind wander.

One thing I kept coming back to was my brother's words the night he had flipped out on his girlfriend Rebecca and turned up at my apartment. Words about love, needing a woman, wanting her, and feeling protective of her. I knew nothing of love, didn't believe in it, never had, but the other stuff ... the needing, the wanting, wasn't that how I was with Stella now? I certainly needed her physically, and I was protective of her that was for sure, my little trampling session in Claridge's had proved that.

Fuck. Squirting some shampoo into my hand I began vigorously massaging it into my scalp with stiff fingers until my skin felt tender. How the hell had everything in my life suddenly got so bloody complicated? Before Stella had come along my life was simple; business was my focus, with sex merely as a nice distraction and always with no emotional ties. Scowling I rinsed my hair with equally as much force and ground my teeth together. Perhaps it was time to distance myself from Stella and try to get my life back to normal.

As I continued my shower I realised that as much as I disliked the thought of apologising I needed to do just that, not to Stella, but to my brother. I'd seen for myself what a wreck he'd been since splitting with Rebecca so maybe I *had* been wrong telling him to finish with her. He'd always been the more normal out of the two of us, so as crazy as it sounded to me, maybe he did love her.

Admitting I was wrong was never easy, but I made the decision to call Nicholas first thing in the morning, perhaps it wasn't too late for him to call Rebecca and try to make things right.

Chapter Five - Stella

I chewed on my lip until I tasted coppery blood in my mouth and then winced as I remembered how Nathan hated it when I did that. Releasing my lip I puffed out a heavy sigh and shook my head as I finally accepted what had happened to cause my nervous state – against all my better judgements, I had gone and fallen for Nathan. How bloody stupid was I to enter an intensely physical relationship with someone and believe that I could keep emotions out of it? I smacked myself across the forehead for being such a naïve loser and noticed several of my office colleagues look over at me with curious interest.

'There was a fly,' I lied feebly, but to be honest unless they were blind they must have noticed my changing moods recently and know that something was up with me. Not that any of them knew me well enough to really care. That's one of the perks of being the boss, I suppose, I could keep an aloof distance from my work mates and selectively choose the few who I got closer too without anyone really noticing.

To really top off my bad mood Nathan had called me yesterday and told me he had to work out of town this weekend so we wouldn't be seeing each other. He'd sounded genuine, but brusque enough that I couldn't help but wonder if his sudden cancellation had anything to do with my slip last weekend where I'd asked if I could call him Nathan instead of Sir. Letting out a groan I closed my eyes at my massive blunder – I was his contracted submissive, not his girlfriend, what the heck had I been thinking letting my post-orgasmic brain blab out something stupid like that?

As much as I might want to try and deny it, the fact remained that I liked him. I winced at my pathetic understatement. I more than liked him if I was being brutally honest with myself. And I wasn't just talking about the sex, although to be fair the sex was out-of-this-world good. But there was just something about him, some kind of weird connection I felt with him that I just couldn't seem to escape, although God knows why I felt this way, the man clearly had issues and what with his demanding personality and stroppy-ness he was hardly a prize catch, was he? Pursing my lips I sighed. Even with his oddities I would put him firmly in the 'prize catch' category. The glimpses I'd had of his softer side; his small smiles, occasional teasing, and boyish hopeful looks just made me instinctively grow more attached to him every time I was lucky enough to see one.

Crap. How did I let this happen? Nathan was a miserable bastard most of the time so what the hell was I doing developing feelings for him because of a few minutes of his 'nicer' side? Did I envisage that he would suddenly realise how amazing I was and change himself for me? Not really, I wasn't that deranged; he'd reached the age of thirty-one with this behaviour so he was hardly likely to change now, was he?

I whacked myself on the forehead again, and it made a rather loud slapping sound this time which drew even more raised eyebrows from the office outside, so with a growl I got up and slammed my door shut so I could berate myself in peace. What should I do? If I walked away from Nathan now and stopped our contract I'd miss him, I knew I would, but if I continued with it and fell deeper for him it would hurt all the more when he ended it, which let's face it, at some point, he would. He'd drop me faster than a hot rock as soon as he realised I had feelings for him.

One thing was now blindingly clear, Nathaniel Jackson,

with his no-relationship policy, is not the type of guy a woman should go falling for, this much I knew for sure. Fuck, I was totally buggered, whichever way I looked at it I was going to be the sorry faced loser in this situation. What a prize idiot I was for ever getting myself tangled up in something so frigging messy.

Chapter Six - Nathan

It had been two weeks since my apology phone call to Nicholas, suggesting he tried to patch things up with Rebecca, and in return I'd had to endure two weeks of constant calls from my brother telling me how deliriously happy he was now they were back together. Yes, it had shocked me too, but even after having a major breakdown which involved some heavy-handed use of a cane, somehow my lucky son-of-a-bitch brother had managed to persuade Rebecca to take him back.

To be honest, Nicholas's enthusiastic happiness was starting to grate on my nerves. I'd repeatedly told myself that my annoyance was because I didn't believe in 'love' or 'normal' relationships, but recently every time Stella popped into my head my reasoning seemed to get a bit blurry and my mood took a significant dive for the worse.

The pencil I'd been absently fiddling with snapped in two at this last thought, and as I stared down at the fragments of splintered wood in my hand I knew I had no-one to blame but myself for my recent stress, because it had now also been two weeks since I'd seen Stella. Usually her weekend visits helped reduce my stress levels, but after my mini meltdown where I'd convinced myself that I was getting too involved with her I'd called and cancelled last weekend together, feigning a business trip away.

I'd hoped that the time apart would cool things down between us, but it hadn't fucking worked at all, she was still on my mind constantly, except now I hadn't had the pleasure of her in my bed to go with it. *Fuck*. I threw the broken pencil towards the bin aggressively and let out an aggravated grunt when the pieces hit the wall and scattered onto the floor. What the hell was wrong with me? My virtual obsession with Stella was even distracting me from work, something that had never happened to me before. A woman come before my business? Ha, not likely – not until Stella, that was.

Standing abruptly from my desk to distract me from my confusing thoughts I ran my hand over my hair to smooth it and then glanced at my watch. It was Friday afternoon, but I probably had a few hours until Stella arrived so I toyed with the idea of going to visit Nicholas to see my lovesick brother in person.

It might be a disastrous idea, but perhaps actually witnessing what Nicholas had with Rebecca would either show me it was possible for damaged people like myself and my brother to love, or prove once and for all that the way I lived was infinitely better. For the sake of my crumbling sanity I hoped to God that it was the latter.

Just twenty short minutes later and I was at Nicholas's town house in Primrose Hill. I loved the unadulterated, modern qualities of my penthouse apartment, but I couldn't dismiss the beauty of his more traditional house either; with its bay windows and ivy-clad frontage it really was rather lovely. Perhaps in some way our choice of housing was a further reflection on our characters, I mused as I jogged up his front steps; me stark, stern, and impenetrable, and Nicholas more open, warmer, and normal. Perhaps that's why his relationship was working with Rebecca, even with his troubled past maybe I would always be the more broken brother.

Apparently seeing my arrival the front door swung open and I was rather glad of the distraction from my troubled thoughts. Mr Burrett, my brother's personal assistant, showed me straight up towards Nicholas's piano room with a polite nod.

After pushing the music room door open for me Mr Burrett scuttled off and I was left looking at the sight of my brother sat at his piano, grinning down at a woman cradled in his lip. Fucking hell, cradling her in his lap? Jesus, I'd never cradled a woman in my lap unless my dick was well and truly buried inside of her.

My eyes narrowed at the sight before me. 'Nicholas, am I interrupting? I can come back later.' I knew my voice sounded cool, but seriously, get a frigging room! Ignoring my brother's soppy expression I allowed my gaze to settle on the woman currently residing in his lap. She certainly was pretty, that was for sure, with long blonde hair, large bright eyes, and very delicate features. Yeah, OK, so I could see why Nicholas was attracted to her. Smirking I took in the flush on her cheeks, quite apparently I had been close to interrupting something more than just an innocent snuggle too.

Nicholas looked across and threw a wink my way, clearly he was feeling like a smug bastard today. But then seeing as he was the one with a beautiful woman nestled on his lap I suppose he had the right to be. Then my brother stood up, allowing the woman to slide down his body in a way that was really far too erotic for me to want to witness, but as she tried to step away I noticed how Nicholas wrapped an arm tightly around her waist and held her against his side protectively, something she obviously appreciated as she snuggled in closer to him.

Blowing out a breath between my teeth I tried to stabilise my emotions with a countdown from 5 to 0 in my head. Christ, it was peculiar to witness my brother like this – acting like a Goddamn regular boyfriend – unconsciously I found my head giving a minute shake of disbelief and I couldn't help but narrow my eyes as I continued to absorb the odd scene in front of me.

'Not at all, it's good to see you, Nathan.' My brother

glanced between myself and the woman gripped to his side before smiling broadly. 'Nathan, this is Rebecca,' Nicholas said proudly, trailing his hand down her arm to her apparent enjoyment, 'Rebecca, this is my brother Nathan.'

I watched in amusement as her throat bobbed and worked, apparently trying to swallow down a dose of nerves before she spoke. 'Hi. Nice to meet you, Nathan,' Rebecca mumbled in what I took to be a falsely bright tone. Knowing that Nicholas had now discussed the details of our shared childhood issues with Rebecca, I couldn't help but think from her tone that Rebecca either didn't like me very much, or was just plain scared of me, which was a possibility because my frosty demeanour had been known to shake even the most unmovable of souls in the past.

'Likewise,' was all I said in response. Let her stew for a bit, I was a cold mean bastard, no point changing the habit of a lifetime. Except recently I didn't seem to be quite as cold or mean as I used to be, I thought, as my eyes narrowed. This was one of the reasons I was here, even I could see that I was softening up recently, I just didn't really understand why.

An awkward silence hung in the air as I continued to look in fascination at my brother doing his 'Mr Normal' impression with the woman who had apparently changed his life so completely. Frowning I wondered just how they'd managed to work through their problems – using a cane on her without her consent must surely have left some unresolved issues – and yet here they were seemingly attached together like glue.

Suddenly my eyes were drawn to Rebecca as she stepped away from Nicholas's side, breaking the silence. 'I think I'll get a cup of tea, would either of you like a drink?' she asked in a seemingly cool tone. Still not my number one fan then.

'Coffee please, you know how I like it,' Nicholas said

with a peculiar smile that made me think it was a private innuendo of some kind. God, when had I ever seen Nicholas this light hearted and relaxed? Never, that's when.

The change in my brother was obvious even in just these few minutes, leading me to believe that this Rebecca was obviously important to Nicholas, so I decided to try and make a bit of an effort with my behaviour. 'Coffee for me too, black, no sugar.' I replied briskly with an attempt at a smile. I say 'attempt' at a smile, because in all seriousness it wasn't a facial expression I found the need for very often, unless I was on a charm offensive and hoping to get a woman into my bed of course. Although in reality my charm expression would probably be described as a smirk, not a smile, and usually resulted in women melting by my feet. Unfortunately, today my smile seemed to terrify Rebecca because she promptly fled from the room.

Once Rebecca had left I propped myself on the side of the large armchair and looked towards my brother curiously. 'You look happy, Nicholas,' I observed, keeping my tone as blank as possible. I didn't want Nicholas to know about the bizarre confusion I was experiencing of late. I was his older brother, his supposed role model, he might think less of me if I told him the myriad of emotions I was experiencing over Stella. Besides he had enough on his plate at the moment dealing with his own issues with Rebecca, he didn't need to be wading through my crap as well.

'I am. You have no idea how it feels to be accepted by Rebecca for who I am. She's amazing.' Nicholas shook his head in apparent disbelief at his luck. After his description of his 'freak out' with the cane I have to say I was also thinking him pretty damn lucky to have got her back too.

'Obviously the peace talks went well?' I enquired, still curious to know how they'd gotten over the cane issue.

'Yeah, eventually. The time I've been spending with that anger management councillor has really helped. Rebecca listened to all my crap about growing up with dad beating me and she was just awesome, Nathan, so fucking supportive of me. I seriously can't believe I'm so lucky. Thanks for persuading me to go and talk to her.' I nodded my response and watched as my brother tilted his head and observed me for a few silent seconds as if about to divulge some great secret, 'You really should try the vanilla thing, Nathan, it's great.'

His words almost mirrored my own recent curiosity, but vanilla – *normal* – and me? In response I merely grunted, my fucked up personality and a vanilla relationship hadn't ever seemed like a very possible combination for me. I had always lacked interest in the basic things needed to make a relationship like that work, like friendship, support and trust. I wouldn't tell Nicholas just yet, but lately even I was starting to question my beliefs on this particular topic.

Disliking the way the conversation had turned on me and churned up my internal confusion again I pushed off from the arm of the chair and walked over to clap my brother on the shoulder. 'I'm glad you're happy Nicholas, really I am, but it seemed that perhaps I made Rebecca a little nervous. I'm just going to pop to the kitchen and clear the air between us.'

Nodding his agreement Nicholas turned to sort through his piano music and I jogged down the stairs towards the kitchen. As I approached the door I saw Rebecca stretching up to reach for something on a high shelf in a cupboard. Even though she was my brother's girlfriend every male fibre in my body demanded that I pause briefly to observe the view. And what a view it was. With a smirk I crossed my arms and continued my perusal, I could definitely see why my brother was attracted to her; Rebecca was pretty and had a fine figure, although it was perhaps a little too petite for my taste. My mind suddenly flooded with images of Stella, her lush curves flushed and naked and needy. Now Stella, on the other hand, whilst still slim, also had those curves at her hips and waist that I just adored. A scowl pulled my brow together as I caught the wayward direction of my thoughts – Jesus, I was thinking about her again! I really was turning into a sap like my brother.

Getting a grip over my disobedient brain I gave a soft cough to make Rebecca aware of my presence as I stepped into the kitchen and stopped by the far counter. Whatever Rebecca had been reaching for flew from her hands as she gasped in shock and spun around to face me. Yep, she was definitely scared of me.

Glancing down I saw teabags scattered across the floor and couldn't stop a small smirk from tugging at my lips from her jumpiness.

'Hi, Rebecca,' I said calmly, hoping to soothe her. My eyebrows rose as I took in a small tremble in her hand. Interesting, perhaps she was more than a little scared of me, what the hell had my brother told her about me? I wasn't that bad, was I? But then I shifted on my feet, suddenly feeling uncomfortable as I realised he'd probably told her the truth – that I was a selfish, ignorant arsehole – a realisation that I was only really coming to grips with myself recently.

Dipping her head to hide her face from me Rebecca bent to collect the scattered teabags as I once again used one of my tried and tested countdowns to calm myself. 'Hi,' she replied in a particularly high tone.

'You have no reason to be nervous.' I offered in a generous attempt to calm her.

'I'm not nervous,' Rebecca replied snappily and this time I openly grinned at her stubborn response. Yes, I could definitely see why Nicholas liked this woman. Luckily she was still bent over the teabags so hadn't seen my smile, but how funny that both myself and my brother obviously liked women with a stubborn streak.

'That's good.' I murmured softly, still smiling. 'I merely wanted to apologise for the bad advice I gave Nicholas when I told him to leave you.'

Standing up with a handful of crushed teabags and a box that had now seen better days Rebecca looked genuinely shocked by my words. 'OK. Accepted,' she acknowledged with a shrug after a significant pause.

Observing the woman who had tamed my brother I could see what a good match they were and felt something a lot like jealousy shift inside of me. 'Clearly you are good for him,' I conceded with a nod.

Just then I became aware of my brother entering the doorway behind me. He was no doubt coming to check that I was behaving myself around his girlfriend. I smiled again at the thought of one of the Jackson brothers having a woman in his life who could be given the title of 'girlfriend', it was just positively surreal.

'Just checking you two are playing nicely,' Nicholas observed dryly before stepping into the kitchen and moving to stand at Rebecca's side protectively.

'We are, don't worry,' Rebecca assured Nicholas with a smile and I decided that perhaps my apology had gone some way towards making her like me a like bit more. Or should that be dislike me a little bit less, I wondered with a small snort.

I watched Nicholas's face soften as he gazed down at Rebecca and saw her relax against him and slip an arm around his waist. It was fascinating. How would it feel to be that protective of a woman? To be so attached to them that you needed to stake a claim over them in public?

It was a whole new concept for me, but suddenly I realised that it was almost exactly what I'd done to Stella when I'd seen her out in the wine bar with her brother. Trying to work out exactly what my seemingly possessive behaviour meant I decided to give it some more thought when I was back at home and alone. Christ, my brain felt like it had massively malfunctioned lately, nothing was clear to me anymore.

Keen to observe the new relationship between my brother and Rebecca some more I decided on the spur of the moment to invite them over. 'Perhaps you two would like to come for dinner at my place tomorrow for a proper catch up?' I suggested, 'How about supper time, say about seven o'clock?'

'Sounds good.' Nicholas agreed with a nod. I didn't miss the slightly panicked expression on Rebecca's face, but managed to contain the amused smile that nearly broke on my lips as a result of it. I'd win her over eventually – history had proven that women could never stay mad at me for long.

Chapter Seven - Nathan

After my visit to my brother yesterday I'd be lying if I said I wasn't left intrigued by his relationship with Rebecca – intrigued, and as much as I hated to admit it ... slightly jealous. This wasn't something I was used to, I didn't do standard displays of jealousy; if I wanted something I simply went out and got it. Fast car? I'd buy it. Business deal? I'd work every angle to ensure I put forward the best proposal to win the bid. Woman? I'd smile and charm my way into her panties quicker than a frog could hop.

But seeing what Nicholas had with Rebecca, a genuine real affection and need for one another, it had left me blindsided. I just hadn't expected to see him so ... happy. When I'd left his house yesterday it was the first time in my life that I'd felt genuine burning jealousy swirling in my stomach, and the reason for my jealousy was clear to me – I couldn't buy or charm Stella into feeling a bond like that with me, it had to be from her side, her heart, and the realisation that it was totally out of my control and potentially unavailable to me had hit me harder than I had ever expected.

So now here we were, it was Saturday night and my brother and Rebecca would be arriving at any minute for dinner. I had invited them over so that Stella and myself could observe their relationship and see if we might somehow, against all my previous beliefs, be able to do something similar. Fuck, the more I thought about it, the more I realised that this was quite a monumental moment for me, I, Nathaniel Jackson, dominant and all round self-absorbed dick, was actually considering a relationship outside the bounds of a dominant/submissive one … I quite literally never thought I'd see the day.

Not that I'd told Stella any of this, I'd just asked her to join us for dinner. No, I might be breaking all my rules on other fronts today, but I was still shit at any form of vocal emotion, conversations about relationships included. Looking in my bathroom mirror I straightened my collar, brushed my hair back with my hand, and loosened off my neck to try and ease my tension. Put me in a boardroom in front of twenty potential clients and I could talk the hind legs off a fucking donkey, but discuss the way I was 'feeling' … Christ, no. Far too prissy. It made me feel queasy just thinking about it. Not my thing at all.

Selecting a nice pair of solid platinum cufflinks I made quick work of fastening them through the soft cotton of my Armani shirt, and then made my way towards the lounge.

Something strange shifted in my stomach when I glanced towards the fireplace and saw Stella standing there awaiting my arrival. Sucking in a breath through my nose I absorbed her appearance. She looked beautiful, but then I suppose thinking about it she always did, had I really been such a self-absorbed arse before that I hadn't noticed enough to tell her?

Her dress tonight was a simple black number, just touching her knees and low enough in the front to give a good hint at what lay beneath. Not that I needed a hint; I had Stella's perfect body committed to memory now. The off the shoulder design gave me a complete view of my most favourite body part – the fragile column of her neck and the light spray of freckles that lay there, and I instantly wanted to walk over and run my tongue from her collarbone to her earlobe. To be honest if it wasn't my brother coming around tonight I'd be tempted to demand she change into something less revealing so that no-one else got to see what was mine.

90

I grimaced, but was she mine? That was the fucking million pound question wasn't it? I knew she wanted me, the heat that rose in her cheeks whenever she looked at me made that clear, as did her keenness to please and the explosive chemistry between us, there was no hiding that either, but did she *need* me? Growing up with a father who demanded no eye contact had left me severely deprived in the ability to judge emotions relating to trust and care, so I really didn't have a fucking clue how Stella actually felt about me outside of the bedroom.

The problem was, I was starting to fear that I *needed* her. I had no fucking idea how it had happened, but during the two week gap where I hadn't seen Stella I'd pretty much figured out that as well as wanting her physically, which I did almost constantly, that I had most definitely started to need Stella too. I needed her to keep me stable when work was shit, needed her to flash me those shy smiles reserved only for me, but most of all, I needed her to keep on making me feel like I might actually have a chance of being somewhere near normal for a change.

Glancing across at her now it occurred to me that Stella was probably feeling pretty confused right now, not only had I all but demanded that she join us for dinner tonight, but I'd not given her any further guidance at all. Grimacing I shook my head at yet another failure on my part. God, I was such a prick. If I had any hope of making something more of my relationship with Stella I needed to get my hopeless arse in gear and start thinking about her feelings for a change.

Stella

As it often did, my breath caught in my throat when Nathan entered the room. It was like his unfair handsomeness somehow sucked my breathable air away and left me floundering like a fish out of water, an effect that thankfully he seemed to be completely unaware of. His ego was no doubt big enough already, he didn't need me and my pathetic swoons adding to it.

Tonight Nathan had gone for his smart-casual look, which meant navy suit trousers and a pale blue shirt but no jacket or tie. That was just fine by me; his tailored shirts looked glorious without any other trimmings, and showed off the tautness of his shoulder and chest muscles to absolute perfection.

I loved the shirt he was wearing too, it was secretly one of my favourites, in a pale blue almost the exact same shade as his eyes; it made his blond hair seem to glow and his striking gaze even more intense than usual. In fact I'd had many a fantasy about that particular shirt, mostly featuring me wearing it, and nothing else, whilst he made love to me for hours on end. Giving myself a mental thwack on the forehead I rolled my eyes, who was I kidding? We didn't make love, we *fucked*, and if I wore anything during that process it would be at Nathan's request and would usually involve lace suspenders or high heels, and certainly not his shirt. Sighing, I glanced at him again; it might only be a fantasy, but it was still a nice one to have.

Great, I was drooling already and our guests hadn't even arrived yet.

A frown settled on my brows. *Guests*. Christ, I was nervous. Nathan had invited his brother and his girlfriend, Rebecca I think, around for dinner tonight and he had requested – demanded – that I join them. This was a first for us. Nathan had had dinner guests before, all business-related, but he'd always told me I could have the night off or make use of the gym or home cinema to keep myself busy. I wasn't entirely sure what to expect tonight, or why he wanted me there, and Nathan hadn't really given me any indication of how he expected me to act either. Hence my fully-fledged nerves.

Just as I was plucking up the courage to ask Nathan what I should expect from the evening the doorbell rang. My eyes closed in frustration. Great. I was out of time now and would officially have to wing it. From our brief introduction the other week I knew Nicholas was aware of the type of relationship I had with Nathan, and from the snippets of conversation I had heard from his brother's visit I also suspected Nicholas might be involved in the domination scene himself, but would his girlfriend be a sub too? Making my way towards the sofas I exhaled a long, calming breath. Sod it, I'd just keep quiet and see how things panned out, go with the flow so to speak.

Just a few seconds later Nathan returned with his guests. As Nathan hadn't told me otherwise I remained standing and kept my eyes mostly averted, but on one of my quick, curious glances I noticed that Nathan's brother looked a whole hell of a lot better than he had when I'd last seen him. Crikey, he was actually very handsome; in fact, back in the day before I'd developed a thing for blonds, specifically those called Nathan, Nicholas would have been exactly my usual type; tall, dark, broad, and handsome as sin. It was funny how a few months could make such a difference to my outlook, before Nathan I'd never even dated a blond, now I couldn't imagine why.

My reverie was broken by Nathan who appeared by my

side and did the introductions. 'Rebecca, this is Stella,' Nathan said smoothly, indicating between the two of us with a swift hand gesture and thankfully sticking to my name and not referring to me as just his sub.

Glancing up briefly I saw that Rebecca was taller and probably skinnier than me, if I'm being honest, and rather pretty in a girl-next-door kind of way. Nicholas nodded to me in greeting and I flashed a small smile, but it died on my lips as I then watched him give Nathan the oddest of looks. What had that been about? It was almost as if he'd asked *'What's Stella doing here?'* and to be honest I was now wondering the same damn thing.

After handing Nathan a bottle of wine Nicholas and Rebecca moved further into the room and took a seat on the black leather two-seater next to the fireplace. Nathan sat opposite on the white couch, but after Nicholas's strange look I was frozen to the spot, my stomach lurching and I felt off-balance and flummoxed as what to do next. It wasn't like Nathan ever made me sit on the floor by his feet or anything, but we never exactly sat on the sofa and had a cosy chat together either. In fact, come to think of it, the only times I'd ever been on this sofa was when Nathan was in a sexual frenzy and screwing me until I screamed his name.

Great, so now as well as standing here like a complete loser I was also bright red from thinking about our amazing sofa sex sessions. God, I wished I could escape to my room and the stack of good books I'd selected from Nathan's reading room earlier. What I wouldn't give for a bit of quiet time and Jane Austen right now.

Staring at my entwined fingers was getting quite boring so I flashed a quick glance at Rebecca again. She was sat close to Nicholas, their thighs touching intimately, looking like a regular girlfriend, so perhaps she wasn't a sub then – or if she was she was a lot more used to social gatherings than me. All of a sudden she gasped quietly and her head flicked up to look at me with wide eyes that showed a sudden and complete understanding of the situation. Somehow from that one shared look I suspected that Rebecca now understood the dynamics of my relationship with Nathan. Not only that, but from the look on her face – like she had swallowed some week-old fish – she didn't agree with it either.

This really was rather unfair, between them Nathan and Nicholas could have had the decency to let Rebecca and I in on the whole story before we all got together, at least then I wouldn't be standing here feeling like a complete prat and she wouldn't be looking like she wanted to vomit all over Nathan's expensive rug. The only small saving grace was that at least we were both feeling uncomfortable, I suppose.

My awkward stance was broken as I heard Nathan speak to the right of me. 'Sit' he ordered softly, patting the seat next to him and looking up at me with a hint of a smile pulling at the corner of his mouth. My attention was firmly distracted from Rebecca as I tilted my head curiously at Nathan's request. This was certainly different, but then this whole evening was feeling fairly experimental so I might as well just run with it. Sitting down I perched myself on the front of the soft leather sofa and once again joined my hands in my lap and averted my eyes. Well, if nothing else came of this evening I was at least going to demand a reward from Nathan later for my exemplary submissive behaviour.

Taking me completely by surprise I felt Nathan's hand rub my shoulder before gently pulling me back so that I was leant against the cushions of the sofa with his arm lightly draped around my shoulders. *Crikey,* I gasped in surprise and then only just managed to hold back a small giggle – I felt like I was a teenager on a first date where the guy pretends to yawn just as an excuse to put his arm around a girl's shoulders. Not that that had actually ever happened to me, but as a girl I'd been reliably informed by the playground gossips that it had been common practice amongst most teenage boys in my school.

'Eye contact is permitted,' Nathan whispered in my ear, his breath hot on my sensitive skin, making me want to lean into him. But hang on, eye contact was permitted? That was *incredibly* uncharacteristic for Nathan and I immediately raised my eyes to his and found him gazing straight back at me with his big blues. A sigh slipped past my lips at just how stunningly blue his irises were. Like a clear sky on a beautiful summer day. I suddenly felt a little breathless. Full-on eye contact. Crikey, this really was new. Nathan never liked eye contact, not with me, and from the little I'd experienced of him outside his apartment, not with anyone else either. I had no idea why, because his eyes were just stunning, but clearly there was a reason, he'd even hinted as much himself.

After the best few seconds of my life though, Nathan flashed the briefest of winks and then looked away again, loosening his shoulders with a roll as if the extended contact had be immensely difficult for him somehow. Perhaps he had meant that my eye contact was permitted with our guests, and not him.

Did he really just wink at me? Mr Cool As Ice Bad Boy Jackson, *winking*? Wow, another first. I should probably be making a list of these so I didn't forget the momentous occasions. Blinking several times I tried to clear my head and refocus on the evening ahead of us, after all, we had guests sat opposite us and I was totally ignoring them and instead practically swooning over Nathan. Normally at parties I was quite a chatterbox, the centre of attention probably, especially after a few glasses of wine, but tonight in these unfamiliar circumstances I was more than happy to sit back and observe.

'So how was the traffic on your drive over today?' Nathan asked his brother with a smile. The casual chatter started easily and I felt myself relax slightly into my unusual situation of sitting with Nathan's arm around me. Whether it was a conscious action or not I don't know, but his fingers were gently rubbing circles on my exposed shoulder and as my skin heated from his attention I decided that, actually, I quite liked this position. Trying to strengthen my resolve I took a deep breath. I better not get too used to it, no doubt once his brother had left we'd be back to business as usual.

Rebecca seemed nice, she was quiet like me for the most part, but every now and then I would catch her flashing Nathan and I odd glances as she obviously tried to work out what was going on between us. Out of the corner of my eye I noticed that Nathan was also watching Rebecca very carefully, and for a few seconds I felt the stirrings of an ugly green-eyed monster rise within me, but the more I looked, the more it appeared that he was looking at them as a whole, a couple, rather than at Rebecca herself. Perhaps Nicholas's relationship with this woman was quite new and Nathan was sussing it out to decide if he deemed her good enough for his precious brother.

Nathan and I might not sit and converse regularly in our weekends together, but in the times we had talked, Nathan's love and protectiveness for his brother had been quite apparent and I suspected that if he saw Rebecca as unsuitable in any way, then Nathan would be quite forthright in telling Nicholas so, and probably Rebecca too.

My throat tightened briefly as I tried to imagine what it would be like if Nathan felt that protective of me. I suspected given my growing attachment to him that I'd quite like it. He'd had his little freak-out in Claridges a few weeks ago, but I didn't really count that as being protective of me, it had more likely been a display of his possessiveness, marking his territory, and claiming what was his, perhaps. With a small sigh I quickly dismissed the stupidly fantastical thought of Nathan ever truly 'caring' about me and looked back at Rebecca just in time to see her turn rather pale.

Something had obviously upset Rebecca, her face was now white as a sheet, although seeing as we hadn't eaten or drunk anything yet to upset her stomach I couldn't think what might be the cause.

Suddenly stumbling to her feet Rebecca looked distinctly like she might pass out, or throw up, or perhaps both. 'Can I use your bathroom, please?' Rebecca asked urgently. Gosh, poor thing she looked dreadful. Perhaps she'd eaten something bad at lunch? But then seeing the brief flicker of her gaze as it moved between myself and Nathan and narrowed I realised the cause of her discomfort could well be us.

'Of course. Stella, show Rebecca the bathroom please, and bring back some drinks for us all afterwards,' Nathan instructed me.

Standing up quickly in case Rebecca vomited like she looked like she might at any second, I led her to the guest toilet and was about to say a few words to help relax her, I don't know exactly what, something like *'Yeah I'm his submissive, but it's what I chose and he's amazing in the sack so it's all good ...'* but as it turned out I didn't get the chance because after flashing me a quick watery smile and a mumbled 'thanks' Rebecca practically leapt into the bathroom and slammed the door behind her.

Poor woman. What I had with Nathan wasn't exactly your usual run of the mill relationship so I could see why it would make her uncomfortable. I was sure that if she just knew the facts she would no doubt feel much better about things, but I didn't feel I knew her well enough to interrupt her in the bathroom, so reluctantly, I made my way back to the lounge. As I arrived at the sofas again I frowned. Nathan was still reclining casually, but Nicholas now looked on edge and nervy, sat forwards on his seat and chewing on the inside of his lip in a look I knew oh so well from his brother. Barely ten seconds later, Nicholas stood up and without saying a word strode in the direction of the bathroom, presumably to check on Rebecca.

Blimey, it seemed that both the Jackson brothers came with drama in their lives. What a family. Rolling my eyes I headed to the kitchen and popped open a bottle of chilled white wine from the fridge which would act as a perfect palate cleanser before our dinner. Then pouring four glasses I carried them back into the lounge and retook my seat beside Nathan who was staring out across the darkening London skyline, seemingly lost in his own thoughts.

Once again his arm snaked out and slipped around my shoulders, and once again I found the move incredibly amusing, but also rather endearing. He didn't say anything, but to be honest, given Nathan's lack of skills in casual conversation it was probably just as well as it may have spoilt what was a lovely moment for me. Instead I enjoyed the silence and lost myself in my girlish fantasies and simply enjoyed him being just a teeny-weeny bit romantic for a change.

'Are you unwell, Rebecca?' Nathan asked directly as Nicholas and Rebecca re-emerged into the living room a few minutes later. It was probably just as well they had come back when they did, because the way Nathan had been casually running his fingers from my shoulder to collar bone in a teasing trail had had me melting and desperate for him to throw me down and take me, regardless of how socially inappropriate that might have been with a house full of guests.

'I was a little dizzy,' Rebecca murmured in what sounded to my highly tuned girl's ears as an out and out lie. 'But I feel much better now, I'm probably just hungry,' she concluded with a smile aimed at me which was a little more convincing. Perhaps Nicholas had worked some Jackson magic on her in the bathroom, I thought with a smirk, knowing that sexy time with Nathan certainly always left me feeling more relaxed.

'Well it's just as well dinner is served then,' Nathan replied giving my shoulder a quick appreciative squeeze and making me smile shyly. 'Stella's been working very hard to prepare us a nice dinner,' he added as we all made our way to the dining table and the floor to ceiling windows with my favourite view over London and the River Thames.

I wasn't going to admit it to Nathan, but I'd had a bit of help with dinner. Actually quite a lot of help ... when he'd headed into the gym this afternoon I'd known he'd be busy working out for at least two hours and I'd snuck Kenny in to help me prepare the food. I can cook, but I'm talking spag bol or chilli con-carne, not dinner party stuff meant to impress. Kenny on the other hand is a like a non-cook's dream – he doesn't even need recipe books to prepare the most amazingly tasty dishes. After he arrived and I'd picked his tongue up from the floor – he was rather impressed with Nathan's apartment – Kenny had dumped down three carrier bags of shopping and with me as his sous chef had whipped up a beef Wellington, creamy mashed potatoes, broccoli, and deliciously rich gravy before whizzing from the apartment making me promise to give him a full tour next time. All I'd really had to do tonight was keep an eye on the beef whilst it cooked and steam the vegetables just before serving. All that was done now and I had to say it really smelt superb. I owed Kenny big time.

Once the table was laden with enough food for a small army my awkwardness suddenly returned again. What should I do? Serve everyone? Serve Nathan? Just sit down and stuff my face? I really had no idea. When Nathan and I ate together at his apartment I always served him first, then myself, but it wasn't a submissive thing as such, it just made sense because he usually cooked and started a quick clear-up whilst I served, then we would sit and eat together.

Thankfully it seemed that Nicholas was better at reading people's emotions than Nathan because he suddenly piped up to help me out, 'Shall we all just dig in?' he enquired, flashing me a smile, apparently well aware that I was stuck about what to do next. It hit me again how handsome he was, not only that, but how easy he was with eye-contact, the complete opposite of Nathan. How strange that they grew up together and yet had such different habits. Once again I wondered why Nathan averted his eyes, but sadly I guessed it was one of many stories I would never find out.

'Excellent plan, brother,' Nathan agreed, but I still decided to play it safe and allow everyone else to serve themselves before I took any. Blimey, Kenny had excelled himself, even the cooking temperatures and times he'd given me were spot on because the beef looked amazing, pink on the inside with the pastry a delicious golden brown around the edges. I definitely owed him a drink or two in way of thanks.

As amazing as the food looked my stomach just wasn't feeling in the mood to eat – it was probably the build-up of stress from today, plus the fear in the back of my mind that after cancelling a weekend together Nathan was going to finish with me soon. He was just so unpredictable that I never knew where I stood with him. No sooner had this unsavoury thought crossed my mind however, Nathan leant in close to my ear and surprised me by placing a hand on my thigh and rubbing it soothingly. 'You are doing very well, Stella.' he murmured, his breath tickling against my neck and almost making me groan with pleasure. As simple as his words were they flushed away my doubt and made me relax almost instantly. 'Also, I didn't get a chance to say it earlier, but you look very beautiful tonight.' A small gasp of pleasure slipped from my lips, probably betraying just how much his words meant to me, but I risked a glance at him and instead of his usual averted gaze I was rewarded with a full contact blue-eyed gaze for a second or two that sent heat rushing to my cheeks and made me smile shyly up at him.

I felt a bit like I was living in some alternative universe, normally our weekends were spent alone, mostly in silence or in the bedroom getting down and dirty, but tonight Nathan was like a different man. Yeah OK so he still wasn't Mr Conversational with me, but the glances, the smiles, the *winks*, I was feeling quite spoilt for attention, and I was loving every single minute of it.

Conversation at dinner mostly focused around Nathan and Nicholas as they discussed recent business news and indulged in some chat about their shared love of fast cars and Nicholas's recent purchase of a new Aston Martin DB9. I'd never heard of the model, but I knew Aston Martins cost a pretty penny, so I assumed Nicholas's piano career was doing rather well. Rebecca was chatty enough, but the way her eyes kept flicking between Nathan and I indicated to me that perhaps she still wasn't sure if she liked our set-up. In fact the glares she was sending Nathan were positively deathly, as if maybe she thought he was forcing me to be with him. Initially her blatant hostility toward him coupled with Nathan's complete obliviousness to it made me want to giggle, but as the meal went on I found myself wanting to defend him, though perhaps that was something not to be tackled at the table.

After we finished eating I got the perfect opportunity to do just that. I began clearing away the bowls, something that Nathan usually did, but he was so absorbed in a talk about the latest Grand Prix – I'd literally never seen him so animated on a subject – that he didn't notice me stand, but instead Rebecca stood to assist me. 'Let me help you clear the dishes, Stella,' she offered, collecting some bits and pieces off the table and following me. Now was my chance to talk to her whilst we were away from the brothers.

Dropping my sweet, silent submissive pose I flashed Rebecca a broader smile and caught hold of her arm as she passed me at the sink. 'I can see your shock, Rebecca. I can tell you don't approve of Nathan and me, but it's not like you think. I want to be with him. Actually, I chose this lifestyle by myself; you might not believe it but I sought him out and I like living this way,' I explained plainly, deciding to keep it short and sweet so we weren't interrupted.

I watched as Rebecca's eyes widened in shock, probably at how easily I'd read her mind, and then saw a flush of embarrassment colour her cheeks. My work here was done. She believed me, and would hopefully be able to relax and enjoy her evening knowing that I was also happy. More than happy actually, given Nathan's uncharacteristic affection tonight I practically felt like I was floating on cloud nine at the moment. Rebecca opened her mouth to speak and I realised she was probably about to blurt a million questions at me, not something I wanted to do within earshot of Nathan, so I gave her arm a friendly squeeze, fired one more of my trademark winning smiles at her, and then disappeared back toward the table.

Perhaps if things continued with Nathan, then Rebecca and I would get more opportunities to spend time together and we could talk about things more fully. It would be nice to have a female to talk to about it all – Kenny was a great listener, but he was just as kinky as Nathan, if not more so, so he was hardly a voice of reason or clarity when I needed one.

Since my brief talk with Rebecca the rest of the meal passed in a much calmer mood. Rebecca had appeared more relaxed, which in turn had seemed to soothe Nicholas. It was quite sweet how in love they obviously were, but deep inside I couldn't help but feel a trace of jealousy. It would never be like that for Nathan and me, no matter how much I might wish it, I was his submissive, he was my dominant and we had a written contract that stated that very clearly.

Ignoring my niggling longing for more with Nathan I decided that, actually, the evening had gone far better than I'd expected. I'd felt almost showered in attention from Nathan, but my bright outlook was dashed as we closed the door after seeing Nicholas and Rebecca off as an awkward silence immediately fell between us. I wanted to say something, or do something to ease it, but I was worried that I might have been reading too much into his little gestures tonight and might overstep the mark now if I spoke by gushing something far too emotional and telling.

Nathan's mouth opened as if he were going to speak, but then it snapped shut a second later and I watched as light-hearted Nathan closed up to be replaced by the shuttered man that I was used to. A sigh slipped from my lips as I visibly saw him change in front of my eyes. My messed-up mercurial man. So tonight had all been a show to impress his brother then? Some kind of sick one-upmanship? The idea made me feel excessively depressed, not to mention used.

Closing my eyes briefly I opened them again to find Nathan staring at the floor. 'I need to check my emails, it's late, you're probably tired, so why don't you go to bed and I'll see you in the morning.' Pursing my lips I held in the desperate words that were perched on the tip of my tongue. So now in addition to the return of his bad mood he was dismissing me without any kind of sexual stuff. Nathan never, ever went to bed without something sexy happening first so this wasn't a good sign at all.

Hiding just how crushed I felt I glumly made my way to my bedroom and miserably brushed my teeth whilst feeling ridiculously disappointed at how the evening had ended. Pulling off my dress I threw it on a chair before flopping on the bed and removing my high heels and flexing out my toes. The only positive was that I was tired enough from cooking and the stress of hosting that I began to fall asleep almost as soon as my head touched the pillow, which would at least stop me dreaming nightmares about Nathan leaving me or throwing me out again.

I wasn't entirely sure what had woken me, but I was suddenly sitting up in bed rubbing sleep from my eyes and frowning as I wondered what had pulled me from sleep and caused me to leap upright. My room was lit only by the pale light of the moon seeping through the curtains and casting eerie shadows on my furniture, so fumbling for my bedside lamp I clicked it on and looked around through sleep blurred eyes. All was normal, nothing had fallen down and disturbed me. How odd, perhaps it had been …

'Nooooo! Don't touch him!' A savage cry rang out from somewhere in the apartment and interrupted my thoughts making me yelp in surprise. Clutching at my chest my heart rate accelerated rapidly and goose pimples flooded my skin. Bloody hell, that shout had been loud and anguished, *and Nathan.*

Jumping from my bed I didn't stop for a robe or slippers, I just ran from my room barefoot and clad only in my sleep shirt headed straight down the corridor to where I knew Nathan's room was. I'd never been inside before; he'd explained his need for extreme privacy at the start of our agreement and I'd adhered to it … up until now. But if he was in trouble I had to help, *I just had to*, so when I reached his door and heard another muffled yell from inside I didn't hesitate and I flung the door open immediately stumbling to a halt in the complete darkness of his room.

Jeez, he must have some serious blackout blinds in here because I couldn't see a frigging thing. Behind me the

106

swinging door bounced off the wall and closed with a loud click cancelling out the pale light from the hallway completely immersing me in inky blackness. Extending my hands I felt around blindly, hoping to find a wall or a light switch. My heart was hammering so hard in my veins I thought one might burst from the pressure, but then, over the course of the next few seconds my pulse spiked even further, as events unfolded quicker than I could properly follow; first I heard muffled movement from somewhere in the room, then without any warning I was being gripped around the neck and forcefully pushed backwards until I hit the wall painfully hard. 'No, Father!'

What the hell? My head throbbed from where it had connected with the wall and my breathing was laboured from both the hands around my neck, and the winded sensation in my lungs. God I wish I could see so I knew what the hell was going on.

'No ... don't touch him ... beat me, not him!' It was Nathan's voice, somewhere close to my face, close enough that flecks of his saliva hit my cheeks as he shouted and his hot breath fanned across my lips. His voice sent an immense shiver through me, it was more gravelly and tortured than I'd ever heard it and I suddenly suspected that he was somehow still asleep. 'Please ...' a sob escaped his throat, '... not Nicholas ...'

Nathan's grip on my neck was so tight by this point that a strangled choking sound escaped my throat as white specks of light started to spin in front of my eyes as I struggled to stay conscious. Flailing wildly as I desperately tried to pull in air I just about managed to kick out with my legs and make contact with his shins, which abruptly eased his hold on my neck and brought a string of expletives flowing from Nathan's mouth as he seemed to finally wake up. *Thank God.*

'Ow, fuck! What the bloody hell?' One hand left my throat and there was more fumbled noise in the dark shortly before soft lighting came on all around us. Blinking several times in the light I wheezed and sputtered as I sucked in much needed oxygen to my system before looking up to find Nathan, naked as the day he was born and staring down at me with his mouth hanging open in total horror.

'Holy shit … Stella?' Rubbing a hand across his eyes as if clearing them, Nathan then stared at me again, his eyes cloudy with confusion. 'Stella! Fuck! I'm so fucking sorry … I was dreaming and I thought you were my father coming into my room again and I …' Nathan's teeth actually cracked together as he brought himself up short, obviously deciding that he'd already said too much.

Tension radiated from every muscle in Nathan's body and as he suddenly dropped his gaze to the floor I watched his chest heaving as he tried to control himself. As I clung to the wall and continued to stare at him an awful realisation dawned on me, just his few words about his father, combined with the chilling ones he'd uttered when asleep, *'Don't touch him … beat me, not him'*, were enough for me to get a pretty good idea of what he must have gone through as a child. Some kind of punishment or abuse from his father given to both him and his brother, from the sound of it.

Bloody hell, if my guess was correct it would certainly explain a thing or two about Nathan's domineering ways. Maybe he was taking control now because he'd never been able to when he was younger, perhaps it even explained his need for giving out some mild punishments of his own every now and then. It also explained just why he was so protective of his younger brother too. *Fuck.* I could hardly take it all in. This day just got crazier and crazier.

Now the lights were on and Nathan seemed marginally recovered from his nightmare I was fully expecting him to send me away back to my room, but instead he chewed furiously on his lower lip as he raised his wide eyes to my throat and gently ran his fingers around my neck checking for damage. He looked utterly broken. 'I'm OK,' I whispered softly, instinctively knowing he needed my reassurance at that moment. Flattening my palms on the coolness of the wall to hold back from the temptation of reaching out to soothe him, I instead risked a small question. 'Are you?'

His expression was tortured, eyes so filled with sadness and half-hidden by a frown, as his hand continued to rub my neck with feather light touches, but he remained silent. I could almost hear the cogs of his mind spinning as his thoughts seemed to run wild. He didn't answer me directly, but he didn't send me away as I'd expected either, instead he finally sighed, lowered his hand, and then made quite a random request seeing as it was the middle of the night. 'I need a shower, come with me.' It was said as a demand, but somehow it almost seemed like Nathan was pleading with me to go with him. Like he *needed* me.

'OK.' I accepted his outstretched hand without hesitation and allowed him to lead me to a frigging unbelievably huge bathroom – Kenny would die if he saw this place; twin sinks, Jacuzzi tub, and a walk-in shower big enough to hold at least six – where Nathan started the water and after pulling off my T-shirt he promptly dragged me under as soon as it had warmed.

'I want to bathe you,' Nathan murmured, then picking up a sponge and shower gel he began to soap me all over my body. It wasn't in any way a sexual act, he just seemed to need the task to focus his mind away from whatever horrible dream had been trapped in there a minute ago, but it was lovely to feel so close to him for a change without it being about sex.

Tilting my neck to give him better access to the skin below my ear I noted that I now had the answer to a question I'd been wondering for a while; the scent of his that I always craved wasn't an aftershave, it was this shower gel. It was masculine and musky and Nathan, and I rather liked knowing that I would smell like him for a while after this.

Nathan dropped to a crouch and began lathering my legs, he was so incredibly thorough with his washing that I was left quite amazed. 'You are very hygienic,' I whispered softly as an observation, thinking of how he always scrubbed his hands too, but at my words Nathan halted in his washing of my knee and looked up at me with an expression of utter torture on his face. *Crap*, what the hell had I said wrong now?

Standing up stiffly Nathan pushed his wet hair off his face, paused for a second and then turned silently to exit the shower, but reacting to his anxiousness I placed a gentle hand on his forearm and stopped him. 'It's OK, I don't mind. Cleanliness is good.' I joked lightly. 'I'm sorry if I've upset you.' I added softly, cursing myself, this was twice tonight that I'd done something that had made Nathan look like he had seen a terrifying ghost of some sort, but I had no idea what to do about it or how to make it better.

Closing his eyes Nathan clutched at the wall with a fisted hand and shook his head, apparently struggling with whatever it was that he was seeing behind those beautiful lids of his. After an age of watching him visibly tense and tremble he finally turned to me, his eyes lowered to the tiles, 'It's not you,' he murmured, 'but you're right, I am obsessive about being clean.' He paused, drawing in a huge deep breath, looking like he wanted to say something further and I held my own breath in anticipation, desperately trying to hold myself back from prying.

'Being with my brother tonight brought back a lot of memories for me …' he paused and swallowed loudly, running his free hand across the stubble on his chin, but I didn't even dare breathe, he was about to open up to me and I didn't want to do anything to spoil it. 'My dad used to be really strict with me and Nicholas when we were kids, he'd come to our rooms and ... and beat us regularly, but you probably guessed that from what I said in the bedroom.' he paused and a look of torture flashed on his features as he shook his head repeatedly, 'There were so many rules: no friends, no eye contact, and always the punishments ...' He heaved in a huge breath and squeezed his free hand into a tight fist by his side, 'When you came in tonight I heard the door close and because I'd been dreaming about Nicholas I immediately thought you were dad coming to my room like he used to ...'

His gaze briefly flicked to my bruised neck and then my eyes and his regret was so obvious, if unspoken. 'I didn't mind it so much, I think it was Father's way of shaping me into a tougher person, but Nicholas couldn't cope like me.' Nathan ran a hand though his hair again, pushing it back from his face so it curled around his ears before rubbing furiously at the back of his neck. His next words were spoken in a rush as if he desperately needed to expel them all at one, 'It went on for years, but one day my brother tried to commit suicide to escape the beatings ... I was the one to find him.' Nathan dropped this shocking line in a voice that was so gravelly and thick that I barely recognised him, then paused staring into space, his face completely blank and lifeless.

Blimey, I had completely abandoned the no eye contact rule now and was openly staring at him, not that it helped because his eyes suddenly squeezed tightly shut. 'Nicholas had slashed his wrist with some scissors. I carried him to the car and drove him to the hospital.' Nathan choked slightly and coughed, but I suspected he was desperately trying to hold back tears, 'I was covered in blood. Nicholas's blood.' Shaking his head I watched as Nathan started to tremble and goose pimples sprung up on his skin so I gently took his hand and guided him back under the warm water of the shower, adjusting the taps to make the water ever hotter.

'When I was finally finished with the police and doctors that night I went for a shower but his blood had dried and it took so long to clean it from my body. *So fucking long*,' he sighed and clenched his fists tightly at his sides until the knuckles went white, 'I kept finding traces of it under my nails and on my skin for days ...' He stopped speaking suddenly, his lips closing and turning white as he rolled them into a thin, tight line between his teeth. Somehow I just knew that Nathan wasn't going to say any more, not tonight anyway, but I was completely at a loss for what to do. I mean what do you say when someone drops a bombshell like that on you? It sounded like his feelings towards his father were complex to say the least, but just this one conversation totally explained his obsession with averted eyes, cleanliness, and discipline, not to mention his protectiveness of his brother. Talk about an enlightening couple of minutes.

Looking back at Nathan I saw he was completely lost now, shutting down and gazing sightlessly at the floor whilst rubbing his hands together as if trying to clean them. He was a shell of the Nathan I knew, and it was obvious that he was hurting deeply, but I didn't know what to do to bring him back to me. I thought about how Nathan always said that actions spoke louder than words to him, and I suddenly knew what to do.

Picking up the sponge that he had used on me just minutes earlier I squirted some soap on it and began to wash him thoroughly all over his body just as he had me, careful not to miss any centimetre of his beautiful skin. Hopefully this was what he needed tonight, to feel clean and not tarred with thoughts of his brothers blood on his skin.

Normally something as intimate as this would have had me panting like a dog in heat, but he was so despondent that all I could think about was trying to soothe my poor, distraught man as he just stood there completely vulnerable, staring at the ground and letting me have my way.

I cleaned every single scrap of skin that I could; around his knees, the arch of his foot, behind his ears, you name it, I cleaned it, although I deliberately avoided his groin – I didn't want him to think I was trying to tastelessly initiate something sexual. Next I shampooed his hair and thoroughly rinsed it, him tilting his head back on my soft commands but otherwise remaining still, and then when I was done with his body I gently applied pressure on his shoulders and eased us both down onto the floor of the shower. With the water still pouring around us like warm rain I reached up for the soap and nail brush and shuffled myself closer to him so that I was sat directly in front of him with my legs crossed. Talk about a peep show – I was completely naked and openly exposed to him, but I disregarded any embarrassment I might have felt, he needed me right now. Besides, it wasn't like he hadn't seen it all before anyway.

Reaching forwards I placed my hands over his and he stopped with the washing gestures and clenched them into fists instead. I could have taken this as a sign to leave him alone, but luckily I'm pig headed so I persevered and took one of his hands in mine. Patiently I began unclenching each finger one by one then I gently and thoroughly washed each digit, careful to use the brush and clean under his nails too, and then repeated the same treatment to his other hand before acting on impulse and clambering a little awkwardly into his lap. Given how wet and slippery we both were this was actually a lot harder than I first anticipated, especially seeing as Nathan was still sat silent and frozen in place like a statue.

Once I was in place and comfy enough I leant my cheek down onto his shoulder and placed one hand on his chest in what I hoped was a reassuring gesture. We didn't generally do anything 'snuggly' together, so I really wasn't sure how this would pan out, he would probably freak out and ask me to leave, but to my surprise after a second or two Nathan's arms came up around me and pulled me against his body, cradling me to his chest and even briefly nuzzling his face into my hair.

I was pruning up from being in the shower so long, and I could see from where Nathan's hands were settled on my arms that he was too, but this was too important a moment to break just because I was looking a bit wrinkly. As if reading my mind though, Nathan briefly leant his head into the top of mine and then began to stand. Did he kiss the top of my head just then? It certainly felt like it, but that would be a very un-Nathan-like gesture, mind you, everything I'd seen about him in the last hour was unusual, he was open and defenceless and in need of me, whereas usually his stark, firm exterior gave the impression that he didn't need anyone, let alone a woman.

Joining my arms around his neck I let Nathan carry me from the shower and place me on the counter between the twin sinks. I glanced at each and both were immaculate and I briefly wondered if he had a favourite or just used which ever took his fancy each night. Without saying a word Nathan turned and scooped two large, fluffy towels from a rack behind him and then began to thoroughly rub me dry before doing the same to himself and then hanging the towels back up.

Once again in silence he turned to me, his hair a dishevelled mess that no doubt matched mine, and then after offering me a small, shy smile Nathan wordlessly scooped me into his arms for the second time in five minutes and carried me to back through his bedroom. With my arms around his neck and my face leant against Nathan's strong, warm chest I decided that I could quickly learn to love this position. A tinge of disappointment crept through me as Nathan by passed his bed and instead headed down the corridor to my room, but this was soon overshadowed by the realisation that he was so effortlessly carrying my size fourteen bum as if I weighed nothing at all. Perhaps all of Nathan's sexual gymnastics had caused me to shape up even more recently.

Instead of depositing me in my bed and leaving as I thought he would, Nathan crawled in behind me and tugged me hard up against him so we were spooning with my back pressed firmly to his front. 'Bad dreams in the other room, can I stay?' he murmured against my hair, and I think my heart just about broke for him. Reaching up to link my fingers with his I nodded, afraid that my tight throat might give away my highly emotional state.

'Of course,' I finally croaked, wriggling myself back for a more firm pressure against him as we both began to drift off to sleep.

Chapter Eight - Stella

The following morning I woke up feeling like I'd been hit by a freight train of emotions. Last night had seen both massive highs and incredibly wrenching lows and I almost felt hung-over from all the thoughts trying to fight for space in my brain. 'Well rested' certainly wouldn't be a phrase I'd be using today, that was for sure; my skin felt tight across my face from the lack of sleep, and I was a little achy from all the time spent crouched on the floor of the shower cubicle, but none of this could distract from the hope I felt inside me this morning.

Even though Nathan and I hadn't had sex last night it felt to me like a sudden intimacy had developed between us that far exceeded anything we'd done together in the bedroom. To be perfectly honest I was now wondering where on earth we would go from here, but I was secretly hoping that perhaps after opening up to me Nathan might start to feel more of the connection between us that I did.

The bed was so comfortable, but even though I just about felt refreshed enough to get up and get on with my day I didn't want to open my eyes yet. He'd be gone, I was sure he would. Nathan never stayed a full night with me. But if I kept my eyes closed I could breathe in the scent of him that hung in the air and in my mind could pretend he was still here with me. I know Nathan had definitely stayed most of the night because I had woken several times and found him still wrapped around me snoring gently. In fact at one point I'd been too hot, but as I tried to shuffle away to a cooler part of the bed Nathan had growled against my shoulder and tugged me firmly back against him. I have no idea if he'd been awake, or merely acting subconsciously in his sleep, but it had been so thrilling that I'd spent the next five minutes lying in the pitch black, grinning like a kid and trying to acclimatise to sleeping with a few extra degrees of body heat attached to me. It had been worth the effort.

Finally I braved a few blinks and let the soft morning light permeate my lids. From the warm glow coming though my curtains it looked like it was going to be a beautiful day. Propping myself up on my elbows I finally forced myself to glance across the bed and confirm the inevitable; Nathan was gone. Flopping back down I let out a heavy sigh that vibrated my lips like a long, loud raspberry. Reaching over I was surprised to find his pillow still warm and my eyebrows shot up in surprise. Nathan hadn't been up long then. Wow, he'd survived most of the night in my bed! I couldn't help it, in celebration I rolled over and buried my face in his warm pillow and inhaled the delicious smell of my complex, troubled bad boy.

Would I ever wake up in the same bed as him? An accepting grimace twisted my mouth – probably not, seeing how private and closed off Nathan was, I doubt he'd ever let me see him relaxed and sleeping, he'd probably think it would make him look vulnerable or something. A huge sigh puffed out of my cheeks at this thought, stupid overly proud man. But my disappointment at his departure didn't distract me from the bone deep sadness I felt for him after all I'd learnt about his childhood last night.

I tried to clear some of the residual mush from my brain by rubbing my hands vigorously over my face in the hope that it might wake me up more fully and help me make sense of last night's events. I'd learnt so much about Nathan that I barely knew where to start and some of it was really confusing for me to grasp. Nathan's relationship with his father certainly seemed to be an extremely complex one, when he'd spoken of him it had almost been with a grudging sort of respect, respect for a man who he had so desperately wanted to please that he'd allowed himself to be beaten daily. Shaking my head I blew out a long breath and pulled the duvet more firmly around myself. Jeez, it was so sad that he'd had to think like that as a child when the love of his parents should have been given freely and affectionately.

I'm really not sure how I'd held back my tears last night – Nathan had been so lost as he'd shared his history with me, but somehow I just knew that pity was not what he'd want to see from me, but I felt wet warmth on my cheeks now as several tears finally escaped and soaked into the pillow. Daily beatings would make most boys hate their fathers, but it seemed that somehow he'd convinced himself that his father's punishments were a tool aimed at helping him improve himself, something I struggled to comprehend because I came from a loving, supportive family. Although having said that, maybe it was Nathan's way of convincing himself that his father loved him, and that the beatings were somehow a display of that love. Making a low humming noise in my head I nodded, I'd put money on the fact that he endured the beatings hoping that if he did, his father might just love him a little more for it. It was such a horrible thought that more tears sprung to my eyes now as I tried to imagine what he'd gone through in his younger years.

Rolling over onto my back I wiped my eyes with the back of my hand and flopped an arm over my head to stretch, and then realised that last night's shower time was in all likelihood why he was gone from the bed this morning. After his confessions Nathan was probably feeling a bit exposed right now, possibly even regretting his uncharacteristic openness with me. But his behaviour hadn't made me think of him as weak, quite the opposite in fact; to deal with issues as life changing as an abusive father and the near death of your brother made him just about as strong a character as I could ever imagine.

It would be like walking through a minefield, but somehow I was going to have to prove to Nathan that his confessions hadn't made me think negatively about him in the slightest. If possible I now felt more for him than ever, but with a sigh I suspected that my complex dominant wouldn't want to hear my soppy confessions about that subject either.

Nathan

Last night had been a real game changer for me in more ways than one – first observing Nicholas and Rebecca and seeing them genuinely happy together had been an eye opener, I'd really never believed that type of happiness could be had by myself or my brother after our fucked-up start to life. Truthfully, seeing how amazing they clearly were together had completely freaked me out and I'd ended up screwing up a perfectly good evening by rudely sending Stella away to bed so I could try and sort out my tangled thoughts. Not that being on my own had helped in the slightest, I'd ended up thrashing around in my bed with nightmares about my father taunting me relentlessly instead of distracting myself with Stella and her willing little body.

Huffing out a sigh I closed my eyes as I remembered how I'd woken up gripping Stella around the neck and pressing her violently against the wall. Fuck, when she had unexpectedly arrived in my bedroom in the middle of the night she'd scared the shit out of me at first. In my dream my father had been about to beat Nicholas again and I'd been trying to intervene, and to be honest I'm amazed I hadn't done her some serious damage when I'd grabbed her in my sleep. But shit, the time we'd spent in the shower together had blown me away. Stella had soothed me in a way I'd never expected, listening to me and taking care of me like she really meant it. Fuck, it was so confusing that I didn't know what to do or say to her. Luckily I did know one person who might be able to help.

After gazing at Stella's sleeping form for several

seconds I had reluctantly dragged myself from the warmth of her bed and slipped back to my room where I ripped open the curtains to let the streams of early morning light disperse the lingering remnants of last night's disturbing dream. The room felt clearer now, so I headed into the bathroom to shower but as soon as my feet hit the cool tiles I stopped abruptly as memories of last night rushed back to my mind. Stella had been in here. She was the first woman ever to enter my bedroom or my bathroom, let alone share my shower, they were my private living spaces, a rule I'd firmly adhered to until Stella had come along and burst into my life.

Licking my lips I stepped up to the sink area and placed a hand on the counter where her naked arse had sat last night when I'd dried her after the shower. Closing my eyes I thought about her glorious body, open and willing, just for me. We hadn't had sex last night though, it hadn't seemed necessary for some reason, holding her close had been enough, and feeling her heartbeat against my chest as she melded willingly into my arms and fell asleep had just been fucking phenomenal. Shaking my head in exasperation at the sudden changes in me I expelled another breath and steadied myself with a countdown from 5 to 0.

Now that morning was here and my vision was lit with the bright bulbs of my bathroom, my near constant desire for Stella returned ferociously as my cock sprang to life at the image of her naked form sat on the counter. Now this was a more normal reaction for me, I thought as I eyed my expectant hard-on, *this* type of emotion I could deal with.

Christ. I really needed to sort my head out before I saw Stella again, God only knows what she thought of me after last night. Most of the stuff I'd told her was only known by myself and my brother – and possibly Rebecca now, if Nicholas had shared our history with her. Looking down at my erection as it bobbed hopefully I grimaced and shook my head, then stepped into the shower before flicking the jets to cold and dousing my morning hard-on under an icy flood of water.

Seeing as it was Sunday morning the traffic in central London was quite light so I cut through the sleepy backstreets towards the University College Hospital, before heading north and following the edge of Regents Park to take me to my destination. All in all I made the trip from my apartment in Docklands to Nicholas's house in Primrose Hill in just under twenty-four minutes, not bad going at all.

I pulled my Audi around to the back of Nicholas's house where a small driveway gave a private entry to the rear door of his property. The Audi TT might just be my 'around town' car, and certainly didn't compare to my brother's new Aston Martin, but I still didn't trust leaving it on a main road in central London with the risk of scratches from idiots not concentrating on what they were doing.

After ringing the bell I fidgeted on the spot, eager to get in and seek the advice I needed, but to my growing impatience Nicholas took an absolute age to answer the door. Tutting my frustration I glared at my watch in agitation and baulked slightly when I saw how early it was. Shit, it wasn't even 8 o'clock yet. I'd been so preoccupied with my own thoughts that I hadn't realised it was well outside of respectable visiting hours, especially for a Sunday morning. Weighing up my choices with a grimace I decided to stay. Well, I was here now and I'd no doubt already woken them when I'd rung the bell so I may as well stay, I thought, ringing the bell again and adding in a brisk knock just for luck.

After another few minutes ticked by laboriously I heard sounds of life from behind the wooden door. After two locks clicked back and a chain was removed Nicholas finally opened it up, looking decidedly dishevelled in jeans and a rumpled T-shirt, his hair a messy mop on his head. I raised an eyebrow and smirked at him, if it hadn't been so early in the morning I would have labelled his look as 'thoroughly well fucked,' but seeing as it was barely half past seven in the morning his crumpled looks were more likely down to my rude interruption of his sleep.

'Early enough for you, bro?' he enquired with a twist on his lips as he stood back to allow me to enter.

'Yeah … sorry Nicholas, I didn't realise the time until I got here,' I apologised lamely. Now I was here I felt awkward. Nicholas was my little brother; yeah, we might both be grown men now, but I suddenly had reservations about sharing my thoughts about Stella with him. What if it turned out that Stella didn't share my feelings? I didn't want him to see me fail at something so monumental – I was supposed to be *his* role model, not the other way round. My sudden indecision made me pause, and so for the time being I kept my mouth shut and pretended my visit was merely a social call. A very anti-socially early call, I thought with another twist of my lips.

After yawning so cavernously that I again felt guilty for waking him, Nicholas set about putting on the coffee maker and I suddenly became aware of someone else entering the room. Turning, I saw Rebecca had joined us. She looked more presentable than Nicholas did, with her hair brushed and smoothed down, but I noticed that she wore no make-up yet – not that it affected her looks in the slightest. In fact she was possibly more attractive in her natural state like this.

Suddenly I couldn't suppress my urge to get this stuff off my chest any longer as a brilliant flash of inspiration hit me; it wasn't Nicholas who could help me sort out my issues – it was Rebecca. She'd effectively tamed my brother, surely she could advise me?

'I need to speak to you,' I announced abruptly, eyeing

124

Rebecca as she tensed at my words. Simultaneously from the corner of my eye I saw Nicholas mirror her tension and turn from the coffee maker with a frown.

'Whatever you want to say you can say in front of Rebecca,' Nicholas replied in a cool tone, eyeing me with a look of suspicion that I didn't understand at all.

'Not you, Nicholas, I want to speak to Rebecca,' I said calmly. 'In private.' I added, turning myself towards her again but keeping my eyes averted. I couldn't help myself, I almost chuckled when she took a step back in surprise. I wasn't completely stupid, I'd noticed her hostility towards me at dinner last night, I'd assumed it was due to her lack of understanding over my relationship with Stella, but seeing this reaction today perhaps it was more like a fear of me. Whatever it was she needed to get over it because I wanted her advice and I would damn well get it before I left here today.

Nicholas strode over the kitchen and slung an arm around Rebecca, still eyeing me dubiously. Ah, so that was what his look meant! A grin wanted to break on my lips, but I suppressed it – if he thought I was trying to steal his girl he couldn't be more wrong. Leaning down, he dropped an overly possessive kiss on Rebecca's lips and then headed back to the coffee maker, 'Five minutes,' he said to me firmly. 'Then I'm coming in,' he promised as he turned back to the coffee.

Five minutes should be plenty of time to say what I needed to – it wasn't like I was the world's greatest talker when it came to emotional shit. Turning abruptly I headed for the downstairs lounge where I immediately set about pacing in front of the fire place. Damn it, now I was here with Rebecca I didn't even know where to start.

A huffed, anxious breath escaped my lips before I began. 'You can't tell Nicholas about this,' I warned in a low tone that instantly made Rebecca begin to back away from me again. Fuck it, terrifying the woman wasn't going to get me the help I wanted, I needed to seriously chill the fuck out. Perhaps if I softened my voice that would put her at ease? Keeping my eyes averted I stepped closer, reigned in my voice to a whisper and started at the only logical place, the beginning.

'Nicholas has told you about our past?' I questioned urgently, god I hope so because that was one shit storm of details I didn't want to be getting into right now, talking about my childhood last night with Stella was more than enough reminiscing for me right now.

'Um, yes,' she responded, looking thoroughly confused and a tiny bit petrified.

'Nicholas had it a lot worse than me as a kid. Dad used to hit me too, but I always thought he was trying to make me better, punishing me so I could learn, you know what I mean?' I asked, thinking back to my childhood and how I'd been sure that Dad had been doing what he thought was best for me. Doing it because he loved me. Something solid and uncomfortable seemed to stick in my throat as I thought about how desperate I'd been for my father to love me and be proud of me, wincing, it took me several large swallows for me to clear it.

It was only when Nicholas began getting the same treatment with the belt that I had begun to doubt things really, but I'd never understood if it had actually been wrong, or if perhaps Nicholas just hadn't been able to see the positives of the punishments and cope with it like me.

'Uhh, I suppose so.' Rebecca replied hesitantly and I immediately knew she didn't understand. No-one would. Only I knew how it had felt, like a singular, all powerful way of gaining my father's acceptance.

'My parents never expressed their love for one another. All I saw was my father's dominance over the household, his unyielding strength – they were united in some strange way but never affectionate.' My voice was clipped as I thought about my childhood in that small, sterile, stifling

126

house of ours, but there were certain things she needed to understand before I asked for her advice. 'Never loving,' I finished with a frown and a shake of my head as images of my father and last night's dream clouded my head again.

'OK ...' Rebecca said softly. 'Where do I fit in to this, Nathan, what did you want to talk to me about?'

There was no point skirting the issue any more, I may as well get straight to the point now, just like I would in a business meeting. 'I want what you have,' I stated calmly and simply.

Watching carefully I saw Rebecca's eyes widen in surprise and then confusion. Clearly she didn't understand me so I elaborated as best as I could. 'I want to be like you and Nicholas. I can see he's happy, *genuinely happy* with you, Rebecca, and you with him. When you sat together last night I could literally see the love passing between you, it was amazing. I've never witnessed that before. I'm not sure I'm capable ... but I want it.' My eyes uncharacteristically flicked to hers and she boldly held my gaze as she processed my words.

'With Stella?' she enquired, the astonishment clear in her voice, which was a fairly natural response given who she was talking about I suppose. To be honest I was pretty fucking astonished to be expressing this shit too.

I choked out a half bark, half laugh at her last question. Of course with Stella! Who the fuck else would I be talking about? But I didn't say that out loud, thankfully I suppressed my outrage and answered calmly, 'Yes. But I ... I don't know how,' I confessed, feeling suddenly vulnerable and wholly uncomfortable. This was the difficult part, I wasn't in control anymore and that terrified me.

'Tell her.' Rebecca said simply, with a shrug as if it were the simplest thing in the world.

'No.' I shook my head defiantly, my words growling from my throat again, 'Words mean nothing very little to

127

me. As a child, my mother would always say she loved us, but then when Nicholas was hurt it was always me cleaning his injuries,' I winced briefly as I thought back to that awful day when I'd found Nicholas bleeding out. His pale blue bedroom carpet had been almost black with blood around his naked body. A bone jarring shudder shook my entire body, tensing my muscles and leaving me with an uncomfortable ache along my spine.

'I need to *show* Stella that I want to be with her, what do I do?' I demanded softly.

Pausing as she considered my question I watched Rebecca roll her lips between her teeth as she thought, just as Stella often did. 'Well, if I were you I'd start by ripping up any 'submissive' contract you have with her.' My eyebrows rose at her mention of a contract, clearly Nicholas had told her more about my relationship with Stella than I'd expected. 'Take her out for a meal in public together, buy her flowers, hold her hand, kiss her, make her feel special, make her feel like an equal.' She reeled off a list of things that I'd never done before with anyone and I felt myself sinking deeper and deeper into a terrifying well of uncharted territory. Holding hands? Flowers? *Fuck*.

An image of my brother from last night sprung to my mind, 'Touch her like you and Nicholas last night?' I asked, remembering how he'd held her hand at dinner and in return she'd kissed his knuckles. 'When he held your hand and you kissed him?' God, I felt so fucking clueless, but my embarrassment about talking to Rebecca had gone now, replaced by my desperate need to learn what I needed from her.

'Yes, exactly like that,' she agreed with an encouraging nod and a smile. Perhaps I was winning Rebecca around at last.

Chewing on my lip I asked a question that had been going round and round my head since I'd laid down and

128

cradled Stella to sleep last night. 'Do you think she likes me?' I was well aware just how open that question left me, not to mention how juvenile I sounded.

Rebecca paused for a second narrowing her eyes before rolling her shoulders and answering, 'Well, obviously I've only met Stella once, but yes, I think she likes you, Nathan, in fact she told me she wants to be with you,' she confirmed, 'and when she looked at you her eyes lit up, that's always a good sign.'

Eyes lit up? What the fuck was she, the Blackpool Illuminations? My back straightened at this bizarre news and I stepped closer to Rebecca to demand more details. 'Her eyes lit up, explain what you mean?' I mumbled, confused by the idea of such a concept. Rebecca shifted uncomfortably and I realised that by invading her personal space I'd made her feel intimidated again without even meaning too. God, I really was a heavy handed jerk, wasn't I? I seriously needed to lighten up if I wanted to make a go of things with Stella, I couldn't have her scared of me too. In fact the thought that Stella *could* be scared of me was enough to turn my stomach.

'People can smile but you know it's real if it reaches their eyes. When Stella smiled at you it reached her eyes.' Rebecca explained simply. Reached Stella's eyes? My nostrils flared as I huffed out an impatient breath. I really was no clearer on what Rebecca was talking about, but apparently my confusion was obvious because Rebecca let out a sigh and then gave me a sympathetic look which I didn't care for too much.

'OK, watch me smile,' she instructed patiently. So I did, skimming my gaze all over her face. Her lips had curved upwards but that was about all I could observe as different from before.

'Now watch again and see if you can see a difference,' she told me. There was a pause where she did nothing, but then suddenly Rebecca's whole face shifted in one smooth motion. Her lips curved upwards again, but this time her eyes changed, crinkling at the corners and warming somehow. I could tell a liar in my business boardroom from a mile off, but bloody hell, how had I never been aware of this stuff before?

My eyebrows had risen significantly, 'I see it ...' cocking my head to further examine her, I had a huge urge to reach out and touch what she was feeling, but thank fuck some of my sense remained and I managed to keep my hands at my sides before I made a complete prat out myself. 'Your cheeks have flushed and your eyes are ... *twinkling*.' I muttered disbelievingly. 'When did Stella look like this?'

'As soon as you told her eye contact was permitted,' she shrugged, and I tried to cast my mind back to last night, we'd been sat on the sofa ... yeah, actually now I think of it, something had felt different about that moment with Stella, significant somehow. '... and at the dinner table when you whispered something to her she had looked genuinely thrilled.'

It was rare for me to blush, but I did now as I remembered the moment Rebecca was referring to, I'd reached under the table and stroked Stella's upper thigh as I spoke to her and it had made me get an instant hard-on that had lasted for the remainder of the bloody meal. Talk about inconvenient.

'Can I ask what you said to her?' Rebecca blurted out rather tactlessly, making me frown.

I wasn't massively keen to share my secrets, but seeing as Rebecca was doing her best to assist me with my questions I should probably try and loosen up a bit. I looked away and cleared my throat several times before answering, 'She doesn't usually socialise with me if I have company, but I was intrigued by your relationship with Nicholas and wanted her to see it too. That was the first time she's joined me for dinner with guests so I said she was doing very well.' I admitted pausing awkwardly, 'and I told her ... I told her she looked very beautiful.' I missed out the part about the raging hard-on – Rebecca didn't need to know *that* much detail.

Suddenly grinning at me, Rebecca practically danced on the spot with apparent glee. 'Do more things like that, she'll love it,' she encouraged me enthusiastically, stepping forwards and patting my arm reassuringly. 'Don't be afraid to tell her what's in your head,' she advised, and I immediately cringed at her words. There was no way I was telling Stella some of my dark, perverted thoughts about her and the many things I wanted to do to her lush little body.

Just then Nicholas opened the door and disturbed us. I disliked eye contact, but always made an exception where my little brother was concerned and I immediately caught how his eyes instantly hardened as they settled on where Rebecca was touching me. Smirking I felt slightly reassured by the fact that jealousy was obviously a Jackson family trait and then shifted myself to hopefully alleviate his concern.

Nodding briskly to Rebecca I turned for the door determined to head home to Stella and try out some of Rebecca's advice. 'I will, thanks Rebecca. I gotta go.'

Just before I reached the door I heard Rebecca gasp and then call out to me, 'The good stuff, Nathan, only tell her the good stuff!' she cried, and I couldn't help but grin at just how well she'd read my very own thoughts about my depraved mind.

Chapter Nine - Nathan

The whole journey home I'd debated what to say to
Stella – how to broach the subject of our relationship, or
what I should do first, but even with nearly twenty five
minutes thinking time in the car I was still undecided as I
reached my apartment block and entered the underground
parking garage. Exiting my car I beeped the lock on my
Audi and then strode towards the lift, anxiously chewing
on the inside of my lower lip. The silver doors opened
immediately, giving me no extension on my thinking time,
then after typing in the code for the penthouse I leant back
against the mirrored wall and continued my pondering.

Thinking back to Rebecca's advice I narrowed my eyes
as I considered my choices with regards to how to
approach Stella. *Kiss her* – well that wouldn't be an issue,
I loved kissing Stella. I could get right on that one straight
away. *Hold her hand* – it wasn't something I did
frequently, but it would be easy enough, too. *Make her feel
special*. I smirked, I was pretty confident that I already did
that in the bedroom, but somehow I didn't think that was
what Rebecca had been referring to. As perplexing as the
idea seemed, I was going to have to work on what I could
do to make her feel special other than through sex, but I
really had no idea where to start.

By-passing that for now I considered the other things
Rebecca suggested. *Treat her like an equal*. I did that
already, didn't I? But my teeth clenched hard as I thought
more about it – seeing as she was my contracted
submissive Stella probably didn't view our relationship as
particularly equal at all, I realised with a scowl.

Jeez, this was so much harder than I thought it'd be. There was so much to consider it was starting to make me feel rather inadequate, not a feeling I liked one bit, so I instead concentrated on what I *could* do. *Take her out for a meal in public together*, we often ate together at my apartment so it would be easy enough to upgrade that experience to a restaurant I suppose, but as it was only 9.30 in the morning it would have to wait. *Buy her flowers*, fuck no, my nose wrinkled at the thought, I might want to change the direction of my relationship with Stella but I wasn't a fucking wimp.

A grimace creased my brow in my mirrored reflection of the lift doors and I shuffled on my feet in agitation. Perhaps this was my whole bloody problem: like the selfish pig I was I had been thinking about myself again, not Stella. If I wanted to make a go of things with Stella I would have to start thinking about her feelings for a change, instead of being selfish and ignorant like usual. Would *she* like it if I bought her flowers? Fuck yeah, she would probably love it, wouldn't she? Slamming my hand on the button panel I reversed the direction of the lift with a scowl and decided to make a quick trip to the flower stand on the corner of the street.

How was it that I could stand in front of a room full of businessmen and not give a damn what one of them thought about me, but the idea of seeing Stella again after being so vulnerable in front of her last night had me completely terrified and practically shaking all over? My shower confessions had probably been my biggest moment of weakness in my entire life, spewing my entire pitiful history in one go like a pathetic little wimp. *Fuck*. And for some reason I chose to do this in front of the woman I now wanted to extend my relationship with? God, I was such a loser. What would she think of me after my confessions? Would she think any less of me? Christ, if I was any more nervous I think I would actually throw up.

Clutching the stupid bouquet of flowers that I'd bought for Stella, supposedly the best in the shop – and they'd better have been for the extortionate price I paid – I finally plucked up the courage to enter my own apartment and face her.

Stella

The metallic sound of a key in the apartment door jolted me from my troubled thoughts and almost caused me to drop the coffee mug in my hand. After waking to Nathan's warm but empty pillow I had been feeling quietly hopeful that maybe we'd turned a bit of a corner last night, that perhaps I wasn't the only one developing feelings beyond the stupid contract we'd agreed on weeks ago. But then when I got up and discovered him gone from the apartment the doubts started to settle in thick and fast – his absence couldn't have indicated anything good so he probably did regret last night as I'd first feared.

It was Sunday so technically one of our days together, but with Nathan gone I hadn't known whether to stay or go, and as such had pretty much spent the last half an hour standing and staring at the coffee maker, deep in thought wondering if I should cut and run whilst the going was good or stick around. Now it was too late because behind me I could hear the door opening and Nathan's footsteps entering the apartment and heading straight for the kitchen. Taking a deep breath I turned to face the music.

Out of all the sights I might have imagined coming through the door on Nathan's return though, it certainly wasn't this. Nathaniel Jackson, casually dressed in a white T-shirt and jeans, looking rather rueful and carrying the most enormous bunch of flowers I think I have ever seen. Bloody hell, it was like he had half of Chelsea Flower Show in his arms. They were stunning; sunflowers, yellow roses, irises, jasmine branches … blimey, I was stunned into complete silence as I stood blinking and gaping at him like an idiot.

'Um ... these are for you,' Nathan murmured awkwardly, sounding embarrassed and unsure if I'd actually want them. For me? My shock grew again, and by this point I was pretty sure my mouth was hanging open in surprise rather unattractively.

'Do you like them?' He sounded affronted that I hadn't said anything yet, so I made an effort to quickly snap my mouth closed and nod. Almost immediately I winced as I remembered how much nodding pissed him off, so frantically forced my tongue to moisten my lips so I could put my mouth into action. 'I love them, Nathan. They're beautiful.' My voice was all girly and whimsical and soppy-sounding, but I couldn't help it, this was the most romantic thing anyone had ever done for me ever, let alone non-romantic, dominate-you-in-the-bedroom Nathan.

Stepping forwards I took the gigantic bouquet from him and staggered towards the kitchen sink to deposit them on the counter, which given its size was actually quite difficult. Gazing down at the glorious blooms I suddenly felt tearful, my eyes welling up as tears threatened to spill over down my cheeks, which was ridiculous and would no doubt freak Nathan out, so to hide my watery eyes I leant forward and buried my head in the gorgeous scents coming from the flowers.

Once I had control over my girly emotions I lifted my head and risked a glance at Nathan, half expecting him to be rolling his eyes at me, or scowling his trademark dark look, but instead I caught what looked quite a lot like a smile on his lips. Wow, whatever next!

'Do you have a vase?' I asked, really not expecting him to say yes. I couldn't imagine a man like Nathan buying flowers just to make his house look and smell nice. In fact, given his uncomfortable stance I wondered if this was the first time he'd ever bought a bunch of flowers in his life. Scoffing, I shook my head. *Don't flatter yourself,* I thought sourly, mentally giving myself a ticking off. With his charm and bedroom skills Nathan had no doubt 'flowered' his way into many a woman's knickers in his time. The thought was distinctly unpleasant, but instead of lingering on being a jealous harpy I instead focused on the fact that today Nathan had bought them for me, and they were glorious, and probably very expensive.

'Shit, I didn't think of a vase,' he muttered, looking momentarily crestfallen. 'I think there might be one around here somewhere – Miranda my cleaner bought some flowers for the table last Christmas.' Let's hope so, otherwise this stunning display was going to spend the next week prettying up the kitchen sink. In silence Nathan and I both began searching through the various cupboards until eventually I spotted a dust-laden vase right at the back of a cupboard full of pans. Poor Miranda, she must have used it once and given up on him.

Busying myself trimming the ends of the stems I then filled the vase with water, tipped in the little sachet of plant food, and set about arranging the flowers as elegantly as I could. 'Wow, they really are beautiful, Nathan. Thank you,' I said softly, standing back to admire them again with a happy little sigh. Clearing his throat gruffly Nathan turned away and started to fiddle with the pile of post on the kitchen counter and I smiled – even though he'd bought the flowers for me apparently he wasn't comfortable with my gratitude just yet.

'We're going out today,' Nathan suddenly said, still focusing his gaze on the letters in his hand, although he didn't really seem to be reading them.

'Oh ... OK.' This was new too. We never went out together, apart from that one visit to Club Twist a few weeks ago. We never did anything together except sex and eating, but that was mostly done in companionable silence, and always at the apartment.

Possibly hearing my hesitation, or my surprise, Nathan

closed his eyes and frowned as if considering something very hard, 'That is, if you would like to?' he added, sounding like the words were particularly hard for him to say.

I had a choice? I always enjoyed our Sunday sex sessions – by then, Nathan was always less fevered and so the sex was a little more like lovemaking, slower and attentive and lovely, albeit with a few handcuffs or blindfolds thrown in the mix, but going out and spending some time with him would be totally new, and getting to know him better was a rather exciting prospect.

'Um, yeah, that would be nice,' I replied, immediately hoping we weren't just going to repeat our last excursion and go back to Club Twist. I wasn't keen to bump into Dominic again, I'd thought Nathan was going to kill him last time, but seeing as it wasn't even lunchtime yet a trip to the club didn't seem particularly likely. 'Where are we going?'

Once again Nathan tensed his jaw as if selecting his words very carefully. 'You choose,' he offered, sounding almost reluctant. *What?*

'My choice?' I squeaked. I couldn't help it, I was stood frozen in the kitchen staring at him like half of his brain was hanging out of his nose. What had happened to him? The dominant Nathan I knew never asked for my opinion and he was certainly never considerate like this. He was almost acting as if his brain *had* been pulled out of his nose.

'As long as we can get ice-cream I don't care where we go,' he added shrugging out of his jacket.

'Ice-cream?' God, I sounded like a complete imbecile repeating all his words back at him, but I was seriously struggling to grasp this new reality that I had been thrown in to. First flowers, and now ice-cream? Where the heck had Nathan been this morning to make him so different?

'Yeah, it's hot outside today. Ice-cream would be nice,'

Nathan murmured. 'I'm going to change, be ready in fifteen minutes,' he ordered. But as he stepped towards the kitchen door I heard him sigh and pause, dropping his head as he did so. '*Please,*' he added, before walking from the kitchen, leaving me standing stock still and gaping at his retreating figure.

What in the name of all things holy was going on? Was I missing something? Was it National Be Nice To Your Submissive day? Shaking off my haze of confusion I hastily made tracks up to my bedroom to change, deciding that whatever the reason for Nathan's odd mood I may as well make the most of it.

Slipping into some lovely new ivory lace underwear – a replacement set from Nathan for the panties he tore up at my office – I stepped into a pale yellow sundress, grabbed a cardigan just in case, and then after touching up my light make-up I headed back to the kitchen.

As quick as I'd been, Nathan had still beaten me to it; he was still in his jeans but he'd changed his white T-shirt for a navy blue polo shirt which did devastatingly good things for his pale blue eyes. Blimey, talk about sinfully sexy. And all mine. For today anyway.

We walked to the lift in silence and it wasn't until the doors closed that he spoke again. 'So, where are we going then?' he asked, tossing his car keys lightly in his hand. He wasn't smiling, but I thought perhaps I could hear a trace of humour in his voice as if he too found it strange to be asking me my choice in matters.

'How about Greenwich Park?' I offered – it was just the other side of the River Thames from here and if we took the Docklands Light Railway I knew we could be there in less than twenty minutes, plus there was great little ice-cream parlour near the entrance that I was fairly sure would satisfy Nathan's demand for icy goodness.

Nodding, Nathan stepped from the lift in the direction of his car but I took hold of his arm and stopped him, a smile popping to my lips. 'We don't need to drive Nathan, its only three stops on the train.'

'The train?' Nathan sounded almost appalled by my suggestion and I couldn't help myself, I laughed at him. Loudly. Which of course immediately echoed off the concrete walls of the parking garage like surround sound. *Oops*. First he looked mightily pissed off, then slightly offended, then determined to shut me up and I promptly stopped laughing as he stepped forwards with a particularly menacing look on his face. I expected a telling off, or a harsh word about my behaviour, but what I got instead was a long, firm kiss on the lips which quickly heated to something far more passionate as his tongue pushed into my mouth and whipped me into a needy frenzy within seconds.

Abruptly pulling himself away from me I staggered slightly from the dizzying sensations of Nathan's touch and he grinned down at me. 'Who's laughing now?' he smirked darkly, before grabbing my hand and dragging me and my wobbly legs towards the pedestrian exit. 'Come on then, woman, introduce me to the delights of the London public transport system.'

He wasn't joking either, from the baffled way that Nathan stared at the ticket machines in the station a few minutes later it was clear that he very rarely used trains, if ever. He literally lived a two-minute walk from the station! How the other half live, eh? I suspected that if we had had to wait for a train I would have endured several smug comments from Nathan about the usefulness of a car, but thankfully even though it was a Sunday with reduced service we walked straight onto a carriage and were on the move just eight minutes after leaving Nathan's apartment.

The train was smooth and quick and gave me some time to try and work out what on earth had happened to Nathan this morning to cause this radical change in his personality. After five minutes I was still totally clueless.

He literally seemed to have evolved overnight, not that I was complaining; with the flowers, smiles, consideration, and hand-holding I was feeling rather giddy with happiness at the moment and decided to just let the day play out.

Once we drew into Cutty Sark station there was just a short walk before we entered Greenwich Park, each with a large cone stuffed with delicious Cornish ice-cream. It was perhaps a little early for ice-cream, but seeing as Nathan was so intent on fulfilling his need I didn't mention the time and happily joined in.

As we meandered along a path in silence it came to my notice that there was something rather erotic about the way Nathan licked his ice-cream, not that he seemed aware of this, but every time I watched his tongue lash up the soft, creamy cone I couldn't help but imagine him doing that to my neck, my breast, or perhaps somewhere even lower down on my body.

I was practically fixated on the movement and I think perhaps I may have moaned out loud, because suddenly Nathan stopped eating his ice cream and turned to stare at me intently.

A smile curved his top lip. 'Oh, Stella. That's a very naughty thought.' Nathan murmured softly, a flash of desire darkening his eyes and causing me to flush instantly. How the hell did he know what I was thinking?

'You can be so transparent when you want something.' he added, stepping closer so his head was dipped right next to mine and I could smell the sweet strawberry ice cream on his cool breath. Transparent? Right now with desire thumping between my thighs like a steam train I felt pretty flimsy on my legs too.

'If we weren't in public I'd like nothing more than to drip this ice-cream on your hot little clit and take my time licking it off very, *very* thoroughly. Would you like that?'

Oh-my-God-yes. And right now I didn't really care who

was watching, his few simple dirty words had made me so needy that I had to grip his shoulder to steady myself and squeeze my thighs together to try and find some relief. Seeing the shift of my legs Nathan chuckled, apparently rather pleased with himself, dropped a quick ice-creamy kiss on my lips and then started walking again whilst humming a little happy tune. Bastard! I was ready to combust and he was strolling casually away!

Thankfully after a second or two of deep breathing my sanity returned and I decided that a police warning for public indecency would possibly spoil the day, so I got my libido under control and caught up with him feeling slightly calmer. I couldn't believe he was humming to himself either, it was just such an un-Nathan-like gesture. Cutting across the grass we walked in a happy silence as we ate our ice-cream and then once the cones were gone and our fingers were clean – thanks to the clean wipes in my handbag – Nathan took hold of my hand and started to pull me up a path to the left.

'I want to show you something,' he said as way of explanation, but to be honest I didn't care where we were going; I was out in London, it was a beautiful day and to top it all off I was with Nathan, and he was in a ridiculously good mood and holding my hand.

Jeez, this was all so weird that I felt a bit like I was having a seizure or a massive brain malfunction; first the flowers, now a walk in the park with hand-holding? *Hand-holding?* I had to concentrate all my effort into acting normally, when all I wanted to do was gawk at Nathan and check his forehead for a fever that might explain his sudden behaviour shift.

'This is the Old Royal Naval College,' Nathan said, pointing to the huge building we were approaching, although to call it a 'building' didn't really cut it, it was a sprawling mass of white columns, domes, and beautiful windows that looked more like a palace than a college.

This was one of my favourite parks in London and so I'd walked this particular path many times before, but although I'd admired the building I'd never known what it was. 'It was designed by Sir Christopher Wren over three hundred years ago,' he added, but when I looked over to Nathan I saw he was lost in a world of his own, his eyes meandering over the building almost lovingly. 'I got my inspiration to go into architecture from his work.'

Crikey, I had learnt more about Nathan in the last two days than I had in the rest of our time together and I greedily soaked up all the information he was giving me. 'Why?' I enquired.

'He's one of the most highly acclaimed architects in British history, I want to be like him.' A simple answer, but it was typical of Nathan to aim to be the very best, in fact I couldn't imagine him any other way, somehow his confidence, which bordered on arrogance a lot of the time, really suited him. No doubt he planned on being even better and more famous than Christopher Wren one day too.

'Well, I guess you've pretty much achieved that, I mean you own one of the most successful architectural companies in London,' I said, suddenly realising just how true it was, and just how insanely successful Nathan was.

He gave a vague grunt that I took to be agreement, then gazed at the building one more time, letting out a happy sigh before he finally turned back to me. My eyes had been on him as he turned and he seemed particularly embarrassed when he caught me looking at him, so he turned away, clearing his expression as he began walking along the path that I knew led to a small boating lake and children's play area.

Walking beside him I glanced down at our hands which were still joined and couldn't help but smile to myself. I still had no idea what had gotten into Nathan today, but as the warmth of his skin soaked into my palm I had to say I liked it. Probably a bit too much, actually, if he went back to his usual stroppy self tomorrow I knew I would miss this more relaxed version of him terribly.

Pausing alongside the small lake we stood in silence for a while and watched a group of ducks greedily fighting over some bread that a young family were throwing to them. 'Shall we sit?' Nathan asked, indicating the grass behind us and I nodded – a little spot of sunbathing would go down a treat. The only disappointing thing was that we had to break our hand hold to sit down, and Nathan didn't reconnect it afterwards. It had only been a hand hold, but I realised that I missed his warmth now that it was gone.

'So do you play rugby then?' I asked, indicating to the polo shirt that he was wearing. It had the number 22 on the area over his heart above the letters HRFC, which I assumed stood for something Rugby Football Club, and the same two digits emblazoned on the back in much larger font. I couldn't imagine a more formidable or terrifying opponent than Nathan on the rugby pitch; he was so tall and well-muscled that tackling him would probably be like running into a brick wall.

'I used to,' he replied, shifting himself back so he was reclining and leaning on his elbows.

'Why did you quit? Too busy with work?' I mused, pulling at a blade of long grass in front of me and absently running it between my fingers.

'No,' he answered, giving no more information than that, but it was the tone of Nathan's one word that caught my attention, it was suddenly cooler and when I glanced across I saw a dark look on his face. Shit. Obviously I had somehow put my foot in it – again. I shifted awkwardly on the ground, unsure how to get back the easier air that had been between us earlier.

'Sorry,' I murmured, not quite sure what I was apologising for, but feeling the need to do it anyway.

Several moments passed and I started to chew on my

lip nervously, how had such an innocent question ruined the entire day? Puffing out a breath I stared at the lake wishing I could get in one of the little hire boats and float away.

'No, I'm sorry, Stella. You weren't to know that it was a sore point for me,' Nathan said suddenly. Turning to look at him I saw an anxious expression on his face, his lip chewing much more vigorously than mine had been. 'I started playing rugby in high school, my father wouldn't let Nicholas or I go out after school with our friends but we were allowed to participate in after-school clubs.' Nathan sat himself back up and looped his arms around his bent legs hugging them to his chest. 'I joined as many clubs as I could, just to get some extra time away from the house.' He was opening up again, I just couldn't believe it, but I shelved all the questions forming in my mind and let him get it off his chest, 'I was pretty good at rugby and when I joined college I got straight onto the team. I'd only been playing for them for a few months when ...' Nathan paused, swallowed loudly and ran a hand through his hair, his agitation obvious, '... when the stuff with Nicholas happened.' He finished in a low tone. 'After Nicholas's suicide attempt my parents were arrested and charged with child abuse so we were on our own. I was eighteen, Nicholas was sixteen, so technically we were legally old enough to be independent, but the trauma specialist who treated Nicholas deemed him to be 'vulnerable' and wanted him in foster care until he was eighteen so he could stabilise emotionally.'

Shaking his head Nathan looked well and truly lost in his memories. 'I couldn't let us be split up, not after everything he'd been through, so I said I'd look after him. It took a bit of convincing, but eventually I was allowed to be his official guardian until he turned eighteen. I knew we'd need more money than council benefits would provide so I quit college that very day and managed to blag my way onto a paid apprenticeship scheme at a local builder's.' Nathan glanced at me briefly, a sad reflective look in his eye, then looked away again, 'So, no more college meant no more rugby, but to be honest the job kept me so busy I didn't have time to miss it.'

Wow, another huge piece of the puzzle had just been filled. Nathan really had sacrificed everything for his brother and I couldn't help but feel immensely proud of him. 'You're incredible, you know that?' I whispered, well aware that I was probably about to get all mushy on him which he would hate.

'I'm not,' he said dismissively as I had expected. 'I did what anyone would do for a sibling in trouble.' He said it liked he believed it, but I couldn't agree, Nathan might hide himself under some controlling, dominant façade, but beneath it all I was starting to get glimpses of the man he really was; caring, considerate, and loyal, even if he didn't seem to realise it himself. Unfortunately it was just making me fall for him even bloody harder.

Deciding not to push him anymore about his brother I changed the subject slightly. 'So the job with the builders, I guess that led you towards the architecture career then?' I asked, hoping at least this was a safe topic.

'In a way, yes, I'd known since I was young that I wanted to design things, it had started with building stuff from Lego and then developed into drawing, and by the time I went to college I was doing all the right courses to get me onto an architecture degree at university. Obviously the stuff with Nicholas stopped that, but when I realised I needed to get a job I still wanted to try and pursue my dream.'

Taking me completely by surprise Nathan looped an arm around my shoulders and pulled us both backwards so we were laid on the grass, him on his back staring up at the clear summer sky, and me tucked in at his side with my head resting on his shoulder.

Snuggling a little closer I smiled to myself. If this was one of his tactics to avoid eye contact then it was just fine by me. Although now I knew the reasoning behind his averted eyes – his father's rules – perhaps I could start to coax a few more glances from him in future. I'd barely had time to register the new positioning, or what the heck all this strangely affectionate behaviour meant, before he was speaking again.

'The apprenticeship with the builders was just a stepping stone for me, soon I was wangling my way into all sorts of meetings and giving opinions to some of the leading people in the industry.' I smiled, I could so imagine Nathan doing that, he was normally pretty quiet around me, but the times I'd heard him on business calls he was cool, precise, and incredibly persuasive. 'Pretty much as soon as I qualified from my apprenticeship I had a job offer from an architecture company that I'd worked with.'

Wow. Relaxing against Nathan I decided to go all out and put my arm on his chest where it wanted to be. I kept myself tense for a second or two, but after a minute had passed and he hadn't freaked out or flipped me off of him I assumed that he didn't mind my fingers there and relaxed, splaying my hand across his warm shirt just above his heart. 'And the rest is history, as they say,' I murmured.

'Pretty much.' Nathan agreed softly beside me. 'The architecture company trained me up, I had a great time there, but four years ago I decided to branch out on my own. I've been incredibly lucky with the speed of my success.' He finished quietly. His uncharacteristic flood of conversation seemed to dry up for the time being, but seeing as he'd shared so much with me in the last two days I was content to enjoy the silence and just lie with him.

We lay like that for some time. I was taking the time to absorb all that had happened between us and I assumed

Nathan might be as well, until I realised that my hand had been working without the knowledge of my brain and was now circling patterns on to Nathan's chest. As my finger brushed across his flat nipple I felt it tighten below my fingertips and a small growl rumbled from his chest.

Smiling at my accidental tease I feigned innocence and repeated the action, causing another longer, lower growl to resonate through my ear. 'How come it's fine for you to touch my nipple in public, but if I did the same to you I'd be breaking some serious etiquette laws?' he grumbled against my hair. A grin pulled at my lips and suddenly feeling daring I flicked at his nipple with my fingernail, forcing a gasp to escape his lips.

'Right, that's it!' Nathan growled and then in the blink of an eye he had flipped me over onto my back and was completely covering me with his body as his lips found mine in a heated kiss which had my earlier lust reignited in seconds.

After plundering my mouth until I was almost feverish with desire he lifted his head, shifted his body slightly and gazed down at me – with a full eye contact, lust-filled stare – and then smiled lazily as if we were just a couple laying in the sun together. Using himself as a shield so no-one else could see, he forced one hand between our bodies and managed to zero in on one of my nipples where he wasted no time in tugging and tweaking it to a tight bud and causing me to writhe below him and moan softly.

Then, just as quickly as he had pounced on me he was gone, standing up, brushing the grass off his jeans and casually offering me a hand to help me get up looking completely unruffled by our make out session.

'You look a little lop-sided,' Nathan commented smugly as his eyes slid to my chest. Glancing down I felt my cheeks rush with colour, he was right, one of my nipples was normal and hidden behind the material of my sun dress, but the other, the one he had just plundered so ruthlessly, was erect and straining at the fabric, desperately seeking another touch. *Bastard*.

'Come on then, let's grab some lunch and head home,' Nathan said, sounding mighty pleased with himself. *Git, git, git*. Even though it was sunny and warm I pulled on my light cardigan to cover my helplessly wanton nipple and then followed him with as much of a scowl as I could manage. I probably wasn't very convincing though; with Nathan in this good a mood it would be impossible to stay mad with him for long.

Stopping to eat a deliciously fresh sushi plate from a little café near the park exit we sat in companionable silence and ate, occasionally expressing a liking for a particular piece, and then after paying the bill we headed for the train again.

I was feeling incredibly light hearted and content by the time we took our seats on the deserted carriage, with a small smile playing on my lips that I was just unable to hide. Especially seeing how out of his element Nathan looked sat opposite me on the train. It was so amusing; he was sat stiffly in his seat and his eyes were darting around, taking in his surroundings like a child might do when experiencing their first ever train journey.

Turning away from Nathan before I laughed at him, pissed him off, and ruined the afternoon, I sighed happily. The last two days had been incredible. Nathan had opened up to me, shared things, taken me out and made me feel ... well, special, I suppose. But in the back of my mind a danger siren was starting to ring and I shifted uncomfortably in my seat. I needed to be really careful here, I already had more complicated feelings for him than I should, but with Nathan behaving like this, almost boyfriend like, it was hard not to get carried away with fairy tale romance images in my head. Oh dear, I suddenly had a sinking feeling that I may well be a lost cause where Nathaniel Jackson was concerned.

Trying to distract myself from my unpleasant thoughts I gazed out of the window across the view over London. The Thames was calm today, shining in the sun and in the distance through the buildings of Canary Wharf I could just about see the white of the Millennium Dome. God, I loved living in London. 'I love the views down here,' I murmured, lost in my own world for a minute or two.

'Me too,' Nathan agreed, but there was something in his tone that snapped me from my dreaming and I turned to him to see a sudden blaze of desire in his eyes. He wasn't looking at the view – he was looking at me. And judging from the heat in his eyes, he liked what he saw. A lot. *Blimey*. My heart accelerated in my chest and a tingle ran across my skin, seeing him so affected by me would never lose its excitement.

Even though there had been a sexual undercurrent buzzing between us all day – there always was when we were together – it had now spiked up a notch or two as I realised Nathan's intentions. He wanted me, and going on the expression on his face he wasn't planning on waiting long either. I licked my lips as I gazed at his heated expression and it suddenly struck me that Nathan was once again using direct eye contact with me. Perhaps last night's confession had somehow made it easier for him to look at me because he'd been doing it all day today – another new development which I loved – and as I let myself get dragged into his blue depths I felt my insides heat even further.

'The view really is superb,' he murmured. 'But it could be better,' he added as he sat back on his seat, crossed his arms across his chest, and gave me his best down and dirty look which made me gulp loudly.

'Take off your panties,' he ordered suddenly in a low, dark tone. *What?* I choked on my breath and my eyes flew wide open in shock, was he serious? Oh God, one look at his expectant face and I knew he was serious. What the heck was it with him and demanding for me to remove my underwear in public places? First my office, and now a train! Apparently cuddly, conversational Nathan was hidden away again as dominant Nathan came back in full force. Actually, in a way I'd kind of missed him and his stupidly crazy demands.

'No!' my reply slipped from my tongue in an embarrassed mumble.

'No? But surely you remember what happened last time I wanted a pair of your panties?' he enquired softly. My answering swallow was so loud it must have echoed around the empty train carriage. Yikes, he wouldn't rip them off in public would he? Just as I thought this Nathan began to lean forward in his seat and reach for me – crap, he bloody well would as well!

Scrabbling my legs shut I held out my hands in a desperate bid to stop him and shifted on the seat so I was as far away from him as possible. 'Wait! But … but … we're in public,' I stuttered, stating the rather obvious fact and hoping it might deter him.

'So? No-one else is on the train, and there are no security cameras.' Nathan said with a nonchalant shrug.

Crikey … what to do? The rational, sensible, law abiding part of me was saying no, but the edgy, risky, sexy part of me that Nathan had brought to the surface was screaming yes, yes, yes! My lower lip was getting a good working out as I chewed on it frantically trying to decide what to do, but to give him his credit Nathan merely sat back, giving me some time to make my own decision – there was no denying the hopeful look on his face though.

Maybe I could do this one little thing for him as a show of gratitude for the effort he'd been making in the last two days to open up? Who was I kidding, taking your knickers off on a train was not a *little* thing – it was a frigging massive thing! And illegal. Talk about indecent exposure! On the positive side, at least I was wearing a sundress so it wouldn't actually be that hard to do …

'What's it to be Stella? Will you take my dare, or my punishment?' Nathan murmured darkly, interrupting my internal debate. His punishment? Actually I usually quite liked Nathan's punishments, but there was no denying the fact that I really wanted to please him today. With one final glance down the carriage to check there definitely weren't any other passengers that I was about to flash, I shifted myself forwards to the edge of my seat and then looked Nathan directly in the eye. His gaze had filled with lust at my shift and I couldn't help but feel emboldened by the approval I saw in his expression.

Placing my hands palm down on my thighs I shifted my sundress up several inches and then in a show of immense bravery – or complete stupidity – I flicked the hem up, revealing most of my legs before I briefly raised my bum off the seat, slipped my fingers under, and found the waistband of my knickers. Pulling them down to my knees I retook my seat before completing the last stage of the removal and kicking my feet out of them. Then in a moment of madness I looped one leg hole of the panties around my index finger and swung them round like a mini lasso. Nathan was completely entranced by my display, but as I did my victory lasso he laughed, a lovely deep rumble of a laugh, and looked me directly in the eye.

'Well, Stella, I enjoyed that immensely.' Reaching out he removed my knickers from my hand and took a few seconds to meticulously fold them into a neat square in his palm. 'It's a shame I don't have a front pocket,' he remarked wistfully, then caressing my panties one last time he sat forwards and tucked them in the back pocket of his jeans. I couldn't help myself from smiling, did I have no shame? Nope. Not where it came to Nathan anyway.

Leaning forwards Nathan propped his elbows on his knees and looked at me as if he were about to share a national secret with me. 'If we were in my car now I'd make you pull that cute little dress right up around your waist so your lovely hot arse was directly on the leather of my seat. Are you hot down there, Stella? Hot for me?' he asked with an urgency in his voice that was reflected in my suddenly needy panting and the way my fingers were now clawing at the scratchy material of the train seat.

'Yes.' My word was thick and husky, but oh so true – just his few words had set me off throbbing between my legs like I was ready to explode. In previous relationships I'd hated it when guys used dirty talk to me, it had been a complete turn off, but with Nathan? It was like flicking a detonator switch that immediately ignited my lust.

He smirked at my reply. 'I'd love knowing that you were making my car seat wet with your arousal. I'd love the way your scent would linger on the leather for hours afterwards, it would make me hard every time I got in the car. Do you know that? Do you know how much you affect me?' he demanded.

Oh God, I think I was about to climax just from his words alone. 'Yes … the same amount you affect me,' I replied breathily, with a lick of my lips to try and moisten my parched mouth.

Blinking at me several times Nathan shook his head very slowly, 'But we're not in my car,' he stated on a heavy breath. 'Because someone wanted to take the train today.' I was flashed an imperious look before he threw himself back in his seat, 'Fuck, just how long is this fucking train ride?' Nathan then exclaimed, twisting to look out of the window and suddenly not looking as cool and calm as he had just a minute ago when he was teasing me.

Hmm, perhaps I could do a little teasing of my own to fill the last few minutes of the ride. Sitting back in my seat I raised my right leg and propped it on the edge of Nathan's chair between his thigh and the wall of the train. I knew that with just a slight adjustment of the front of my dress Nathan would have a complete view up my legs, but was I feeling that naughty? You bet I was. I was so aroused and needy and seeing as he had started this game in the first place I wanted him to be just as frustrated as me.

The change in my position had drawn Nathan's eyes away from the window and his focus was now solely on me. Using one single finger I pulled the front edge of my skirt up several inches and watched in fascination as Nathan's expression changed from curiosity, to shock, to downright dirty approval.

I giggled, half from embarrassment of just how slutty I was being, and half from his amusing response. 'Fuck, Stella.' He ran a hand over his face trying to clear his surprise, then looked back between my legs with an expression of pure desire on his face. 'Do you want me to blow my load here on the fucking train?' he asked in a strained tone as he lifted his hips slightly and adjusted his groin within the tight confines of his jeans.

He must be rather uncomfortable now, poor guy, all his large aroused manhood stuck within that denim. I smiled deviously, his obvious arousal only adding to my thoughts of naughtiness. Very slowly I shifted my finger lower until it brushed across the soft skin of my inner thigh. A choking sound came from Nathan's throat and I grinned as I saw his hands balling into fists at his sides with the effort not to touch me. Apparently he did draw the line at train sex, which was good to know for future reference.

Knowing we were just seconds away from our station I decided on one final tease for him and briefly ran my finger down the warm crease of my folds, a small moan escaping my lips at just how good it felt, not to mention how wet I was. Jeez, without my panties on I'd practically be dripping on the walk home. But before I could finish my planned seduction Nathan let out a growl, ripped my hand away from my clit, pulled my dress down, and immediately sucked my finger into his mouth. *Bloody hell.*

The look in his eyes as he ran his tongue around my finger was one of pure unadulterated arousal and I bit my lip as my own body thrummed along with his.

Just then the train pulled into our platform and Nathan stood up, literally hoisting me from my seat by my wrist. His foot tapped manically as we waited in strained silence for the doors to open and then as soon as they had he was off, dragging me from the train and down the platform. 'Do you have any idea how close I was to taking you on that bloody train?' he barked, sounding so frustrated that I couldn't help but smile, 'Next time we go out we take my car. No more fucking trains. That way when you decided to act like a little temptress I can park in a private place and fuck some sense into you.'

I'd never seen Nathan this impatient; his laid-back demeanour of earlier was gone, replaced by his more characteristic bolshiness, but I didn't mind, when Nathan was focused on well and truly sexing me up I could do nothing but hope that the walk home went quickly.

Shoving my Oyster card impatiently onto the barrier I let out a yelp of shock as Nathan came up behind me and in a split second had slid a hand up my skirt and rammed two fingers right inside of me. Holy shit! I sagged forwards as the delicious pressure of his pumping fingers curled inside of me, hitting perfectly against my G-spot; it was just as well there were no station staff around otherwise I might be getting that warning for public indecency after all. 'So fucking wet,' he murmured against my ear, but then his fingers were gone and he was reaching around me with a growl to take my card from my shaking hands and let me through the barrier, following shortly behind me.

With my wobbly legs and trying to stop my skirt blowing up in the breeze I struggled to keep up with Nathan on the short walk home and by the time we reached the bottom of the steps to Nathan's apartment building his frustration with my speed was becoming apparent. 'Move. Faster.' he complained through gritted teeth, but then replacing his frown with a grin he suddenly bent down, scooped me up over his shoulder, and began to stride on again. 'Better,' he stated over my yelp, smoothing my dress down with one hand so at least my bum wasn't exposed to the world.

Well, this was certainly quicker. Tucking my hands into the waistband of his jeans to support myself I looked around from my upside down position and saw the man on reception giving us a strange look that just made my grin even bigger. Once we were in the lift I thought Nathan would let me down, but he didn't, instead one of his hands began impatiently tapping out a drumming rhythm on the wall as he waited for us to reach the top floor whilst the other began fiddling under my skirt again, making me giggle and writhe around on his shoulder. Well two could play at that game, so I pushed my hands inside the back of jeans, down inside his boxers, and gave his firm bum a damn good fondle of my own.

We made it into his apartment within two seconds of exiting the lift and then Nathan strode straight for the bedroom – *his bedroom* – another new development for the day, before he tossed me down on the bed immediately following and covering me with his big, hot body.

I couldn't help but get excited as Nathan loomed over me. He was just so powerful and domineering that it flicked all the right switches within me. 'Well, Stella, you got me so worked up on the train that I'd thought I'd have to take you fast and hard when we got home.' My heart rate accelerated at the prospect and I drew in a shaky breath pulling my lower lip in between my teeth and biting down. Getting control over his breathing Nathan tilted his head, examining me as if he'd never seen me before. 'But now that we're here I think I might just take my time.' Oh goody, fast and hard was fun, but drawn-out sex with

Nathan sounded even better.

Supporting his weight on one hand Nathan reached up and flicked my lower lip free of its confines. 'No biting on this,' he reminded me as his mouth lowered to meet mine. I had fully been expecting a bruising, fierce kiss, but what I got instead was oddly tender and sweet. Not usual for Nathan at all, but equally as arousing for me, if not more so. His body was still covering me like a blanket and pressed so tightly against me that it was almost difficult for me to breathe, but I didn't complain, in fact I relished the contact. Usually Nathan would have me restrained in some way and unable to touch him whilst he drove me wild, but following the trait of the day Nathan's sexual routine seemed to be following a different route to usual as well.

My hands became greedy and began exploring Nathan's hard muscles; roaming across his bunched biceps as they held his position above me, tracing the shape of his shoulder blades, and finally following the line of his ribs until I hit his belt. I never got to undress Nathan, he would dispose of my clothes and then do the same to his, but seeing as everything was different today I decided to go with my instincts and I took hold of his polo shirt and pulled it out of his jeans. The material was warm where it had been tucked inside and I wanted nothing more than to pull it over his head, but our bodies were too close to allow me the space to do it.

As if sensing my thoughts Nathan rolled us over so I was straddling his hips and then sat himself up so we were chest to chest, where he immediately captured my mouth again. When he finally pulled back his gaze was heavy lidded and I noticed we were both breathing heavily, almost panting, and we'd barely got started on the tiring stuff yet! Dropping a quick kiss on my lips he leaned back a bit and raised his arms slightly as if inviting me to remove his top. Was this a trick? I decided not to question everything and took hold of the hem of his T-shirt and pulled it over his head in one swift move, leaving his hair in a mussed pile on his head and his glorious chest within licking distance. Instead of licking him I licked my own lips, and he chuckled, apparently reading my thoughts once again.

'Touch me, Stella,' he murmured, but it wasn't a demand or an order like usual – it was just the soft, needy words of a lover and after a brief swoon I immediately complied, pressing him back on the bed and then leaning over to explore his body. Instead of going straight to the temptation of his chest though, I decided to do a bit of kissing of my own and I cupped his jaw with one hand and lowered my lips to his, my tongue seeking entry to his mouth by running along the seam of his lips in a swift lick. He gave a soft groan and opened his mouth as his hands came up to rest on my hips, his fingertips digging into the flesh.

After a truly dizzying kiss I began to work my way down the column of his neck, dropping kisses and licking up the delicious salty taste of his skin until I was next to one of his hard nipples. Just a quick flick of my tongue had it tight and I grinned at his response before repeating the same treatment to the other side of his chest.

Shifting my hips down so I was sat on his thighs I began working the buttons of his jeans but paused when he propped himself up on his elbows, watching me inquisitively. Had I overstepped the mark? Looking up at him I bit on my lip and paused, 'Is this OK?' I asked cautiously, my hands mid-grope on his bulging groin.

'Christ yes, Stella, keep going.' My apprehension was swept away by a huge grin and my fingers once again set about freeing him from the constriction of his jeans. Considering just how excited he was this was a little trickier than I first anticipated, but with some help from Nathan and a good deal of wriggling I finally had him naked and hard below me.

'I think there is a little unfairness in your clothing levels compared to mine,' Nathan observed wryly as he fingered a section of my sundress and gave it a gentle tug.

'Really? There are certain advantages to being naked though, for example, if you're naked I can do this ...' I dropped forwards and placed a wet lick across one of his nipples, causing him to moan and arch from the bed, 'Or this ...' Shifting down I repeated another lick, but this time running my tongue from the tip of his cock right down to the base. This move definitely got more response than just a simple moan as I found myself bucked into the air and then seconds later I was pinned below a very aroused, very frustrated mass of blond male.

'Enough teasing,' he panted, 'I need to get you naked *right now* ...' My sun dress was gone so fast I barely felt him move me – in fact I'd be surprised if I found it in one piece tomorrow – my bra quickly followed suit and then we were naked and sprawled on his huge bed in a tangle of legs and arms and lips.

Leaning up on one elbow Nathan paused for breath and positioned himself between my legs, so instinctively I averted my eyes, but to my surprise Nathan nudged my chin with one thumb, 'Look at me, Stella,' he whispered, and as I made eye contact with his big blue pools of lust he thrust into me in one long, smooth motion, causing me to cry out and clutch at his back.

Everything about today with Nathan had been different, even now he moved within me with a slower, gentler pace than usual and I couldn't help but feel that this was also new, if I didn't know about our contract I'd have almost believed we were making love, not just fucking.

The entire afternoon had been like one long foreplay session and now with Nathan increasing the speed and depth of his thrusts I could already feel the build-up of a climax in my abdomen. 'Wait ... Stella, wait for me,' Nathan murmured, and then after just a few more of his harder thrusts I felt him hardening even more inside of me as his eyes once more sought mine.

'Now?' I asked, desperately hoping he'd say yes, because there was no way I'd be able to hold it off much longer.

'Yes ... together ...' he panted, his strokes getting less controlled as he neared his climax, and then I was lost to the pleasure of an immense orgasm as it washed over me in wave after wave of delicious spasms, clenching around Nathan and causing him to spurt his release into me on a loud shout.

Holy fuck. Talk about intense. We'd done so much together in the bedroom, but that had honestly felt like our first time together, it had been so much more intimate and passionate than anything else we'd done that I was feeling pretty blown away by it all.

Thankfully, in his post-orgasmic state Nathan didn't seem to notice my teeth working my lower lip as my brain tried to make sense of what the heck had just occurred between us.

Nathan was the first to break the silence as he rolled off to the side and pulled me over to rest in his arms. 'I ... I've enjoyed today, Stella,' he sounded almost hesitant as if embarrassed to admit it. 'And ... and I wanted to thank you ... for listening ... last night.' I could sense how uncomfortable his mention of last night made him, so I stayed mostly quiet, just murmuring 'Any time,' careful not to spoil the moment by getting too deep.

His hand began running up and down my arm gently and I shivered with pleasure and snuggled closer to his incredible warmth. 'I wish I didn't, but I have to be away on business this week, I'll be back next weekend though. Stay at my place as usual next Friday if you like, I'll get home as soon as I can on Saturday morning.' Oh! My eyebrows rose in excitement, he sounded quite keen, surely that was a good sign? Maybe I could invite Kenny round on the Friday night for a DVD and a takeaway so he could get a proper look at Nathan's apartment.

'I had planned to take you out to dinner tonight,' Nathan murmured, and I'm fairly sure I could hear a smile in his voice. '… but I think perhaps now that we are both naked maybe we'll just order a takeaway later. Unless you're hungry now?' A smile spread on my face, it was nowhere near dinner time yet, but I knew exactly what I wanted to do to pass the time.

'I am hungry, but not for food,' I whispered, lowering my left hand under the sheet to where I found Nathan already hard and ready for round two – as I had suspected he might be.

'That's my girl,' he murmured darkly, rolling me over and lunging down to kiss my neck.

His girl? Holy crap, I wanted to ask Nathan to rewind his last sentence and give it to me in writing so I could treasure it forever, but my words were lost as his mouth travelled up my jaw and lowered to my lips distracting me from logical thought once again.

Chapter Ten – Stella

I was trying desperately hard not to breathe too deeply or loudly and spoil the unexpectedly lovely moment that I had found myself in when I woke up. Blinking several times I squeezed my eyes shut and then opened them again just to check that I was definitely awake, and that this was real.

Yep, as surreal as it seemed, I was awake and this was definitely real. It was morning – the morning after our lovely trip to Greenwich Park – and Nathan was still fast asleep in the same bed as me. *His bed.* This had never happened before, I'd always woken up and found Nathan gone in the mornings. Christ, I was so excited by this new development that my heart was beating so fast and so loudly that I was worried it was going to wake him – in barely a split second my poor ticker had literally gone from restful and sleepy to wide awake and pounding like a sledgehammer.

What was making it even more special for me was Nathan's positioning – he wasn't just asleep in the same bed as me, he was asleep and draped *all* over me. Like he had craved me in his sleep and moved closer until he was almost smothering me. His head was on my chest, using one of my boobs as a pillow, his right arm was laid on my stomach, and his right leg was flung over both of mine as if to stop me escaping. He needn't have worried on that front, I was so ecstatic right now that I wasn't planning on going anywhere any time soon.

The minute he woke up I knew it. I felt his breathing shift slightly, becoming shallower as awareness came over him, and his eyelashes flickered against my skin as he blinked. I stopped breathing altogether, waiting for him to realise where he was, panic and leave. But to my amazement he didn't. There was a brief tensing of Nathan's body, but then I felt a long warm breath fan across my chest as he let out a sigh and snuggled in closer, his hand shifting to my hip and rubbing gentle circles on my massively oversensitive skin.

Oh my God. Nathaniel Jackson, my so-called dominant and bad boy, was snuggling. *Snuggling.* I quite literally never thought I'd see the day.

Just when my little bubble of happiness had begun to grow in my chest to obscenely joyous levels I was brought back down to earth with an enormous thump. Nathan's hand ceased massaging my hip as he paused and his whole body tensed. Had he been half-asleep before and only just realised where he was and who he was with? From the tension he was now holding in his frame it certainly felt like it. With his body still rigidly stiff his fingers left my hip and slowly made their way up my body until they reached my neck, then he shifted himself carefully – apparently still thinking that I was asleep – and began to undo the choker around my neck.

Oh God. Nathan was removing my collar, the object that claimed me as 'his'. Without that what were we? We were nothing, he'd as good as said so to me in the past. There could be no other explanation for it – he must be done with me. We were over. I couldn't believe it. He must completely regret everything that happened yesterday between us, perhaps deciding it was all getting too much like a relationship and now as a result decided that enough was enough. I almost sobbed on the spot, but somehow I managed to pretend to be asleep and hold myself together just long enough for him to remove the collar, slip from the bed, and stride from the bedroom.

Flinging myself over onto my stomach I buried my

head into the still warm pillow and let my tears flow silently as Nathan's delicious scent teased me mercilessly. Gradually my tears lessened and common sense broke through my panic – perhaps I was overreacting? Perhaps he had some other reason for removing my collar? I was about to get up and confront him about it when I heard the clunk of the front door closing. Nathan had gone out? As I sniffled pathetically and wiped my runny nose on the back of my hand I remembered how he'd mentioned going away with work this week, and wondered if he'd left for his business trip already.

Frowning, I sat up and ran a shaky hand through my hair as I clutched the sheet to my chest and looked around his huge, unfamiliar bedroom. This should have been a monumental moment, the first time being officially allowed in his bedroom, but instead all I felt was complete confusion mixed with a desperate need to get out and back to the familiarity of my comfy little flat.

Deciding to double check if he really had gone out – perhaps there was a note explaining his actions – I headed cautiously through towards the lounge. Glancing around my breathing halted as I came to a sharp stop in the kitchen doorway as my eyes spotted something on the counter which crushed any remnants of hope I might have had, and made me realise with sicking finality that it definitely was well and truly over with Nathan – my submissive contract lay ripped in half on the kitchen counter, with my beautiful silver choker thrown carelessly next to it.

Closing my stinging eyes my mind immediately flashed back to my first meeting with Nathan at his house when we had discussed our contract and my throat tightened as I recalled his words – *'If either of us wishes to end our agreement we can simply say so and tear up the contract, end of'*. So that was definitely it, was it? End of? My hand instinctively went to my empty neck; it felt so bare as I clutched at the skin with trembling fingers.

After everything that had been happening recently; the shower together, the gentle sex, the walk in the park, his confessions … I'd really thought we'd turned a massive corner. But obviously that wasn't what Nathan wanted, he'd been clear about his 'no strings' expectations from the start, and now after letting myself get carried away with romantic visions yesterday, it was all over.

Not wanting to get caught looking like an emotional wreck if he returned I wasted no time in dashing back to his room and pulling on yesterday's discarded clothes and then heading straight to my room. I spent several minutes gathering every one of my belongings from the space so I wouldn't ever have to return. My head was fuzzy, my chest hurt in a way that I didn't even want to consider at the moment, and tears kept leaking down my cheeks, but I had my plan of escape ready – clear all evidence of my stay and then head towards the door to get the hell out of here as quick as my legs could take me.

Checking under the bed for any more stray clothes I cursed as I dragged my laptop bag out – thank goodness I hadn't forgotten that – but was suddenly filled with horror as I realised it was Monday morning.

'Shit.' I muttered thickly, pausing to close my eyes and grimace. I had to go to work now right after being dumped, what a frigging nightmare that was going to be.

Hoisting the bag over my shoulder I left the room, and then the apartment without even bothering to look back. My neck felt horribly, oddly bare without the necklace and as I stood in the lift my fingers repeatedly traced the skin where it used to lie. Talk about a shitty way to finish things. I couldn't believe Nathan had taken such a cowardly way out and not even spoken to me in person. And to do it on a Monday morning when I had to go to work just made his actions even more fucked up.

168

Chapter Eleven – Stella

Blowing some wayward hair out of my face I searched in my bag for my house keys before finally unlocking the door. A huge breath of relief flew from my lungs as the familiar scents and sights of my flat surrounded me, unfurling my tense muscles and letting me relax at last. Today had certainly been one day at work that I didn't *ever* want to repeat – I'd literally never been more pleased to get home in my entire life.

Dumping my work bag down, I stepped over the holdall containing my things from Nathan's that I'd dropped here before work this morning. Giving it a hateful glance I grimaced, I seriously doubted I'd ever want to wear or use anything from in there again. Way too many painful memories attached.

After the mornings shock of Nathan leaving and dumping me in the most crappy way possible I'd been a complete mess by the time I got to the office – complete with red-rimmed eyes and snivelling nose – and had had to endure a multitude of pitying looks from my colleagues as I'd walked through the agency to my private office. Initially I'd been tempted to take a day off, but in my stubbornness I'd forged on – there was no frigging way I was going to let a man disrupt my life like that. Even if the man in question was Nathaniel Jackson. Besides, what good would a day off have done me? I'd have sat around the flat moping and feeling sorry for myself, when I was perfectly capable of doing the exact same in my office and getting paid for it.

Of course none of my colleagues knew why I looked

like hell, but I'm sure the office gossips had already made up several juicy possibilities by the time my door had closed shut and I'd snapped the blinds together. I did discover one benefit to arriving at work with a miserable, blotchy, snot-covered face though – no-one dared bother me all day – so at least I had been left alone to stew in peace and chastise myself for falling for Nathan. Why hadn't I had a better grip on my heart? Falling for Nathan was beyond pointless, the man was so controlled and unfeeling that he practically needed a written contract to sneeze for God's sake.

Grabbing two bananas I dug my fingernails through the skin, peeled them almost violently, and then shoved them in the blender, before adding half a pint of milk, a shot of vanilla syrup, and slamming the lid on. I pressed the 'on' button just as the front door opened again, signalling the arrival of Kenny home from work, and in a spilt second I was covered in a syrupy, banana mess as the bloody blender lid flew off mid-whizz.

In front of me there was a fountain of banana milk flying everywhere and spattering onto the ceiling and walls. 'Fucking hell!' The words flew from my mouth as I desperately struggled to find the off switch amongst all the milk pouring down the side of the blender like Niagara frigging Falls. I'd always hated this stupid machine. 'Stupid bloody thing!' I very rarely swore out loud, but the combination of being dumped and now soaked had obviously brought out the worst in me.

'Here …' Kenny braved ruining his shirt – his turquoise shirt, might I add – and turned it off for me. Of course he would know where the stupid switch was, he always made his horrible diet drinks using it.

Casting an unamused glance around the splattered kitchen I shook off my sodden arm, sending a thick, oozy trail of milkshake spraying across the lake of banana milk already residing on the counter. 'So ... what's up?' Kenny asked knowingly, standing back and gazing at me intently as he wiped his hand on a tea towel. It would take more than a tea towel to sort me out, I was drenched. Not to mention put off bananas for quite a while; the smell was all over me and suddenly quite revolting. I looked up at him from under furrowed brows, a bit of banana-vanilla milk dribbling down my nose, and sighed heavily. I was dumped, depressed, and drenched, what wasn't up?

'We're going out to get drunk,' I replied, avoiding his question completely.

'We are? But it's Monday night.' The confusion in Kenny's voice was obvious as his brows dipped lower.

'Yeah? So?' I huffed grouchily. My foul mood probably wasn't making the prospect of going out with me for a drink the most appealing thing ever, so I sighed again and confessed my woes. 'Nathan finished our agreement this morning.' I plucked a piece of banana from my hair and flicked it in the bin, but it missed and slid down the wall instead. 'I wasn't ready for it to finish,' I added softly feeling fresh tears prick at the backs of my eyes. What an understatement. I had fallen for Nathan hook, line, and sinker and now he'd finished it I felt like a chunk of my heart had been chewed up, spat out, and trampled on.

'Fuck,' Kenny winced supportively, 'So, what are you waiting for then? Clean that sticky crap out of your hair and let's go drinking,' he said, coming forwards and pulling me in for a special Kenny-style squeeze regardless of the state of my clothes. God, I loved Kenny so much sometimes.

'If your plan for the night was to get drunk, then why were you making a milkshake?' he enquired, leaning back from our embrace and eyeing the blender cautiously.

'Lining my stomach,' I mumbled, burying my head in his chest again.

'Ah, I see. That kind of defeats the whole drinking

thing doesn't it?' he teased, giving me a little tickle on my lower ribs – my most ticklish spot.

'Shut up, Kenny,' I mumbled against his shirt. 'Take me out and get me drunk.'

If I'd looked like crap going into work on Monday, then I must have looked like crap warmed up going into work on Tuesday – with a hangover from hell after 'Mojito Monday' at Mojo's cocktail bar. Turns out that Kenny was right, Monday night drinking was not a good idea. Actually, it possibly goes down as the most God-awful decision I've ever made. Apart from joining Club Twist and seeking out a dominant sexual partner of course – now that really *was* the worst decision of my life.

The remainder of the week dragged by horrendously slowly. I did barely any work and the more I mourned the loss of my 'relationship' with Nathan, the more my mood progressively worsened. I'd been such a super bitch at work in the five days since 'the dumping', that I think my colleagues were actually scared to approach me by Friday.

No calls had come from Nathan either, not that I'd really expected them to. After the cold way he'd ended things he'd made his feelings pretty clear. I still shuddered when I thought about my ripped up contract and discarded necklace. Jeez, even with all his fucked-up-ness I'd have thought Nathan would at least have had the guts to finish with me in person. I'd been tempted to call him on several occasions to give him a few lessons in break-up etiquette, but thankfully this was usually after a few drinks and Kenny had always been there to talk some sense into me.

When all was said and done, Nathan had been my contracted dominant, certainly not my boyfriend, a fact that I bitterly reminded myself of daily. Regardless of his strangely affectionate behaviour last Sunday, feelings and emotions weren't supposed to be part of our agreement, he'd made that perfectly clear from the start. *I* had been the one to break the rules and develop an affection for him, so *I* was the one who needed get a wriggle on and get over him.

Chapter Twelve – Nathan

I'd had a full week away with work, staying in a bloody hotel and even with my determined effort the source of the mystery company that was plaguing my bids was still no clearer. I'd left Gregory on the case in Manchester, where the mystery PO Box was listed, and now finally it was Saturday morning and I was on the road. I hated hotels and the lack of privacy that they afforded you – there was always some busy body cleaner knocking on the door every five minutes. I couldn't wait to sleep in my own bed tonight, but topping that, I couldn't wait to get home and see Stella.

Whilst I'd been away I'd made the monumental decision to lay my feelings out on the table with her. I might not like talking about emotional stuff – in fact just the thought of it was enough to make me shudder – but some things just needed saying in words and after our amazing weekend together I needed to hear Stella say that she wanted to be with me, that she wanted to try a relationship with me. Christ, talk about a shocker. I literally never thought I'd see the day when I, Nathaniel Jackson, dominant, moody arsehole, was actually hoping with every fibre of my being that a woman wanted more than just sex with me.

Shaking my head I smiled at my thoughts. Despite the ongoing work issues, I'd been feeling quite light-hearted all week, something I was giving Stella the credit for, after she had made me feel so alive last weekend.

My final meeting yesterday had run on and on, eventually finishing well past two in the morning, but undeterred I'd driven through the night to get home for the weekend, hoping that Stella had stayed at mine last night as I'd suggested. Smiling, I thought back to last weekend. Being more open around her had been far easier than I'd expected, and seeing her thrilled response to my simple actions like hand holding and eye contact had made me feel far more contented than I'd ever thought possible.

Me, turning into a sappy nice guy, who'd have thought it eh? Although 'nice guy' was a bit of a stretch given the dark thoughts and sexual depravity that often loitered in my head, perhaps 'deviant developing a conscience' was more accurate.

Thinking of nice gestures I made an on the spot decision to stop off on the way home to grab some breakfast for us both as a surprise. Hopefully Stella would still be in bed – nah, scrap that; hopefully she'd be *naked* and in *my* bed.

As I waited for my freshly baked croissants the waitress poured me another glass of orange juice and I settled back with a paper from the counter. Immediately I found myself raising an eyebrow as a photograph in the paper caught my eye. *Nicholas*. More precisely Nicholas and Rebecca at some charity function they'd attended last night. I chuckled to myself and shook my head, my brother hated the semi-famous status he had from his piano career, but to be honest he looked pretty damn happy in the photo as he gazed lovingly down at a resplendent Rebecca. *Lovingly*. Wow, it really was clear in my brother's eyes, but also in Rebecca's too, that they shared a very special bond. Was that something I could have with Stella? Christ, I hoped so.

Instead of heading straight home to Stella with the croissants, I decided to pay another quick visit to my brother for a bit of last-minute advice from his endlessly supportive girlfriend. Normally I hated asking for assistance from anyone, but if Rebecca had managed to tame Nicholas maybe she could give me some final words of wisdom too that would bolster my courage and help me in my talk with Stella.

Fifteen minutes later I realised that I really needed to start wearing a watch, because as I stood on Nicholas's doorstep for the second weekend in a row I checked my phone and noticed once again just how early it was. Damn it. Well, I wasn't going home without speaking to Rebecca first so I may as well use the key Nicholas had given me to let myself in and get some coffee going.

I had possibly – OK, intentionally – banged around a bit whilst setting up the coffee maker hoping to wake Nicholas and Rebecca, or perhaps they were just early risers, because not long after the coffee had brewed I was joined by them, both looking sleep-tousled but happy.

'I saw you two in the papers this morning,' I said as way of greeting, chucking down the copy I'd brought from the café. I watched as Rebecca picked it up and looked at the picture with wide eyes. At a guess I'd say it was her first experience of being in a national newspaper. If she was planning on sticking with Nicholas she'd better get used to it, he was quite a magnet for the journalists now that his piano playing had hit the big time.

Handing them both a cup of coffee I leaned back on the counter and sipped my own drink whilst they skimmed the article. Nicholas slipped an arm around Rebecca's waist and read over her shoulder, looking rather pleased with himself – no doubt as a result of catching himself such an incredible woman. Could I do that? Be with one woman and look that happy? I was starting to think that I could if that woman was Stella.

'Rebecca, can I grab you for five minutes again?' I asked, too impatient to wait for her to finish her entire coffee. I wanted to speak to her and then make tracks home to Stella.

'You can't *grab her* at all, brother,' Nicholas warned me with a glare as his possessive grip on Rebecca tightened. I almost smiled as I thought back to my own over reaction when I'd seen Stella out with her brother. At least now I knew exactly how Nicholas felt.

'You know what I mean, Nicholas. Five minutes' chat,' I explained patiently with a shake of my head. Rebecca smiled up at Nicholas and then shrugged out of his arm to lead me to the lounge again. She certainly seemed more relaxed around me this week, which was good.

Taking up my usual position by the fireplace I glanced around and smirked – this was becoming like our regular therapy room. Not bothering with any preamble I got straight to the point. 'I did what you said. We went out to the park last weekend; walked a while and ate ice-cream. I think Stella enjoyed it. We had sex afterwards, no funny stuff, just normal sex ... it was good ... really good actually.' I almost surprised myself by how true my words were. There had been no kink at all, but still it had been some of the best sex of my life.

'Maybe you should discuss this with Nicholas ...' Rebecca mumbled. I would have totally missed her embarrassment if it weren't for the flush that crept to her cheeks, but I couldn't speak to Nicholas about this, not yet, not until I definitely knew if Stella wanted to try a relationship with me. No, I needed Rebecca's advice, she'd just have to get over her embarrassment and help me.

'No Rebecca, you've changed Nicholas, I see that, I want to change too, I need your advice.' I stepped closer, using full eye-contact as I had with Stella last week. I was actually getting quite good at it. 'I'm fairly sure my father used to be in charge in the bedroom too, my room was next door and I ...' I paused, realising that now it was me who was embarrassed, '... I saw and heard certain, uh ... things,' I finished with a narrowed expression as I remembered back to some of the messed up things I'd seen my father doing to my mother.

Rebecca looked about ready to run from the room so I sidestepped to block her path. There was one question I needed the answer to before she left. 'Do you and Nicholas do any kinky stuff now, any bondage or punishments at all?' I demanded hotly.

'I'm really not comfortable discussing this, Nathan. It's up to you and Stella to set the boundaries,' she murmured awkwardly.

A frown knit my brows together and I scowled down at her, not pleased by her answer at all. Didn't she realise I needed clear, definitive answers? I was just about to demand she tell me, when Rebecca seemed to relent on a sigh. 'Nicholas and I talked about what we both liked and what I disliked and there is certain stuff we don't do any more, but it's a personal thing. You need to sit down with Stella and ask her opinions.'

OK – ask her opinion. I wasn't the world's best talker but surely I could do that if it meant that Stella might stay with me and give me a chance at something more with her? I nodded, running a hand nervously through my hair at the prospect of the conversation I needed to have with Stella. 'Right, ask her opinion, got it. You mean what rules we stick to? Which toys she likes, things like that?'

Rebecca blushed, the colour reaching up to her hairline. 'Er, yeah. You might want to loosen up on the rules bit, Nathan; normal relationships don't use them quite the way you do. She needs to feel like an individual as well as your partner.'

'OK … reassess the rules and ask her opinion on sexual stuff … I'll go and do that now,' I stated firmly, before heading out of the lounge door and practically running into Nicholas who was loitering outside the door with a protective frown on his face.

'Thanks, Rebecca. Bye, Nicholas,' I called as I practically jogged down the stairs to my car so I could head home to Stella.

179

Unfortunately when I got home my excitement about developing my relationship with Stella was brought to an abrupt halt by a slight problem. There was no Stella. In fact, Stella and all traces of her were gone from my apartment – it was as if she had never been there at all. What the fuck?

Chapter Thirteen – Stella

It was Saturday morning and I was lounging on the sofa feeling well and truly sorry for myself. Kenny came sailing into the adjoining kitchen humming a dreadfully tuneless song wearing only a pair of black *Batman* pants and nothing else. Thank God I wasn't hung-over because the sight of Kenny in Y-fronts would quite possibly have prompted a very speedy vomiting session. To be fair to Kenny, he had quite a nice body; it was the Y-fronts that were vomit inducing – I'd always hated them on a man, but then realistically you'd have to be hung like a horse to ever make them look vaguely passable.

As it was I just grimaced, and tutted – if I couldn't see Nathan's near-naked body I didn't want to see anyone else's either. 'For God's sake, Kenny, cover yourself up!' I mumbled grumpily, digging myself deeper into the cushions on the sofa so I was well and truly cocooned in preparation for my day of moping.

Letting out a piercing shriek Kenny jumped a mile into the air, spraying coffee beans everywhere and then turned to me, clutching his chest dramatically. Oh my God, the pants got worse – on the front, right over his groin, was written *The Dark Knight Rises*. How very Kenny.

'Christ, Stella, you nearly gave me a heart attack! What the hell are you doing here on a weekend, you're normally with …' Dumping the coffee on the counter with a loud clatter Kenny smacked himself on the forehead and winced apologetically, 'I'm such an insensitive knob … sorry, I totally forgot you split up.'

Sighing heavily I felt like informing Kenny that Nathan

and I hadn't split up, he'd simply torn up my contract, removed my collar, and buggered off. All information I'd kept to myself at my drinking session with Kenny last Monday night; I bit my lip and kept the mortifying details quiet. And how Kenny had forgotten we'd split up I had no idea, I'd been like a bear with an exceptionally sore head all week. Climbing from the sofa I found the dust pan and brush, knelt by the sink and started brushing up the spilt beans as a distraction to my depressing thoughts.

'It's fine,' I huffed. It wasn't fine, but what else could I say? I fell for a guy who told me our relationship would only ever be about sex and now he's gone I miss him so much that I want to crawl into a pit and die? Perhaps that was a little dramatic. Maybe living with Kenny the drama queen was starting to rub off on me.

'So what are your plans this weekend then?' Kenny asked brightly, 'I bet now you've finally got a Saturday free you've got loads of stuff to catch up on.' Bless him, Kenny was obviously trying to make me feel better, but it wasn't working. I had nothing to do. No a thing. Had my weekends been this dull and empty before I met Nathan?

Our slightly awkward exchange was suddenly interrupted by the chiming of our doorbell, informing us that someone was at the main entrance to the flats. I continued with my brushing as Kenny skipped over to see who it was before staggering back in shock, making a high pitched noise in his throat which sounded rather like a car alarm. 'Oh my God, Stella, it's him!' Kenny whispered, flicking frantic stares between the camera and my prone form on the floor. There was no need to ask who the '*him*' was he was referring to – the horrified look on Kenny's face made it perfectly clear who it was. *Nathan.*

'What should I do?' he whispered again, although why he was whispering was a mystery to me, there was no way Nathan would have been able to hear him; the camera didn't contain a microphone and we were three floors up.

Nathan would have to have ears like a bat to hear Kenny's voice from down there. But they weren't bat like at all – from memory Nathan's ears were pretty perfect, just like the bloody rest of him.

'Ignore it,' I said tightly. Easing my reluctant body from the floor I dumped the wasted coffee beans into the bin before joining Kenny by the intercom. *Fuck*, even through the grainy black and white image of the security camera Nathan looked just as bloody glorious as he would have done in full high definition colour. Glorious but angry, by the looks of the scowl on his face.

Turning my back on the image I squeezed my eyes closed to try and shut down the pain now radiating in my chest. Why was he here? We were over, for God's sake. Was he here to torment me and remind me how much I still wanted him? I'd moved all my things out of my room at his place and left it tidy enough, what the hell could I have done wrong?

Clutching the wall I tried to breathe slowly and ease the pain in my lungs. I'd never been in love before, but given the utter misery of the last week, not to mention the pain currently burning in my chest, what I felt for Nathan must be bloody close. I was so sodding naive to enter a relationship with him and not see this coming. My head dropped until my chin touched my chest. God, I loved Nathan and he'd finished with me. My life really was well and truly shit.

'He looks angry,' Kenny commented, his eyes still latched to the screen. I suspected that whilst being supportive of me he was also getting his fill of my ex's delicious features. 'Don't you want to know what he wants?'

I did and I didn't. It wouldn't be anything good though, would it? After ripping up my contract and removing my choker he'd made his feelings towards me perfectly clear. Nope, I was better off keeping my distance, I'd made it through a week and was well on the way to getting over him. A near hysterical laugh bubbled in my throat – over him? What a complete load of rubbish! I was nowhere near over him, but seeing him in person certainly wasn't going to help so I began to cross the living room away from the door.

'Nope, just ignore it if he rings again. I'm going for a shower.'

Nathan's unexpected appearance at our flat this morning had turned out to be the most interesting highlight of my day so far. Apart from spending an age in the shower distracting myself by plucking, waxing, shaving, and preening every part of myself, I had then retreated back to the sofa and proceeded to watch crappy re-runs on television while also having the occasional little snooze.

I hadn't even had Kenny to keep me company, as it turned out that the *Batman* pants were being worn especially for the male guest he had holed up in his bedroom. That probably explained his forgetfulness about my dumped status too, he'd no doubt been too busy trying to impress his date and had forgotten all about my lacklustre love life.

After he'd made me a coffee this morning I'd not seen any more of Kenny, and thank God I hadn't been able to hear whatever he was getting up to in his lucky pants either, which had been a mighty relief.

By five o'clock I had started to consider the possibility of ordering some takeaway food when there was a loud banging on my front door. The door right behind me, not the intercom, which meant that it was either one of my neighbours popping round or someone had got past security and made their way up here. Another huge pounding on the door made me shriek and I jumped up thinking the entire door and frame was about to come crashing inwards.

'What the hell's going on, Stella?' Kenny squealed, appearing at my side and still only wearing those bloody pants.

'I don't know ...' I murmured cautiously, staring at the now silent front door, and although I had a pretty good idea of who was banging the grain out of my door I still had absolutely no idea why.

Inching closer I looked though the peep hole and confirmed my suspicions. Nathan. Looking really broody as he stared at the floor with his shoulders rising and falling frantically from his exertion. Suddenly as if he knew I was looking his head snapped up and he looked straight at the peep hole, causing me to shriek almost as stupidly as Kenny had earlier.

Advancing on the door in a flash Nathan was pounding again at the same time as speaking loudly, 'I know you're in there, Stella, I heard you, open this bloody door before it falls down.' With the way he was banging I seriously believed it would as well.

Flashing an edgy glance at Kenny I reached for the lock and then biting my lip I tensed my body and cautiously opened my poor abused door.

'Stella, thank fuck,' Nathan said on a whooshed breath. Confusingly he looked rather relieved to have found me, but his relief was shortly replaced by flooding emotion again as his cheeks flushed and his eyes flashed around wildly. 'Where's your fucking phone? I've been trying to call you all day.' My phone ... good question. I hadn't been expecting any calls so I didn't have it with me, it was probably still in my bedroom shoved under my pillow on silent.

At this point Kenny attempted to be my hero, bless him, by walking over to Nathan, puffing out his chest, placing his hands on his hips, and looking up at him. With Nathan being rather tall it was quite a long way up for Kenny, but I suspected that he did this partly for me, partly to get a closer look at my God of a man up close, and partly to impress his boyfriend who was now peering around the door frame watching us all with wide eyes.

'I think you need to leave,' Kenny said firmly, which was quite brave really seeing how emotional Nathan seemed – he was literally vibrating and twitching at the moment, but when Nathan ignored him Kenny took a step closer and I winced, not liking Kenny's chances against Nathan's strength one little bit.

Thankfully Nathan didn't hit him – in fact Kenny's attempted intervention didn't faze Nathan at all, he just placed a hand on Kenny's chest and held him at arm's length whilst Kenny's legs kind of skidded on the spot in a rather cartoonish fashion as he tried and failed to get closer.

As this bizarre scene unfolded in front of me Nathan's icy blue eyes hadn't left mine once, he merely stared intently at me unblinking, as if worried that I might vanish again before his very eyes. The sensation of his undiluted attention took my breath away and sent my body into a tail spin, as all the emotions of the last week reared up and engulfed me again, making my legs weak below me.

'It's Saturday, why aren't you at my place? And why have you moved all your things out?' Nathan demanded in a low tone between deep breaths. OK, *time out*. I might be overly emotional, but it'd be fair to say I was well and truly confused now. He was the one who had torn up our contract and removed my collar, but here he was seeming like he'd completely forgotten that he'd done it. Had he been in an accident? Maybe he had partial amnesia? I couldn't think of any other logical reasons for his crazy behaviour.

'Jesus, I've been going out of my fucking mind, Stella.' He said suddenly on a huge whooshed breath, but at the moment I couldn't respond, I felt beyond speech, I just couldn't comprehend what was going on. One thing I did know, however, was that I didn't want to discuss this in front of an audience, and with Kenny and his friend gleefully looking on like spectators at a tennis match I was suddenly very keen to get out of here.

'I'm a little confused, Nathan ...' I started, but his mind was obviously in overdrive because his eyes flew open wide as his arms began to gesticulate wildly and he spoke over me.

'You're confused?' he choked, looking even more unstable now. 'You're confused?!' he repeated in a higher, almost warbled tone as if it needed repeating. Which it really didn't, I'd heard him perfectly the first time.

'Look ... I think perhaps we need to go somewhere and talk?' I suggested warily.

'You're damn right we need to talk.' Brushing Kenny away like a fly Nathan strode straight past me and down the corridor into my bedroom, leaving me standing by the open door still utterly confused and staring after him. What was he doing now? Ignoring Kenny's excited whispers to his boyfriend I pushed the door shut and quickly followed Nathan to my bedroom. Glancing suspiciously into the room I found him muttering nonsensically under his breath whilst shoving a random collection of things into my weekend holdall, his huge build and bristling tension seeming to dwarf my room to the size of a shoebox.

'What are you doing?' I questioned cautiously, thinking that Nathan might actually have lost his mind.

'I'm taking your stuff back to my house. You're moving in with me,' He grumbled petulantly, stalking to my bookcase and practically sweeping the entire contents of the make-up shelf into the bag. My eyebrows flew up, not from his actions, but from his words - *moving in with him?* He really had lost his marbles.

I stood frozen to the spot, now far too confused to form any logical sentences as he moved wordlessly past me into my en-suite. I heard the sound of more frantic packing coming from my bathroom and shook my head trying to clear my foggy confusion.

Finally Nathan re-emerged, still with an unreadable expression on his face and now moving with the speed of a crazed tornado.

'Uh, Nathan ...' I began, about to ask what the heck was going on, not to mention enquire what he was on about when he said I was moving in with him, but he spun in my direction and the distraught look on his face completely floored me and had me snapping my mouth shut in surprise.

Wide blue eyes gazed back me, almost childlike in their desolate expression. It was difficult to tell, but he looked fearful, almost broken, as he continued to look at me, his lashes blinking long and slow as if he might even be fighting back tears. Holy shit, this sudden transparency in his emotions was confusing me even more. I was stunned into a frozen silence, my heartbeat hammering loudly in my ears making me feel giddy. I was torn between the urge to go to him and throw my arms around him, but terrified that I was reading this situation all completely wrong and that he might still reject me.

Suddenly it was as if Nathan deflated before my eyes; a huge breath escaped his lungs as his shoulders slumped forwards, he dropped my bag to the floor with a loud clattering and then he leaned forwards to brace his palms on the doors of my wardrobe.

Wincing I looked down at my bag. I'd be lucky if any of my cosmetics survived his hasty packing – in fact, after being dropped like that I wouldn't be surprised at all to open the bag and just find a big powdery, sludgy mess smeared all over my clothes. Marvellous.

Licking my lips I cautiously stepped towards Nathan and placed a hand tentatively on his shoulder. He acknowledged my touch with a small grunt, but didn't shake me off as I had expected. Now that I was closer I could see how hard Nathan was fighting to hold himself together, whatever was going on here was clearly upsetting him just as much as it was me because he was breathing in and out through his nose so deeply that it flared his nostrils with every breath. It sounded like he was muttering numbers under his breath, counting down in sequence and just as I was about to speak again he reached zero and then turned to me.

Rolling his shoulders back Nathan loosened off his neck with an audible click that made me wince and then bent to retrieve my holdall.

'Pack some things, Stella,' he murmured, then grimacing he closed his eyes added a quiet, 'Please,' to his sentence. 'We need to talk and it's getting late, bring a bag with you but if you don't want to stay I'll bring you home again afterwards.'

My head couldn't process things quick enough to protest and it felt too big for my body as I nodded my agreement and reached out to take the bag from his clenched fist.

Moving the bag out of my reach Nathan used his free hand to place a thumb under my chin and tip it up so my eyes met his narrowed gaze. 'When you answer me I expect it verbally, Stella, you know that,' Nathan said in a low tone, which caused my gaze to snap up to his. What the heck? That had sounded much more like the Nathan I was familiar with. What was going on? I blinked at him several times and then licked my dry lips as I tried to calm my disorientated brain enough to think of what question to fire at him first.

'Stella …' he growled, obviously not liking being kept waiting by my confused silence.

'Sorry … *Sir*,' I whispered, adding his title because his sudden change in demeanour seemed to require it somehow. But after my two feeble words my mind ground to a halt and I was unable to vocalise anything more. My eyes were still locked with his though as I struggled with my confusion. 'We'll talk, Stella, but not here, your flat mate no doubt has his ear pressed to the door. Come on, grab a few things.' I had no idea what to pack, as far as I had been concerned Nathan and I were finished, but his sudden appearance had made me question that, in fact I was just about questioning everything at the moment. Letting out a huge breath I opened my bag, shoved in a change of clothes and some clean underwear from my drawers, and then turned to leave.

To my surprise Nathan was standing with both his hands gripped in his hair as if he were trying to pull great tufts out of it. Cocking his head to the side Nathan dropped his arms and inspected me closely, his eyes running up and down my body several times before he shook his head, blinked several times, and then took my hand in his huge, warm palm and proceeded to stride back through my flat towards the front door with me struggling to keep up with his long legs.

As we reached the lounge I noticed with an eye roll that Kenny and his house guest were still standing looking rather shocked, but to be honest, I was too, so that that made three of us.

As Nathan yanked open the front door Kenny made a grab for my free hand, trying to halt my exit which caused Nathan to turn and stare at him incredulously, his chest once again heaving and his eyes seeming to flash with jealousy at Kenny for even daring to touch me. As peculiar as these last ten minutes had been, Nathan's apparent possessiveness over me further flared my optimism that perhaps he still wanted to be with me. Stowing these thoughts for later I quickly slid between the two of them before Nathan acted on his jealousy, or before Kenny wet himself in fear at Nathan's rather impressive display of supremacy. His tall frame seemed even more striking than usual when compared to our small hallway and Kenny's shorter height, and suddenly, even though given the current circumstances I shouldn't have been, I found myself rather aroused by Nathan's claiming behaviour.

'Nathan, just give me one second, I'll be right out' I promised in what I hoped was a soothing tone. His eyes turned away from glaring at Kenny and visibly softened as they landed on me. Chewing on the inside of his lip he nodded, 'Fine.' Then scowling at Kenny he huffed from the apartment, taking my bag with him.

I released a huge pent-up breath and turned to Kenny to find him giving me a 'what the fuck' look with his eyebrows raised.

'I have no idea,' I told Kenny as I rubbed my palms over my face and gripped the bridge of my nose, trying to calm myself, and wasn't that just the truth, I was so confused my head was spinning, 'But I'll be fine Kenny. I'll talk to Nathan and see what's got into him. I'll call you if I need you.' I assured my bemused flatmate.

'OK hun, if you're sure?' Kenny asked tentatively to which I nodded. 'By the way, Stella, this might not be the time to mention it, but that man is smoking hot in the flesh, and boy does he know how to throw a sexy strop!' Kenny gushed.

Rolling my eyes I left my apartment to the sight of both Kenny and his friend grinning and fanning their flushed faces. Bloody hell, Nathan even had the 'swoon effect' on men, although given Nathan's stunning looks and effortless sense of style he was exactly Kenny's type so it wasn't really surprising.

The tension in the car as Nathan drove us to his apartment felt thick enough to cut with a knife, but I chose not to try and break the uncomfortable silence, Nathan was the one who had dumped me and then turned up at my place behaving like a deranged lunatic, so Nathan could be the one to explain himself first.

To add to the completely bizarre situation the soothing

tones of Chopin's *Nocturne No.9* were floating from the stereo, calm and lulling and at complete odds to the strained atmosphere between the two of us. His driving was pretty erratic too tonight, a far cry from his usual careful manoeuvres, but I didn't dare mention that either, instead I clutched at the expensive stitching on the leather seat and hoped we'd get there in one piece.

As we pulled up to the gate of Nathan's underground parking he drew the car to a sudden halt and banged the steering wheel several times with the heel of his hand in apparent aggravation. 'Shit!' he exclaimed, making me jump in my seat as I looked at him apprehensively and began to chew on my lip. Turning and seeing my anxiety his features marginally softened and he winced, 'I've been away all week so I've got nothing in the house to eat, you head on up and I'll go grab some food and a bottle of wine and be back as quick as I can.'

I wasn't hungry in the slightest, in fact the thought of eating when I was this nervous actually turned my stomach, but Nathan's words weren't a request, they were a demand and we both knew that regardless of how independent or stubborn I might usually be, at this point it would just be easier to go along with him rather than stamp my foot and argue back. With a heavy sigh and still feeling like aliens had stolen my brain, I climbed out in a daze and headed through the minimalistic entrance foyer towards the lift.

Even though I usually didn't come to Nathan's place in between our weekends together it still felt weird walking in and seeing everything just as I'd left it, but knowing we were over. Or were we? After his dramatic performance at my flat I really had no idea, his sudden appearance had been so disorientating, not to mention his claims that '*I was moving in with him*'. Shaking my head I ran my hands over my face and tried to calm my rampaging heartbeat.

Wandering down to my bedroom to keep my mind busy

I stopped dead in the doorway as I looked at the scene in front of me. OK, so maybe not everything was quite as I'd left it. My mouth hung open as I comprehended what I was seeing, my room had been completely ransacked. What the hell? The bedsheets were flung back and tossed half on the floor, the empty drawers were tipped over and hanging from the unit, and the cupboard doors stood wide open showing the bare wardrobe with hangers scattered everywhere.

Wow, this certainly wasn't the state I left my room in on Monday. The only conclusion I could come to was that Nathan must have gone loopy when he found I was gone. But why? Once again I came back to the confusing fact that he had torn up my contract, but for some reason was now going bananas by trashing my room, turning up at my flat in a fury and dragging me back to his place like some hormonal caveman. It was incredibly confusing and definitely not good for my health if my churning stomach and thumping heart were anything to go by.

I hadn't been in Nathan's apartment long before the doorbell sounded breaking me from my nervous pacing. Had he forgotten his key? Frowning, I headed back down the corridor, realising that there was no way he could have picked up a takeaway and be back this quick. Making my way to the door I looked though the peep hole and grimaced when I saw a colleague of Nathan's that I vaguely recognised from a previous visit. Gregory. Since the problems with his company that Nathan had briefly mentioned to me, I'd overhead him on the phone to Gregory practically every time I had been over. I didn't know for sure, but I assumed from their regular contact that this guy was fairly high up in Nathan's company, but his timing really couldn't have been worse tonight.

Opening the door with a tight smile I stood on the threshold, not particularly keen to let Gregory in – he was the kind of man whose appearance seemed to scream 'smarmy'. I hadn't liked him much when I'd last met him and Nathan had been present, now I was on my own and it made me feel decidedly uncomfortable.

'Stella, what a pleasant surprise,' he said with a grin that was just a bit too smug for my liking.

'Hi Gregory, Nathan's not in at the moment.' Cool, breezy, and straight to the point, that was the best way to handle guys like him.

'I know, I spoke to him on his mobile. I'm here to pick up a contract from him then I'll be out of your way. He said to come in and wait for him.' Oh, he had, had he? Great, so now I was lumbered with Gregory until Nathan got back – could this evening get any worse?

My nerves were frayed enough from tonight's events and now with Gregory's appearance I was feeling decidedly prickly. 'Um, I guess you should come in then. Take a seat.' I offered, limply pointing to the couches behind me. Jeez, in my frazzled state and with my thoughts running riot playing hostess was the last thing I needed tonight.

'I can just go straight to his office and grab it if you like? It'll probably be waiting on his desk.' As much as I wanted to get Gregory out of here as quickly as possible I wasn't happy with the idea of letting him roam around in Nathan's office unchecked, especially with the problems he'd been having with information leaks, so I reluctantly blocked his path to the office and indicated to the sofas instead.

'No, come and sit for a minute, Nathan won't be long,' I encouraged, trying to sound a little friendlier than I had earlier.

'Well that sounds like an offer I can't refuse,' Gregory purred with a sickly sweet smile. Ugh, I only just refrained from gagging and rolling my eyes. Kenny would describe that tone as 'puke-tastic' – something likely to make you puke if you were subjected to it for too long, or too frequently. One thing was for sure, I wasn't offering Gregory a bloody drink, as soon as Nathan had given him the paperwork I wanted Gregory out of here so I could finally sit down with Nathan and sort out the jumble of issues we had to deal with.

Instead of sitting on the couch opposite me, Gregory irritatingly chose to wait for me to sit and then came and sat directly next to me. Talk about uncomfortable. I huffily blew some hairs from my face – God I could so do without this now.

Unfortunately things only went from bad to worse as Gregory's hand slid across the back of the sofa and lightly touched my shoulder. Frigging sleazeball! Although admittedly the sofa was quite small so perhaps it was an accident. I shifted myself further away from him and tried my best to act casual, but unfortunately I was a crap actress so probably completely failed. Within seconds however, I felt the touch of his fingers on me again and shook my head in disbelief. Once I could pass off as a mistake, twice was definitely intentional.

Instead of a discreet shift this time I snorted out an impatient breath and flicked his hand off dismissively like I was shooing an irritating fly. 'Gregory, I'm not interested,' I stated flatly, wondering for the hundredth time what was taking Nathan so bloody long.

'Because of Nathan? You're not exactly a proper couple though, are you? We both know the type of relationship you have.' His tone was lecherous and made me feel quite sick, but all I could focus on right now was Nathan, and wondering if we had a relationship at all – not that I was going to admit that to Gregory. He once again adjusted his position on the sofa to try and close the gap between us, but I moved myself further away again until I was squashed right up in the corner, 'For example, I know you only see him at the weekends, maybe we could meet up mid-week sometime for a bit of fun?' I was completely taken aback by Gregory's line of pursuit; for one thing it was bloody cheeky, but secondly it sounded distinctly like he knew exactly what kind of arrangement Nathan and I had together, which must mean that Nathan had told him.

That was it. I was now officially pissed off. Both at Nathan for sharing our private details, and at Gregory for being a complete knob and trying it on with me when I was in no mood for it.

'I'm not a fucking prostitute Gregory,' I spat, pushing away his roaming hand again, this time with substantially more force.

Apparently my rebuff ran off Gregory like water though – I suspect a seasoned charmer like him was used to rejection from women – but he merely grunted a laugh before trying to slide closer to me again. I'd had enough now and tried to stand up, only to have Gregory push me back down. 'It's not even a real relationship is it, Stella?' he spat, getting right in my face with all his podgy ugliness. 'It's an agreement that says Nathan gets to fuck you each weekend as much as he likes. I wonder if you'll be so keen when he's lost all his money. Don't kid yourself that he gives a fuck about you, Stella, you're just a convenient way for him to get a shag,' he said bluntly, making me shudder at his coarseness and turn away from him with a flinch.

That stung. As much as I shouldn't let his spiteful words affect me, they did, because unfortunately I knew they were probably true – not that I'd let Gregory see that he'd upset me. Turning back to face him as I still struggled to stand up I put on the blankest face I could, 'Maybe so. But it's different now, for me anyway. I'm with Nathan because I want to be, and for your information Gregory, I wouldn't touch you with a fucking barge pole even if you did offer to pay me.' As finishing lines go I was quite pleased with that one.

Raising my chin proudly to see if he'd finally got the

message I watched in disbelief as Gregory literally disappeared before my eyes. Blinking several times I looked at the sofa where moments before Gregory had been lounging with a cocky expression on his face, but it was empty.

One minute he was there, then he was gone.

Just like that.

Behind me I heard a muffled groan and swivelled to find Nathan doing a pretty good impression of the Incredible Hulk as he gripped Gregory's suit lapels and dragged him towards the door of the apartment. Oh, so Nathan had been the cause of Gregory's sudden evacuation from the sofa; that certainly explained his disappearing act.

'Clear your desk on Monday, Gregory, you're done. It seems I can't trust you as far as I can throw you,' Nathan grunted as he yanked open the door, '… and if you ever touch Stella again I swear to God I'll fucking kill you. '

'Jesus, Nathan, calm down, she's your fucking submissive, not your wife for fuck's sake …' but the rest of Gregory's sentence was lost as Nathan punched him firmly in the face twice, probably breaking his nose if the amount of blood spurting out was anything to go by – bloody hell that looked painful – and then slammed the door after him.

Staggering backwards, Nathan shook out his fist with a grimace and then turned to face me with his chest rising and falling rapidly as he tried to catch his breath. Blimey, he looked completely wild, his eyes were blazing and wide, his hair was a messy mop on his head and his shirt was covered in Gregory's blood and un-tucked from the struggle.

'This wasn't how I planned this conversation starting …' he murmured, before shrugging slightly and fixing m with an intense stare, 'Did you mean what you said about us?' he suddenly demanded between panted breaths.

Panic encased my entire body. *Bugger*, he'd heard the

whole conversation. I could literally feel the blood leaving my cheeks as I paled significantly; this completely went against everything Nathan had wanted from our partnership, but after the events of the last seven days, not to mention the past hour, I was a little unsure where that partnership stood at the moment.

My head felt like it was on a see-saw trying to balance out my confusion and all the possible outcomes of this talk – on one side I could lie and pretend I felt nothing for him and he might take me back for our original contract, but alternatively I could tell him I cared about him and he could freak out, officially end our agreement verbally, and throw me out.

I decided distraction was the best tactic here, it would buy me a few more minutes of thinking time, so I stood up on incredibly shaky legs and walked towards the kitchen where I began digging in the freezer before finally reappearing with a bag of frozen peas. If I could fit my big arse in there I'd climb right into the freezer and hibernate for a month to avoid the impending confrontation that was about to go down. I sighed heavily and turned to find that Nathan had followed me, his furrowed gaze firmly locked on mine and his breathing still ragged.

'Sit,' I ordered, indicating to one of the bar stools by the breakfast counter. He raised a bemused eyebrow at me giving him orders, which granted wasn't exactly a regular occurrence, then after staring at me for an age he eventually sat and allowed me to examine his damaged hand. The bruises were coming out already, his skin going a pale blue in places through the blood stains. Biting my lip I tried to ignore the jolt of pleasure that was always present from touching him and instead focused on wrapping his bruised hand in the ice, but a small traitorous sigh escaped my lips anyway.

'There's been a change in the balance of our relationship for me recently, Stella, but did you mean what you said? How you're here because you want to be with me? About it being different between us now?' I faffed around with his hand deliberately delaying speaking, and hoping he couldn't see the guilty flush that had spread on my cheeks, 'Tell me the truth, Stella,' he demanded in a low tone.

Pursing my lips I prepared myself for the worst; regardless of the reaction I expected from Nathan I had to be honest with him now, this had gone on long enough, 'Yes ... but if you want to keep seeing me I'll make sure it won't change anything between us.' Pah! I was lying already! Of course it would change things! I had feelings for him – deep feelings – it changed everything!

'Oh but it does, Stella.' Nathan murmured ominously.

'No, no, everything will be fine, I promise!' I insisted quietly, knowing I was getting desperate and failing to keep the despair from my voice. Pathetic woman!

'It changes everything, Stella.' I watched as Nathan ran an agitated hand through his hair again, practically pulling out a great handful as he did so, and I grimaced. Here it comes, I thought, he's going to finalise things because I've stupidly let myself get attached.

Who was I kidding? I was more than attached to Nathaniel Jackson, I was in love with him. If my life hadn't been about to crumble around me I might even have laughed at how stupid I was to go and fall in love with my bad boy. In fact, I'd have given myself a firm slap around the face for my stupidity if Nathan hadn't been sat three feet away from me.

The noise of his chair shifting followed by Nathan's gruff voice broke me from my startling thoughts. 'Gregory was talking a load of shit, you know, I don't just view you as a convenient shag.' Oh, really? This got my attention and I looked up in time to see Nathan pause awkwardly and once again run a hand shakily through his hair. 'Perhaps at the beginning ... but ... *fuck it*, I'm no good at talking about this shit, do you want a drink?' God yes, a shot or two of whiskey might just get me through this horrible ordeal.

'Let me get it, rest your hand,' I said, pushing him back down and walking to the glass cabinet. This was another diversion tactic, but gave me a good reason not to look at him, I desperately didn't want Nathan to see how heartbroken I was feeling at the thought that this might be one of the last times I spent with him.

My hands were shaking but I managed to grab two glasses and then took the bottle of red wine from him, unscrewing the cap before unsteadily pouring us each a decent measure. Well, if there wasn't any whisky to calm my nerves a big glass of red would have to do.

'Stella there's a reason it changes everything ...' Nathan insisted, returning to our conversation as soon as he had his wine in front of him. Something in his voice made me want to look up, but my eyes were starting to sting and fill with unshed tears so instead I desperately stared at the table as if it held the secrets to the Holy Grail. Suddenly my hand was grabbed from across the table by Nathan's undamaged one and I felt his warmth soaking into me like a healing balm. Unexpectedly Nathan gave my hand a sharp tug, making me lurch forwards and my head shoot up at his surprising move. I was torn between pulling my hand away to help me maintain my composure, or letting him touch me in case this was the last time I ever felt his skin against mine.

'It changes everything because I feel it too, Stella, I want more,' Nathan said in a low tone. Eh? What? Had I heard him correctly? God, I needed a rewind button, but I was fairly certain he'd just said he wanted more ...

'More?' I questioned weakly, wondering what he meant and not daring to believe for one second that he might be feeling the same deeper attraction that I was. Only an idiot like me would go and fall in love with their BDSM buddy, and believe me, Nathaniel Jackson was no idiot.

Without allowing him time to answer, my mind suddenly flashed back to last weekend and the reason I'd been feeling like shit all week. 'But you walked out, last weekend after we spent the full night together ... you took my collar off, tore up my contract and walked out ... you finished with me ...' Irritatingly I let out a small, dry sob on my last four words and ruined an otherwise well-spoken sentence. Then my eyes flicked to the kitchen counter where the contract and collar still lay abandoned and taunting me.

'What!?' Nathan's tone was so harsh he suddenly sounded furious again, causing me to flinch, but as I looked up it seemed his anger was directed at himself and not me. 'Is that what you've been thinking all week?' he demanded, causing me to nod shakily, 'Fuck! I took the collar off because I want more, I want *you*, not just as my submissive, but as my partner. It's the same reason I tore up your contract, I thought after we'd spent that amazing Sunday together that you'd realise why I'd done it ...'

My head was shaking all by itself now. 'But at the start of our agreement you said if either of us wanted to end it we could just tear up the contract ... you tore it up ...' My voice was reedy and thin as I struggled to comprehend what Nathan might be implying from his words.

Grimacing, Nathan seemed to be running his actions through his mind again, 'Fuck ... I can see now how that must have looked to you. God, I'm so sorry, Stella.' Nathan started to reach out for me with his other hand, but a firm look from me had him smiling ruefully and tucking it back under the icepack again.

Sensing something momentous might be about to occur, my eyes were locked on him, intent on soaking up every word and every movement of the next few minutes. Shifting on his stool I watched Nathan chew on his lower lip anxiously and felt a tiny seed of hope take root in my belly. 'Look, the thing is ... I ... I care about you, Stella, the things you said about feeling more for me, I know what you mean because as alien as it is to me, I feel it too,' I very much doubt that he loved me like I did him, but at his words my mouth popped open in surprise no doubt forming a large silent 'O', but Nathan continued, 'When I say I want more, I mean I want to spend more time with you ... I want you to move in with me, talk, share things ... go out on dates.'

'D ... dates?' I stuttered, ignoring his ridiculous request to live with him – it was *way* too soon for that.

'Yes.' Nathan ran a hand through his hair again, which was seriously starting to resemble a haystack. 'I know at the start of our agreement you said you didn't have time for a proper relationship, but I hoped maybe that had changed? Would you be interested in trying something more with me?' The sudden uncertainty in his tone was so clear that I very nearly laughed out loud as every muscle in my body seemed to relax at once.

'It has changed, Nathan, surely you must know that. And yes, I'd really like to try more with you.' I smiled at my own clumsy wording, but Nathan didn't seem to care – the pressure on my hand increased dramatically as he gripped me tightly and practically dragged me round the counter so I was stood between his legs next to the barstool and cradled against his chest by his good arm.

'Thank God for that,' he muttered into my hair, placing kisses against my ear and making me shiver with delight.

'I think it's too soon to move in together though,' I added hesitantly, worried he might explode again. At my words Nathan leaned back and stared at me for several seconds, his mouth hanging open in apparent shock at my refusal, then, grumbling his annoyance he lowered his head to my neck again.

'I'll work on you,' he promised, kissing the skin by my ear fiercely and making goose pimples rise all across my skin. Ahhh … now that was more like it, this was my favourite place to be.

'I'm not saying this will be easy, this is a first for me and seeing as we've started off as a D/s couple I don't know how that will work as a standard relationship,' he said cautiously, before I felt a laugh shake his chest, 'Mind you, you were never exactly great at the whole "Sir" thing anyway.'

If possible my smile broadened. 'I guess we'll figure it out along the way,' I suggested happily. 'But we could probably keep certain elements of that going,' I added with a mischievous tone to my voice. 'I quite like your dominant ways in the bedroom, Mr Jackson.'

I couldn't see his face because my head was tucked against his chest, but I knew Nathan approved of my words because he let out a low, satisfied growl and squeezed me against him even tighter. 'That's just as well, Stella, because although I might want more with you, I think there will always be a part of me that craves domination and control. I hope you can deal with that?'

Could I deal with it? Was I ready for it? Yes, without a doubt. For every part of Nathan that needed to control me, I seemed to have a matching piece of me that craved my submission to him. We were like a perfect pair.

Reaching across I picked up the silver necklace that had been my collar, our symbol of our togetherness. 'Can I still wear this? It makes me think of you.' I asked hopefully, I really liked the choker, and I loved what it represented about us.

'Absolutely,' Nathan agreed, taking it from my hand and fastening it around my neck again before dropping a small kiss on the side of the chain just below my jaw line. 'Mine,' he mumbled, his lips tickling my neck.

'Yours,' I agreed happily, fingering the chain and feeling complete now that I was wearing it again and back in his arms.

There was a comfortable silence for a few moments as we both absorbed the enormity of what had just occurred between us before Nathan noticeably tensed around me. 'Motherfucker!' he suddenly exclaimed, making me jump like I'd be scolded. Pushing out of his embrace I stood back with wide eyes and looked up at Nathan to see his eyes darting around wildly as he obviously considered something in his head. 'What did Gregory say to you about my money?'

Trying furiously to cast my mind back I chewed my lip as I thought. 'I don't know, something about would I be so keen if you lost your money?'

'No ... I'm pretty sure he didn't say *if*, he said *when* ... he's the fucking leak behind all these fucking lost deals!'

Practically pushing me aside Nathan jumped up and dashed to the apartment door, presumably checking if Gregory had already gone, which he clearly had since he left at least ten minutes ago, but apparently in his confusion Nathan wasn't thinking straight.

'Shit, Stella, I'm sorry to do this but I need to make a few quick calls and try to check this out now. Gregory has access to all my current bids so if I'm right this needs to be stopped immediately.' Without another word Nathan spun and stormed towards his office, leaving me behind in a daze and his ice pack melting on the counter.

I wasn't sure if I should follow him, but I couldn't seem to keep myself away, not after everything Nathan had just confessed to me about wanting to try a relationship together, it was just so monumental that I needed to be close to him to make sure it was real. Picking up the icy bag of peas I wandered to his office deciding that if the door was shut I'd leave him to it, but if it was open I'd go in.

When I got to his office the door was open, surely a good sign, so peeping around the frame I saw Nathan was still on the phone. Hearing me approach he looked up and the scowl on his face softened as he signalled for me to enter with a wave of his hand. I held up the ice and gave him a mock chastising glance before crawling onto his lap and gently encasing his damaged hand in the ice again whilst he continued to talk into the phone.

Resting my head on his tense chest it soon became obvious that he was talking to his head of security, someone who seemed to be familiar with Gregory if what I could hear was anything to go by.

'Find him, Stewart, and find him tonight. I want answers first thing in the morning.' With that Nathan leant forwards and replaced the receiver on the table, so I stood up, hoping we might be moving back to the lounge to continue our conversation, or our snuggling – either would be fine by me.

'Shit.' I heard Nathan's murmured curse and glanced over my shoulder to see what the matter was. His gaze was fixed on my back and then dropped to his own chest, which was still covered in Gregory's blood. From the apologetic look on Nathan's face I assumed I was also covered in that blood now too. Ugh. Removing his hand from the ice pack I clearly saw the splatter marks present there too, but Nathan's grimace didn't go unnoticed by me.

Raising his eyes to me Nathan smiled tightly. 'What is it about me and blood on my hands?' he murmured. I was about to launch into a Macbeth quote, but decided this might not be the time for Shakespeare when I saw the lost look filling his eyes. 'I may have ruined your blouse,' he commented softly. It was fine, I didn't even like the blouse much anyway. What I was more concerned about was Nathan, who seemed to be withdrawing away from me to somewhere dark and troubling in his mind – no doubt thinking about the imminent threat to his company. But as I saw him rubbing his bloodied hands repeatedly against his trousers I realised that he was probably also reliving memories of his brother's suicide attempt and the blood he'd had to deal with that night.

Thinking quickly I realised I needed to do something to bring him back to me, then a genius idea sprung to my mind. 'Hey,' I said softly, tipping his chin up so he'd have to look at me. 'After spending a horrible week thinking you'd dumped me I think you owe me some apology sex, Mr Jackson.' Thankfully it worked; Nathan's face softened immediately and a small smile broke on the corner of his mouth as he stood up, stepped forwards and pulled me towards him again.

'Ah yes, apology sex, I seem to recall we were in a toilet last time that happened,' he mused, reaching up to rub his chin thoughtfully. I grinned as I cast my mind back to the luxurious bathroom of Claridges and the delicious encounter we had had there.

'I don't apologise often, Stella, you know this, but I think perhaps on this occasion you're right.' His eyes ran over me, his irises darkening as they did so, oh goody.

'Seeing as we both need a shower we may as well keep up the bathroom tradition,' Nathan commented, suddenly dipping to scoop me up in his arms before striding towards the huge en-suite off the master bedroom with me giggling in his grasp. What a difference a day makes!

Chapter Fourteen - Nathan

I was sipping an early morning coffee and feeling pretty damn content with my lot right now. After the hell of 'losing' Stella yesterday and then realising her misunderstanding about me removing her collar we had talked through our issues in the shower last night – in between several rounds of lazy lovemaking – and were now well and truly sorted and set on our plan to try a relationship together. Jeez, me in a relationship. I let out a long breath and shook my head in amusement. The funny thing was that I wasn't panicky or concerned as I'd thought I might be – I was actually excited about the prospect.

As we'd been lying in bed last night I'd had a phone call from my brother inviting Stella and myself over for dinner the following evening. He'd sounded even happier than usual on the phone and I wondered what had made him quite so jubilant. I guess I'd find out in a few hours.

Stella had been in the bathroom at the time, so I'd taken the opportunity to thank Rebecca for her advice and told her things were going well for me now, although I left out the disaster of Stella moving out because she thought I'd finished with her; that was a stupid misunderstanding I intended to forget all about.

At a little past 9 a.m. I went to wake Stella up, I'd allowed her a lie-in today after I'd kept her awake a fair bit later than usual with some extra-special sex aimed at showing her just how much I cared for her. I hadn't been able to say the 'L' word to her. In fact, I didn't know if I'd ever be able to say I loved her out loud – after my childhood the words had never meant much to me, but the way I felt about her had to be some kind of love I suppose, whatever form of love I was capable of anyway, and I intended to show her that in every possible way. Always actions over words, that's the way I worked, so instead I'd planned a nice breakfast excursion to start her day off with a smile before we headed to Nicholas's later on.

Chapter Fifteen - Stella

It was a beautiful day, one of those days where things really couldn't get any better. The sun was out, the streets of London were warm and buzzing with the excited atmosphere of people making the most of the sunny weather, and best of all I was with Nathan. We were together – as in together like a real couple – and he was in a fabulous mood. Taking hold of my hand he gave it a squeeze and then after giving me a very uncharacteristic, but decidedly lovely, wink, he led me along the cobbled street down the side of the piazza in London's Covent Garden. The outdoor cafés were already doing thriving business this morning, as were the entertainers who'd drawn large crowds as they busily touted for business by juggling or busking on the sun baked pavements.

We were heading to a particular café in Soho for an early brunch to celebrate our new relationship status, according to Nathan 'a hidden gem in London's back streets', but seeing as the weather was so good we'd decided to park a little further out and walk. I smiled when I thought of how loving Nathan had been last night. He hadn't said he loved me in words, but his actions had certainly implied it, and now here we were as a couple. Or perhaps given Nathan's concerns that he was going to mess up, we should be labelled as a 'trial couple'. Nathan might not have complete faith in himself, but after the changes I'd seen in him during our time together, I did – and the more I thought about it, the more I hoped that even if the road got bumpy at times, we would make it.

Pausing to look in a shop window I couldn't help but

stare at our reflection in the glass; my hand was held by my ridiculously possessive and dominant boyfriend, who was currently staring down at me intently as if I might vanish at any second, and I was grinning broadly and obviously feeling rather content with my lot. Don't get me wrong, I knew Nathan was still a dominant personality, he probably always would be, and there would no doubt still be off days where his temper would flare or memories of his childhood would knock him off balance. I wasn't naive enough to think he could simply change his personality over night, but then nor would I want him to. My pride and independence told me I shouldn't like Nathan's domineering personality, but if I were honest with myself, it was one of the key things that drew me to him.

The reality that I enjoyed being with a man as controlling as Nathan had shocked me at first – I was used to my independence and relished the control I harnessed at work – but we'd somehow struck a nice balance; he was definitely less demanding than at the start of our agreement, no doubt because I would rebel every now and my stubbornness kept him on track. In fact, I think my stubbornness was one of the things that made us so good together, I doubt anyone had ever questioned or said no to Nathan before, and I think he found the challenge I presented quite refreshing.

Still staring into the window of the small boutique Nathan tugged my hand to wake me from my daydreaming and I smiled up at him. 'Sorry, I was miles away,' I apologised, leaning up to place a quick, chaste kiss on his lips. A thrill ran through me – I could kiss Nathan whenever I wanted now – a nice bonus of our new relationship status that I intended to repeat as often as I could.

'Somewhere nice with me, I hope,' he murmured as he tried to deepen the kiss by sliding a hand to the nape of my neck and tugging me towards him. The physical pull between us was so strong that I probably would have let him if it hadn't been for the disapproving look I caught from the shopkeeper through the window. Giggling like a randy teenager I gave him one more warm kiss and then pushed against his chest to separate us.

'Come on, hot stuff, cool it for now, we're in public,' I laughed, almost giddy in my happiness as I moved back to his side so we could resume walking.

'Like that would stop me,' he muttered hotly, leaning in close to my ear. God, the man was insatiable. But luckily I was too, and just those few words and dark, lusty tone had me feeling flushed in my cheeks as a throbbing settled low in my belly.

Suddenly, Nathan froze beside me, pulling me to a sharp, jerking stop in the middle of the pavement. The hand that was holding mine went completely rigid and when I turned to him in confusion I saw that his face reflected his tension; a muscle jumped in his jaw line and his eyes were hard and intently focused just ahead of us. Following the line of his gaze I saw a woman with a pram walking towards us, smiling shyly at Nathan.

I had no idea who she was, or what was going on, but I suddenly had a distinctly sick feeling in my stomach. The woman drew to a stop in front of us and flicked a gaze over us both, lingering on our joined hands with a curious look, before glancing back at Nathan and averting her eyes. 'Hello, Sir, it's nice to see you.'

Sir? As the implications of her words hit me I felt the air leave my lungs in a single rushed breath. A huge surge of jealousy landed on me so swiftly I almost staggered. It was official, I wanted to throw up. Luckily I managed to hold back and instead focused on clutching Nathan's hand to keep myself upright. His hold on my hand was equally as tight, but he finally cleared his throat and broke his silence.

'Melissa ... it's been a ... a while.' Shifting on the spot

211

he glanced at me, but the expression on his face was completely unreadable – was it fear? Panic? Guilt? Anger? I had no idea. 'Stella, this is Melissa.' Indicating briefly with his free hand he then gestured towards me. 'Melissa, Stella.'

Melissa, who I assumed from her little use of the word 'Sir' was an old submissive of Nathan's, turned her pale green eyes on me curiously. She was shorter than me by quite a way, skinnier too, and quite pretty, but there was a meekness to her that curved her shoulders in a slump and made her seem a little feeble. Her eyes flitted again to where my hand was linked with Nathan's and I saw her eyebrows shift into a slight frown.

Not knowing what to say or do my gaze dropped to the baby as a distraction, but unfortunately this only made my stomach sink even further as I took in his features. It was probably my jealousy making me ridiculously paranoid, but his luminous blue eyes were almost the exact same colour as Nathan's ... and the blond fluffy hair was basically identical too. He was gorgeous, all soft, chubby, pink skin and innocent youth, but the more I stared at him the more the sickness I'd felt earlier began to rise up my throat, was that why Nathan was so tense, was this *his* baby? Did he have a child that he hadn't told me about?

Nathan having a child wouldn't necessarily be an issue, but concealing it from me wouldn't exactly be the best start to our attempt at a relationship would it? My head was swimming as I suddenly released Nathan's hand from my death-like grip and pretended to be fiddling with my handbag. I didn't re-take my hold of his hand afterwards, I couldn't, not until I knew the facts. Looking at the baby it was obvious he was just a few months old, and suddenly as well as wondering if this was Nathan's baby, a horrifying thought crossed my mind – had Nathan still been seeing this woman whilst we had been together? He'd told me he was monogamous in his relationships, even as dominant and submissive, but if he had been expecting a child with her perhaps that changed things ... had he cheated on me? Was that why he was so tense and had greeted her so stiffly?

What the heck was wrong with me? I'd never felt jealousy like this before, *never*, but the more I looked at Nathan's tense expression, Melissa's curious face, and her baby's annoyingly cute blondness the more my imagination went into overdrive. Realistically I knew I was thinking irrationally, but my mind was awash with questions and I couldn't seem to calm it. Was this his baby? Had he loved Melissa? Why had they split up? Ugh. My brain was moving so fast that I literally felt sick.

Melissa's oddly inquisitive glances made me focus on the issue of whether he might have cheated on me and I tried to remember if Nathan had acted strangely at any point in our time together. But this was an almost impossible feat because Nathan and all his peculiarities was never exactly what you could call run of the mill.

It was fairly far-fetched, but the thought that he might possibly have overlapped myself and Melissa while he had been trying to father a child with her and still continue his sordid sex life on the side with me made me feel really dizzy, and suddenly I was desperate to get away and clear my head.

'Sorry, Sir, I forgot to do the introductions, this cheeky little monkey is Dylan,' Melissa finally said, pushing the pram back and forth a few times to calm the baby's restless murmurs.

It was a marginal relief, but at least Melissa's words seemed to confirm that Dylan definitely wasn't Nathan's baby, so perhaps all my paranoia about his faithfulness was unnecessary. But why had he been so tense when we'd met her? I definitely hadn't imagined the way he'd stiffened next to me. As much as I hated myself for it I still couldn't help but question exactly when Nathan had ended his relationship with this woman.

I'd never thought of myself as the overtly jealous type, but seeing this woman here right in front of me, Nathan's past lover, a woman he had seen naked and had literally been inside of affected me more than I could ever have imagined.

Melissa leant down and lovingly ran her fingers across the baby's cheek. 'Anyway, we're heading to playgroup so I need to be off. '

Beside me Nathan's tension reduced slightly, apparently glad that the conversation was coming to a close, and he nodded his head sharply. 'Bye, then.' he murmured in a tone that was practically devoid of all emotion.

Talk about blunt. Not that I mined, with my brain feeling foggy and confused I also wanted to get away as quickly as possible.

Melissa gave me a curious smile and a nod and then pushed the pram off in the opposite direction, leaving us standing there stunned in the middle of the street. Turning his head Nathan stared down at me intently, his look still impossible to read – was he shocked from the run-in with Melissa, or wary about my reaction? I had no idea, all I did know was that I still felt quite sick and dizzy from the shock encounter and his scrutiny wasn't helping settle me at all.

'That was Melissa ... she used to sub for me,' Nathan murmured, apparently testing the water and gently taking hold of my hand again.

My fingers felt like stiff wooden twigs within his grasp.

The stew of emotions in my brain was so messed up that I barely knew how to react, so I decided to use my custom fall back; sarcasm and swearing. '*Really*? I'd never have fucking guessed, *Sir*,' I spat in a low whisper, making sure to inflict as much emphasis on the last word as possible. Perhaps it was nearly my time of the month and I was hormonal or something, because bizarrely Melissa calling Nathan 'Sir' had actually shaken me up more than seeing the baby. The idea of him in bed with Melissa, or any other woman for the matter, made me see red and feel like going on a killing spree. Although seeing how many women Nathan had probably slept with in his illustrious past it might take me a while to track them all down, I realised with a bitter grimace.

'Stella, calm down,' Nathan warned in a soft growl, but I was way past calming down. Ripping my hand from his, I crossed my arms and looked up at him defiantly, completely unable to get the images of *him* buried inside of *her* out of my mind.

'When were you last with her?' I demanded, keeping my eyes locked on his. In our last few days together Nathan had become so much better at holding eye contact, so if he dropped his gaze now I'd definitely suspect that he was hiding something from me. But he didn't drop his gaze; in fact, if anything it heated by several degrees and made my stomach tighten. He shook his head as if considering something, but then confusingly a smile began pulling at his lips. Reaching out he tried to stroke his hand down my cheek – his touch usually never failed to flare desire inside of me, but not today, right now I needed answers so I dodged out of his way with a swift sidestep and another glare.

'Don't try and distract me,' I said, knocking his hand away and causing Nathan to narrow his eyes, 'When you first saw her you looked terrified, Nathan, like you had been caught red handed. So when exactly did you last see that woman? Was it while we were together?' My voice faded out as bile settled in my throat. If he said 'yes' I'd have to turn and walk away before I threw up on him.

But Nathan didn't answer me verbally, instead his nostrils flared, his eyes darkened with annoyance, and then too quickly for me to dodge he grabbed my wrist and

215

proceeded to drag me down a tiny side street to our left. Actually, it turned out to be more like an alleyway, full of bins and doorways which presumably were back entrances to the shops, but I didn't stop to look too closely because after about ten steps Nathan had me pushed up against a wall and was leaning down over me rather ominously.

I felt completely unhinged, totally irrational, and close to losing it – quite apparently jealousy is not a trait that settles well with me because I beat him to an answer and spoke first. 'When were you with her, Nathan?' I shrieked again, before my courage evaded me, but my answer was met with a growl, as his face turned redder and redder by the second. 'When did you last *fuck* her? Is that more understandable language for you?' I demanded, as gathering tears stung my eyes. Nathan's mouth descended upon mine so suddenly that I didn't have time to think about avoiding it, one of his hands lunged into my hair, twisting it around his fingers and keeping my head from moving as his tongue forced its way inside my mouth, whilst the other hand gripped my hip and held me firmly against the wall.

Even in this situation, with jealousy blurring my actions and countless questions rolling through my brain, I struggled to resist my pull to him and an infuriatingly needy moan rose in my throat at his possessive onslaught. Raising his head just a fraction he gazed down at me, his eyes heated and lusty. 'I fucking love that you get this jealous over me, Stella,' he panted, but seeing me lick my bruised lips and frown he sighed, 'Is that why you're so upset, you think I cheated on you?'

Chewing on my already sensitive lip I was teetering right on the edge of losing all control. I could feel it slipping through my fingers like grains of sand, so I didn't reply – I just stared at him, desperate to hear the answer I needed to hear. 'Well over a year and a half ago, OK? Things ended with her before you and I met, Stella, I

216

would *never* cheat on you.' he informed me, his tone and grip both softening with his last words.

Releasing my tortured lip from between my teeth I found my voice. 'But you looked so guilty when you saw her.'

As tense as the situation seemed to me, Nathan smiled. 'The reason I froze was because I thought you might freak out meeting her.' he paused and ran a hand through his hair, 'Plus it slightly threw me to see her with a baby, for a few seconds I panicked that it might be mine.'

Swallowing loudly I stared at his features and could only see truth reflected in his eyes, which reassured me, but as painful as it was, I needed to find out a few more things. 'Did you want the baby to be yours?' I asked in a pained whisper.

Nathan's eyes opened so widely they almost popped from his head. 'Fuck, no,' he replied with a firm shake of his head and a grimace.

It seemed fairly apparent from that reaction that Nathan didn't like the idea of having kids, not that I'd expected differently, given his own troubled childhood. Finally, as his fingers massaged my hips softly and he continued to stare down at me with wide, pleading eyes I felt myself relax. The release of tension nearly made me hysterical and I had to work hard to keep myself in check and stop myself laughing.

Placing a hand on his chest I could feel his pounding heart beating a heated pattern that pretty much matched my own. Adrenaline was still rushing through my system from our encounter with Melissa, not to mention the dose of desire that Nathan had stoked within me with his earlier kiss.

'Did she live with you?' I whispered suddenly, not sure why I was asking, but somehow finding that I wasn't able to stop myself.

Drawing in a breath, possibly in preparation for his

217

answer, or maybe to calm the raging hard-on that I could feel pressing against my stomach Nathan tilted his head but maintained eye contact. 'Yes ... but only for four months and only as my submissive. Our relationship was always very business-like.' My eyebrows had drawn into a frown, I could feel it, and upon seeing my look Nathan gently moved a hand to cup my face, where he began to soothe away the crease between my brows with soft circles of his thumb.

'She may have lived with me, but she knew very little about me, Stella. I don't wish to upset you, but with Melissa, and the others before, it was just sex for me, nothing else.'

His use of the phrase 'the others' made my stomach twist with another insane twist of jealousy and I instinctively tensed up again. 'Did you love her?' The question popped from my mouth before I could stop it, and I felt him stiffen again. Why was I asking that when I didn't even know if he loved me?

'No. I never loved any of them.' Perhaps sensing that I was on the verge of losing it Nathan lowered his head and kissed me softly, his warm lips scattering kisses on my cheeks, eyelids, and finally lips, his sweet actions going some way to soothing my hurt, 'You, Stella, you're so different ... I ... I ...' But much to my disappointment, whatever he was going to say dried up in his mouth. 'It's my past, Stella, I can't change it, but you must believe me when I say you're the only woman I have ever been like this with, the only woman I have ever ... *cared for* like this, and that's the God-honest truth.'

He'd avoided saying the word 'love' again, but his words meant so much to me that I finally smiled and relaxed feeling the remnants of my jealousy softening and melting away.

As we stood there pressed together I briefly considered telling Nathan that I had fallen in love with him, but

218

decided against it for now – I wanted the words to be said in a time of passion, not a tense situation. Besides, they were just words, did I really need to hear them from his lips? As long as he treated me well and we were happy together what would those three little words really achieve in the long run?

Nodding, I also knew he was right about us and how he viewed our relationship as different. Nathan didn't know it, but when I'd been in the bathroom last night I'd overheard him on the phone to Nicholas and Rebecca arranging tonight's dinner, and to my surprise he'd started talking about me. Quite apparently it wasn't the first time either, because he'd sounded genuinely thrilled as he'd told them that things were progressing well between the two of us.

Relenting, I rolled my lips between my teeth before he reached up with his thumb to stop me with a chastising look. 'OK, I'm sorry, Nathan, I probably overreacted,' I murmured, now feeling rather stupid about my childish outburst.

Pressing himself more firmly against me Nathan leaned down and kissed my ear, drawing the lobe between his teeth to bite it gently and causing me to groan and lean my head sideways to give him better access. 'It's OK. Besides, you can't be jealous of the fact she lived with me, I've asked you to move in twice now and you've turned me down flat.'

Making a little humming noise in the back of my throat I prepared for him to bring up this little sore point from last night again. It was true, I'd rejected the offer to move in with him, but when Nathan said he'd 'asked me twice now', I had to smile, as far as I was concerned, forcibly packing up my things and practically dragging me to his apartment did not count as 'asking me'. So purely out of principle when he'd brought it up again later after our reconciliation I had said 'no' again, which had shocked

219

Nathan no end. A smile lit my lips as I remembered his expression, he'd literally had no idea how to deal with my rebellious response so he'd tried to kiss me senseless instead.

His reaction showed how much he'd progressed in recent weeks, in the good old days of 'dominant Nathan' he'd simply have taken me over his knee for a long spanking and demanded that I agree. Instead he'd looked completely torn, his mouth opening and closing like a goldfish until finally he'd nodded jerkily and hidden his face by kissing my neck. It had been a small victory to me, but one that I suspected wouldn't last long if he chose to really lay on his persuasive talents.

The idea of living with him was tempting, of course it was; I was head over heels in love with him, but it was way too early in our relationship and seeing as I was basically addicted to him already it probably wouldn't be hugely healthy for me. Plus I liked the idea of keeping my flat on; it allowed me to maintain some sense of myself.

The fact that I viewed his flat as just that – *his* – with the idea of his previous submissives living in it with him didn't help either, it actually made me feel rather ill and wasn't somewhere I would chose to move into full time. Seeing as Nathan's apartment was self-designed by him – one of the first developments Nathaniel Jackson Architecture completed after he started up his company – and as such totally adored by him, I'd chosen not to share my dislike of the apartment with him in our time together.

Pressing his groin against mine he pinned me to the wall more firmly. 'Move in with me,' he urged me again, as I'd known he would now the topic had been raised, but I shook my head and ignored the persuasive squeeze he gave my hips.

'No, Nathan,' I replied softly, but seeing the rising stubbornness on his face, possibly accompanied by a touch of hurt, I tried to placate him by adding, 'Not yet,' and then began soothingly rubbing my hand across his chest. It worked, marginally, because he let out a long sigh, but didn't say another word on the subject.

'Come on then, my stubborn little minx, let's get that brunch, shall we?' Grateful that he had let the subject drop for now I nodded, took his hand, and allowed him to lead me back onto the main shopping thoroughfare in search of our food and caffeine fix.

We meandered through the packed streets, but with the lovely weather the atmosphere was relaxed – as relaxed as it gets in the bustle of central London anyway – and after stopping for a bottle of orange juice in a tiny little shop we then headed off to continue our walk to our brunch destination.

We couldn't have been out of the shop more than a minute when I saw an eerily familiar face step from a side street just ahead. The focus of my gaze was deeply involved in a heated conversation with a blonde woman who looked like she was going to cry any minute. 'Christ, you have got to be kidding me,' I muttered, slapping a palm to my forehead and quickly trying to change the direction we were heading in by gripping Nathan's hand and dragging him to the left.

'What is it?' Nathan asked, not shifting a millimetre and pulling me to a standstill. Standing still was not good, we needed to move – preferably hide – so I tried to tug on his arm again, but frowning down at me Nathan simply wouldn't budge. Bloody stubborn man. Glancing to my right I winced, accepted the inevitable, and then looked up at Nathan. 'Let's just say that today is obviously going to be a day full of exes,' I whispered miserably, as Aidan, my previous boyfriend, spotted me and joined Nathan in his frown.

The gods obviously had it in for me today. I mean seriously, what were the chances of meeting not only Nathan's ex, but mine too? It had to be a million to one, but no, lucky me, there was Aidan in all his glory staring at me in surprise across the street.

'Stella?' he called questioningly, looking from myself to Nathan and then back again. 'It is you!' he added, pulling the startled-looking blonde along with him as he came over to speak to us.

I *so* did not need this. Seeing Melissa had been bad enough, but knowing Nathan he'd probably kill Aidan if he made one wrong comment, which was highly likely because Aidan was not the most tactful of men. The woman on his arm smiled weakly at me, still looking upset about something or perhaps just sensing the impending shitstorm, and then looked utterly relieved as her mobile phone started ringing in her hand. Detaching herself from Aidan's arm she smiled apologetically and walked away to speak on her phone.

As soon as his girlfriend had left – I assumed she was his girlfriend anyway – Aidan turned back and stared at where my fingers were joined with Nathan's before glaring at me with a look of pure annoyance on his face. Oh God, here we go. 'I thought you were *too busy for a relationship*,' he sneered, repeating the exact words I'd used as an excuse when I'd finished with him. Shaking my head I didn't even give him the satisfaction of a reply, instead I turned with a crisp 'Goodbye, Aidan.' and started to walk away. To my complete and utter surprise Nathan obediently followed me, but I didn't dare look up at him, not yet anyway.

'Word of advice, mate,' Aidan called to Nathan as we made our retreat, 'She might be hot in the sack, but don't expect any more, she's not the relationship kind.' Aidan's voice was filled with bitterness and if I hadn't been terrified that Nathan was about to kill someone, Aidan or perhaps even me, then I would have politely informed Aidan that the reason I left him was because apart from his bedroom skills which were passable, although nowhere near as good as Nathan's, he was the most boring man alive.

Nathan froze, the hand that was holding mine tightened and I knew he wanted to go back to 'speak' with Aiden. Gripping him as if my life depended on it I literally dragged him away into the crowd. Fucking hell, this day really couldn't get any worse. As soon as we'd got further away from Aidan I wanted to get a big, strong coffee to calm my nerves and then to head home so no more visions of either of our pasts could haunt us. The idea of going anywhere to eat turned my stomach now. Jeez, it had started out as such a beautiful day too ...

'Stella, stop.' There was no way I could ignore Nathan's words, the utter command in his tone was unmissable and I briefly closed my eyes in defeat. He was clearly pissed off, which was probably understandable given what Aidan had just yelled for half of London to hear, but I really didn't want the drama of him screaming at me on the street too if I continued to try and walk away.

I paused, drew in a steadying breath, and then turned to find him glowering at me with a face like thunder. An expression that was probably pretty similar to mine not that long ago when I'd freaked out about Melissa, actually. The irony of this situation, this whole day, wasn't lost on me and I very nearly let out a hysterical laugh.

'Who the fuck was that?' Nathan ground out through clenched teeth, as a muscle in his jaw line went crazy indicating that his level of annoyance was reaching 'high alert'.

'My ex, Aidan,' I replied, deciding not to give any extra details unless he asked for them.

'The guy you were with before me?' he demanded, his grip on my hand now painfully tight and threatening to crush my bones. 'The guy you said made you interested in domination?' His grip might have been tight, but his voice was even tighter. Clearly Nathan was really struggling to maintain his composure at the moment.

Hesitating for a few seconds, my brain desperately tried to think of a way of calming him down. What had he done to me when I'd got jealous over Melissa? He'd dragged me down a side street and kissed me senseless. Hmmm, I was nowhere near strong enough to do that, just getting him this far away had been a struggle, and there was no way I was going to pounce on him in the middle of a packed street, so unfortunately honesty seemed like the only other option.

'Yes,' I whispered. Nathan's face turned from intent and focused, to furious and bright red in the blink of an eye and I winced as his grip on my hand tightened even further as he desperately struggled to draw in several steady breaths through his flared nostrils.

'*Overbearing fucker,*' he muttered, then spinning around Nathan scanned the crowd, presumably to search the crowd for Aidan's retreating figure. I raised an eyebrow, Nathan had obviously decided to overlook the fact that he too was an 'overbearing fucker' at times, and was apparently intent on making Aidan pay for it, but thankfully my less than charming ex had wisely disappeared.

Nathan turned back to me with an expression of pure unadulterated anger on his face. 'We're going home right now. There are things I need to say and do that aren't appropriate for a packed street.' Unfortunately from his gritty tone and taut body language I could just tell that the 'things he needed to say' were not going to be fun-filled, so I sighed and finally succeeded in pulling my crushed fingers free from his grasp.

Wiggling my fingers to restore the blood flow I tilted my chin up at him defiantly. 'You know what, Nathan, today started out so well, but it's steadily turned really fucking shitty. You go home in a mood if you want, but I need a coffee'. Without waiting for an answer I turned and headed for the coffee shop I'd spotted a minute earlier. I'd have a drink, let my nerves calm down, and then maybe head home – to *my* flat, not Nathan's – and wait until he was feeling mature enough to discuss this like an adult. Knowing I'd had a similar temper tantrum less than an hour ago made me feel truly hypocritical, a thought that didn't settle that well in my stomach, so I brushed it off and strode up to the counter in the cafe.

Glancing around I noticed the café was going for the nostalgia theme – the tables were made up with long checked cloths and the walls were chock-a-block with copper kettles, pans, plates, and teapots but I was so dazed and in need of a coffee that I truly didn't care where I was, so ignoring the jumbled décor I placed my order. 'I'll have a double shot cappuccino please,' I told the barista, then cocking my head I sighed wearily, sensing Nathan approach behind me when my skin began to tingle with awareness. Shaking my head to try and alleviate my annoyance I resisted the urge to look at him and instead muttered, 'Do you want a drink or what?'

'I'll have the same as you,' he replied petulantly.

'Make that two large cappuccinos please,' I said as politely as I could given the circumstances. Once the drinks were made – which seemed to take an absolute age of horribly tense silence – we picked up our overfull mugs and headed to the most private booth in the corner.

Sliding in one side I was surprised when Nathan joined me on the same seat. I had expected him to sit opposite so he could fry me with his killer glare, but he didn't, instead he placed his cup on the table, took my hand gently in his, and took in a deep breath which he then released through his nose.

'I apologise for my temper,' he mumbled. *What?* Well, I had not expected that! 'I'm new to this, Stella, jealousy is not something I've ever felt before you,' he admitted, gently running the pad of one thumb across the back of my hand, tracing the feint web of veins there. 'But the idea of Aidan, *fuck,* any man, touching you …' Shaking his head he closed his eyes as his nostrils flared again, his unfinished sentence hanging, but the meaning was clear and oh so lovely to me. He might not be able to say he loved me, but he really did care about me.

'I feel the same, Nathan, why do you think I freaked out so much earlier? That feeling in your chest right now when you imagine me with other men, I get that too, and believe me when I say I have far more to be jealous of than you – my sex life before you was practically non-existent.'

'Except for him,' he added in a cool tone jerking his head towards the window, obviously referring to Aidan. There had been a few others too, but I decided not to add that little detail to the mix right now. Running a hand through his hair Nathan nodded, seemed to loosen his neck off with an audible click and then sat up straighter, 'OK, OK … point taken, my past is far less salubrious than yours, but it is my past,' he reassured me with an intense glance.

'As is Aidan,' I reminded him firmly.

Taking a sip of his coffee Nathan sat back and seemed to visibly force himself to relax and then looked at me, appearing calmer. Wow, he really was making progress lately. 'Tell me about him. When we met you said you broke up with your ex because you wanted different things, but that's all you said.'

'Do we really have to do this?' I asked, folding and refolding my napkin as a distraction and suddenly feeling awkward. Knowing how hard Nathan was trying to keep himself in check discussing my past sex life was hardly going to help matters.

Turning watchful eyes on me he blinked several times as he chewed on the inside of his lower lip. 'Just the basics. You asked questions about Melissa and I answered them truthfully, now I'm asking about Aidan.' So it was going to be 'tit-for-tat' was it? I sighed, well fine, so be it.

Hastily swigging a mouthful of my coffee to give me a brief reprieve from my story I practically burnt my tongue off on its scalding heat. Placing it back on the table with a wince I wondered how I could briefly explain my relationship with Aidan without too many gory details to rile Nathan. Keeping my tone bland I gave my best attempt at short and sweet. 'I met Aidan though a friend, we were only together about five months, we never lived together, but when he started pushing for marriage I finished things.'

Spraying his mouthful of coffee across the table Nathan erupted from calm to furious in a split second, 'You were engaged to that lanky prick?' I was about to grin at his concise description of Aidan, but he shocked me by slamming a hand onto the table so hard that it spilt a huge amount of his drink and nearly tipped my mug over completely.

Trying to give Nathan a moment to calm down I watched in silence as the coffee soaked into the table cloth. He was sucking in deep lungfuls of air through his nose as if literally on the verge of a full blown freak out and I could have sworn I heard him counting down under his breath.

Wow, talk about eruptive anger. 'No, Nathan, I wasn't,' I explained quickly, calmly giving the cafe owner a reassuring smile to indicate things were fine, apart from the ruined tablecloth, which was far from fine, '… he was actually really boring, but he started talking about getting engaged and that's when I told him it was over.'

'So you only stayed with him because you liked the sex with him?' he questioned, his voice low and quiet now. The blunt answer to that was yes, the only reason I'd lasted five months with Aidan was because he'd excited me a little in the bedroom, but seeing as Nathan was a hair's breadth away from an explosion there was no way I

227

was explaining that to him. Instead I turned the subject round hoping to stroke his ego.

'Nowhere near as much as I like sex with you, Nathan.' I saw him flash me a dark glance and realised my words were working. Knowing that dirty talk did it for him I leant in closer so no one could overhear and prepared to put on my most breathy, and hopefully alluring, voice. 'Remember how I told you I'd barely ever orgasmed with a man before I met you?' That much was true, and although I'd enjoyed the sex with Aidan even he hadn't been that great at hitting the right spot for me. 'But you, Nathan ...' I paused to add drama to my little speech, '... you make me come so fucking hard and long that I can barely see straight.' Jeez, I was even turning myself on.

A growl rumbled up Nathan's throat and as he lowered his eyes to meet mine I saw that the only emotion visible now was pure, unadulterated lust. Oh goody, my plan had worked. The hellish encounter with not one, but both of our exes was forgotten. For now anyway. The only small hitch was that we were sat in a public cafe, I was now horny, and Nathan was looking at me like he wanted to devour me on the spot right this very second.

Leaning forwards he slid a hand into the hair at the nape of my neck and pulled me forwards where he placed a surprisingly chaste kiss on my lips. 'I aim to please,' he murmured.

Giggling at our ridiculously dirty conversation I smiled up at him flirtatiously, 'Oh you always please ... *Sir,*' I murmured, adding the title that I probably wouldn't use as much anymore, but today it had the desired effect and Nathan's hand slid from my hair down my body to rest upon my thigh.

With a casual flick of his other arm Nathan brought the tablecloth up so it was covering his hand, then swiftly burrowed under my short skirt and cupped my groin in a no-holds-barred display of his possession. Gasping at his sudden contact through my panties, my eyes flew wide open, but now that his little tantrum was over Nathan simply looked his usual cool and calm self. The fact that he was cupping my increasingly damp groin seemingly having no effect on him at all. No outward effect anyway, but I was fairly sure that if I lifted the table cloth I'd see his arousal making itself clear in his jeans.

Using his free hand he lifted his mug and took a casual sip of his coffee before placing it on an unsoiled part of the cloth and looking at me. 'So, just to clarify, our exes are exes for a reason, yes?' he whispered huskily. To be honest I doubted Nathan would remember he'd made this statement if we ever bumped into another of my ex-boyfriends, he'd no doubt go bonkers again because he was just so damn territorial, but I didn't say that, instead I merely nodded and sluttishly lowered myself down the seat to increase the pressure from his hand. Chuckling at my very unsubtle manoeuvre Nathan clicked his tongue in a chastising sound and then removed his hand and raised his eyebrows at me. 'Now, now, Stella, you know how much I hate it when you nod. I'm going to need your answer out loud, or I stop.'

Swallowing and desperately trying to moisten my dry mouth I nodded again, but this time accompanied it with a breathy response, 'Yes … yes … exes are in the past.'

'Good,' Nathan said, nodding his satisfaction, 'I'm glad we agree on that point, now, where was I …' he murmured thickly, sliding his hand back under the privacy of the table cloth to cup me again and cause me to let out a pathetic gasped moan.

This time instead of merely resting his hand there Nathan began to run one finger firmly up and down, causing me to squirm on the seat. Even through the cotton of my underwear it was almost too much to bear. 'You are mine, Stella. No one else's,' he growled next to my ear.

Good God, I was almost on the verge of orgasm and we

229

were sitting in a crowded coffee shop. 'Say it, Stella, tell me and I'll reward you.' He really did love being in control, didn't he? But you know what? When he made me feel this good I really didn't care!

'Yours, Nathan ... I'm yours,' I gasped, and as soon as I had spoken he slipped two fingers around the edge of my knickers and slid them back and forth across my trembling flesh. 'Christ, Stella, you're so fucking wet for me,' Nathan breathed, pushing his fingers inside me and beginning a slow pumping rhythm that immediately had me struggling to breathe.

As I let my head roll back in ecstasy I noticed a guy on the other side of the coffee shop watching us intently, his gaze was on us, but one of his hands was in a similar position to Nathan's under the table and his arm was slowly moving up and down. Coming immediately to my senses I sat up and let out a noise of choked embarrassment from my throat. Nathan's dexterous fingers had remained embedded inside me as I straightened, but he raised an eyebrow at my sudden movement.

'Oh my God, Nathan, that guy over there is watching us and rubbing himself!' I whispered furiously, trying desperately to dislodge his hand from my groin. To my utter amazement Nathan continued to move his fingers whilst slowly turning his head to survey the cafe. His gaze landed on the man and held for a second before he turned back and examined my face. 'Do you like the idea of being watched, Stella?' Nathan murmured, adding his thumb to the pleasure by slowly rubbing my clitoris. 'Does it make you wetter to know that he's getting off because of you?' Christ, what exactly was the correct answer to that question? I was horny as hell and pretty close to coming and to be honest the idea that the man was watching us was giving me a bit of an extra thrill, but only because we were fully dressed and he couldn't really see anything.

'You're close,' Nathan stated, watching me carefully,

230

and I bit my lip to muffle the moan threatening to escape my throat. 'I'm sorry to do this, baby ...' Nathan said, and I was just about to ask what he was apologising for when he swiftly removed his fingers and stood up. 'But nobody gets to watch you come except me,' he said in way of explanation. 'I'll make it up to you later, I promise.' Then he dragged me to my feet, flashed a smug grin at the watching stranger, and supported my wobbly legs as he guided me outside.

'Well, I think we made his day, he certainly saw enough to help him finish off,' Nathan said darkly as we emerged into the busy street. I was so aroused that all my senses felt amplified; the noise was too loud, my groin too sensitive, my legs too wobbly, and my breathing far too frantic. Clinging to Nathan was literally the only way I was managing to stay upright. 'Nathan ...' I whispered, hoping he'd slow down before I fell down – it probably sounded like I was begging, which in my current needy state I nearly was.

Pausing, Nathan glanced down at me before frowning and pulling me against him. 'I'm sorry, baby, are you struggling?' I had no idea where the 'baby' had suddenly come from, but right now I didn't care and I simply nodded against his chest, desperately hoping he'd take me to a bench where I could sit down and come down from my rampant arousal. I'd never felt this desperately horny before.

Instead of taking me to a bench, I found he'd taken me down yet another London alleyway, as he pressed my back against a cold stone wall, pushing his firm, hard body against my front to keep me upright. 'Let's see if I can ease the pressure a bit,' he murmured. Lowering his head Nathan kissed me softly, his tongue parting my lips and stroking across mine, as one hand made the journey down my body and slipped under my skirt again. We were in an alleyway in London where anybody could walk by at any

231

moment, and yet I did nothing to stop him, I was so turned on all I could focus on was my desperate need to climax.

'Given our location and your horniness we'll make this quick,' Nathan told me softly as he dipped two fingers inside me and took up the same rhythm as before. Curling them he managed to reach my G-spot and as soon as his thumb joined in and rubbed against my slick clitoris that was it, I was a goner. Burying my head in his shoulder I let out a muffled cry and clung to his jacket as wave after wave of pleasure swept through my body. After an orgasm that seemed to last an absolute eternity, Nathan removed his fingers and used a handkerchief to clean between my legs before wiping off his own fingers and grinning down at me.

'I'd ask you to return the favour,' he mumbled eyeing the obvious evidence of his erection pressing against the front of his jeans, 'but I think perhaps here is not the place. Let's head home, shall we?' This time as I mutely nodded my agreement Nathan didn't chastise me for it, he merely guided me to a nearby bench so I could recover, our brunch plans forgotten in the wake of our overwhelming horniness.

A few minutes later, when my wobbly legs had recovered, I took in a deep breath and looked up at Nathan with a coy smile. 'I'm OK now, I can walk,' I said with an embarrassed chuckle. Instead of teasing me how I thought he might, Nathan merely smiled down at me indulgently and then leaned in to place a small, sweet kiss on my temple. 'Good, lets head to the car, I have plans for you at home.'

Chapter Sixteen - Nathan

Stella's mood was just as buoyant as mine as we drove through relatively quiet London streets to Nicholas's house for dinner later that day. My hand rested on her thigh most of the way there, but we didn't say much – to be honest we didn't need to speak to know that we were both feeling pretty damn content at the moment. After this morning's craziness with Melissa and then Aiden we'd headed back to my apartment and indulged in several hours of rather spectacular sex, if I do say so myself. It was amazing what a bit of rivalry can do to you. Even though it was unnecessary, I had spent the entire time focused on making sure that Stella would never ever think about going to bed with anyone other than me.

Reaching Nicholas's road I saw it was free of cars so I pulled the Audi up and managed to bag a space just down from his house.

Jumping out of the car I walked around and opened Stella's door for her like a true gentleman would, smiling down at her and once again thanking my lucky stars for meeting her. 'Nicholas said that Rebecca's looking forward to meeting you again,' I told Stella as she stepped from the car, but any further conversation froze in my throat as I glanced down the road at an odd figure standing by Nicholas's gatepost.

It took me a second to comprehend what I was seeing as I blinked and stared at the tall, broad-chested man before me. 'Dad?' I croaked, not quite believing that my father was really standing there larger than life. Fuck, I hadn't seen him since the night he went to prison. I felt like my body had been pumped full of lead, my limbs went heavy, too heavy for my body almost, and suddenly it became a struggle just to stand upright.

'Hello, son.'

Stella

My heart was thundering in my chest as my eyes flicked rapidly between Nathan and his father. Bloody hell, this could *not* be good. A thick tension descended around us so abruptly that I thought I might throw up from the sudden inability to breathe, or swallow, or perform any basic bodily function. When Nathan had told me about his history I was sure he'd said his parents had been put in prison for child abuse, but seeing as his dad was stood in front of us as large as life I guess he'd either broken out, or his sentence had finished.

He was tall, athletic-looking, and handsome just like Nathan, although his build was larger and more domineering than his son's. I'd been wrong when I'd said I couldn't think of an more imposing figure on the rugby field than Nathan – Mr Jackson had his son trumped on that front; he had the type of frame that would crush you in seconds, and one that you wouldn't want to face off against given a choice. His hair was similar to Nathan's; blond but shorter, and at his temples there were flecks of grey. His eyes flicked to mine briefly and I felt any remaining air leave my lungs. Nathan had an intimidating stare when he wanted to use it, but by God, his father's was ten times worse.

He had only said two words, but already I hated this man with a vengeance for the things he'd put his sons through and I felt my body tensing as if preparing for a standoff. There was no way I could ever beat him in a physical fight, but if he tried to touch Nathan then I wouldn't hesitate in trying.

Nathan was stood silent and frozen like a statue. I understood why Nathan couldn't speak out against his father – after all this was the man who Nathan had wanted so desperately to please as a child that he'd allowed himself to be beaten daily. Not that he'd had much choice. But how could Nathan ever believe that daily beatings were an expression of a parent's love? I guess if you are a young boy desperate to be loved you can convince yourself of just about anything. What a thoroughly depressing thought, not that it helped me right now. Shit, what should I do? What *could* I do? His father was huge and, to be honest, absolutely terrifying.

'I thought a little family reunion might be nice, son, it's been a while hasn't it? Perfect timing that you're here as well,' Mr Jackson smirked in a cold tone that made me wince.

Then without saying another word or even bothering to address me, Nathan's father strode up the steps to Nicholas's house and rang the doorbell.

Nathan cast me a glance that was so devoid of emotion I felt my chest compress – it was like the life had been sucked right from his body – but before I could say or do anything to help him he turned and silently followed his father up the steps.

The door was opened several seconds later by Nicholas, whose face went from a wide grin to an expression of such utter torture that my stomach flipped and the urge to vomit came upon me again.

'Nick.' Mr Jackson greeted his other son with a nod and a sweeping assessment from head to foot, giving him a disaffected look.

'Father?' Nicholas murmured, his voice just as hollow as Nathan's face looked. This was utterly horrible, I wanted to do something but I had no idea what; Nathan had only recently entrusted me with details of his past, I was hardly an expert on his family history and in no position to try and stamp my authority. Really all I could do was take my lead from Nathan and try to be there to support him I suppose.

Behind Nicholas I saw Rebecca emerge from the lounge with a look of horror on her face that reflected mine, from her expression I guessed she also knew about their father and was just as shocked to see him as Nathan and Nicholas were.

'Dad popped round to see us,' Nathan muttered thickly, his eyes focused on the carpet before us. Jeez, he looked like he'd gone into submissive mode, it was really disturbing to see my usually confident man so distraught. 'He wanted to see how you were getting along.'

'Nick, you've done very well with your piano playing. I've read about you in several journals,' Mr Jackson commented. In response Nicholas shrugged slightly, looking just as lost and confused as Nathan. 'You must have got that skill from me.' What an arse this guy was. How the hell were people like him allowed to have kids in the first place?

A horrible silence settled over us. Nathan and Nicholas were staring at the ground helplessly and Rebecca was stood just off to the side with her eyes flicking edgily between Nicholas and his father. Someone needed to do something, but as the newest member to this family group I really wasn't sure it should be me.

Answering all my prayers for action, Rebecca stepped forwards as if about to speak but was swiftly cut off by Mr Jackson as he turned to her, crossed his arms, and smirked. 'And who are you?' he asked swiftly, stopping her before she'd even had the chance to speak one word.

'I'm Rebecca, Nicholas's girlfriend. Fiancée actually.' she stated coolly. Fiancée? That was a new development since we last saw them, but I'd have to think about that later, this situation was just too crazy at the moment to focus on anything other than getting Nathan out of here and away from his father.

Instinctively though, my eyes flashed a glance at Rebecca's ring finger, as I saw Mr Jackson's do the exact same. There was a beautiful diamond sparkling away there and in other circumstances I would have been smiling and cooing over it, but not today, instead I flinched as Mr Jackson made a dismissive noise in the back of his throat and curled his lip snidely.

His dismissive gesture would have put me off, but it just seemed to spur Rebecca on and she stepped closer to him and straightened her back defiantly, 'These three might be too polite to say anything, Mr Jackson, but I'm not. You are not welcome here, please leave.' She sounded cool and calm and at that moment even though I barely knew her, I felt immensely proud of how brave she was being.

In the blink of an eye Nicholas's father went from calm and hoity to absolutely freaking furious and I saw Rebecca flinch slightly at his sudden outburst, '*Who the fuck do you think you are?*' he roared, looking and sounding like he might actually be about to kill someone. Or perhaps all of us, who knew? To my complete amazement Rebecca simply tipped her chin back and stood her ground. Crikey, that girl had some serious backbone.

'I'm the woman who loves your son more than you ever did. I'm the woman who's helped him recover from the fucking mess you left his life in, and I'm the woman who will marry him and make sure you never have the chance to fucking hurt him ever again. Now get the fuck out!' she screeched. As monumental as the words probably were for her and Nicholas, they did not please Mr Jackson one bit and in a flash of movement he was suddenly bursting forwards, throwing me out of his way, grabbing Rebecca by the shoulders and shoving her down the corridor away from us all.

'You need to be taught a serious fucking lesson, young

238

lady,' he growled, dragging her further away as I picked myself off the wall with the help of a stunned-looking Nathan. Nicholas didn't react for a second, almost looking like his father's movements had been too fast for him to register, but then as if a switch had been flicked Nicholas leapt into action, chasing them down and literally ripping his father off Rebecca so she fell into a heap on the floor.

Shoving Nathan and I back against the wall Nicholas then unceremoniously dragged his father down the corridor and threw him out of the open door. Christ, there was a four-step drop outside and I watched in shock as the big man sailed through the air before landing on the path with a loud thump and a curse.

'If you ever touch Rebecca again I will kill you, do you understand? *Now fuck off out of our lives,'* Nicholas roared in a tone so utterly terrifying that I shrunk away from him into the safety of Nathan's side as his arms reached out and dragged me against him. Then within a second Nicholas had slammed the door and was back down the corridor pulling Rebecca into his arms as the banging of the closing door still rang in my ears.

Holy fuck. I couldn't believe what had just happened. Nathan's chest had never felt such a safe place to be and as his arms wrapped tightly around me I willingly gave myself over to his tight hold. From start to finish the whole episode had probably only lasted five minutes at maximum, but the way my heart was thumping I felt like I'd run a marathon and if I hadn't been in Nathan's warm embrace I would have been sorely tempted to lean forwards on my knees to catch my breath.

'Are you OK, Stella?' Nathan murmured next to my ear, placing a shaky hand on my jaw and pulling my eyes up to meet his. He clearly wasn't, looking thoroughly traumatised by the whole situation.

'I ... um ... yes.' I was in shock – who wouldn't be – but physically nothing had really happened to me except a

239

couple of bumps into the wall, and to be honest I was more worried about Rebecca at the moment.

Leaning down to drop a swift kiss on my lips, Nathan released me and then turned and stepped towards where his brother was still cradling Rebecca in his lap and gently rocking her. Thankfully, Rebecca looked fine – in fact she seemed more together than Nicholas, who was looking pretty shaken up too.

'Shit, Nicholas, I'm so fucking sorry for bringing him here,' Nathan exclaimed limply from his position by my side. Although technically we hadn't brought him here, his father had just arrived at the same time as us. 'I don't know what I was thinking …' Nathan shook his head in confusion feeling out for my hand which I willing gave him to hold, 'I guess I wasn't really thinking at all …' his voice faded off.

'Brother, it's OK, I know what a hold he had on you,' Nicholas responded, looking up to meet Nathan's eye intently.

'I see now … it's all clear to me just how fucked up he is … I'm sorry, Nicholas, Rebecca … we'll leave you alone, I'll make sure he's gone,' Nathan ran a hand through his hair and then smiled weakly. 'Engaged, eh? Congratulations, can we have drinks tomorrow? My treat, in way of apologising for this shit and celebrating your good news?' he suggested hopefully.

'Sure,' Nicholas said, but he was too tied up in Rebecca to watch Nathan and me as we left.

Chapter Seventeen – Nathan

Taking Stella's hand as we left Nicholas's house I felt my stomach tense in the anticipation of having to see my father again. After so many years of not seeing him I knew he wouldn't just have left – in fact, I was sure of it. Once I had firmly closed Nicholas's door my fears were realised when I saw him just down the road, leaning back on the hood of my car looking smug and composed and none the worse for his fall down the steps.

Tucking Stella behind me I gritted my teeth and expelled a long breath through my nose to try and calm myself as I did a quick countdown from five to zero in my head, although to calm me enough for this situation I'd probably have needed to start at a million.

'Stay here, Stella,' I instructed her with a quick glance in her direction to make sure she complied. Thankfully she nodded and I watched as she licked her lips nervously. 'Be careful, Nathan.' The concern in her eyes made something inside me compress and even with all the craziness of the last ten minutes piling up around me I couldn't resist leaning down and dropping a quick kiss on her lips, 'I will,' I murmured before turning away.

Jogging down the steps I began to approach my father. Fuck, I felt winded as I looked at him again. He was the man I'd idolised for so long that seeing him now and realising just how fucked up he was felt like a massive kick to the gut.

'Why did you want to come here? To wind Nicholas up? To remind him of the shit you put him through as a kid? You're fucked up, you know that?' I growled, any

241

remnants of respect I might have had for this man had gone when I'd seen how he'd flipped on Rebecca and shoved Stella against the wall. How fucking dare he touch Stella?

'Something like that, perhaps,' my father murmured with a twisted smile curling the corner of his mouth. 'As a pianist it was difficult for me to intervene in his life in any other way, short of breaking his fingers of course.' He laughed humourlessly, 'But a nice little visit seems to have wreaked enough havoc on him for now.' What the fuck did he mean, "intervene in his life"?

'How's business?' my father asked suddenly, that same sick smile curving on his lips. 'Tough times I bet? Fierce competition for contracts?' My heart slowed in my chest as an icy feeling settled in my veins and my vision went slightly hazy. Surely not …

'It was you, wasn't it?' I whispered. Just like that, all the pieces fell into place: my father had been the one paying an insider to get the details so he could undercut me in all my company's bids! Had he been working with Gregory? My security team hadn't been able to confirm Gregory's involvement for sure yet, although it was looking highly likely.

I couldn't believe it, my own fucking father was the one trying to ruin me! 'Why? Why would you do that?' The pain of his deceit burned deep, even after all these years … he was still my dad … how could he do that to his own son?

'What can I say, son, you fucked me over all those years ago by telling the police what I'd done to Nicholas. I'd expected better from you, Nathan. I guess I'm holding a grudge,' he shrugged, 'Not a good trait, I know, but hey, I had a lot of time to think about it all after you got me sent to prison,' he said with a wicked, hate filled smirk.

Standing back I shook my head in shock. Had I seriously wanted to be like him when I was younger?

Right now as I looked at him there alone and filled with bitterness I couldn't think for the life of my why I'd ever thought he'd been so powerful or formidable.

Suddenly something occurred to me. 'You don't even know anything about architecture, how the hell do you plan on completing the projects?' I demanded.

'You're right, I don't know anything about architecture. But the bidders don't know that, and by the time they do your company will already have lost enough money to make it struggle significantly – which will be reward enough for me for the time being. With Gregory's help I put together some very convincing packages, good enough to undercut even you, Nathan,' he bragged with a sick smile. So it *had* been fucking Gregory going behind my back. When my security team caught up with him I wanted to have some serious words with the traitorous bastard.

I'd heard enough. Bunching my right fist I let rip and smashed my bastard of a father square in the face. He staggered backwards with blood flowing freely from his nose and a look of total shock on his face. Apparently he'd still been expecting me to be the subservient little wimp of my childhood. But no more. He had well and truly opened my eyes to just what a bastard he was and I wanted nothing more to do with him, or the hold he used to have over me.

'And this one is for Nicholas,' I ground out, advancing once again and landing another punch, this time to his jaw. Fuck, that was satisfying. The second one floored him and my father moaned on the pavement, leaning back on my car. I felt Stella's hands gripping my arm to stop me from following up with more blows.

'Nathan ... be the bigger man. Walk away,' she whispered. Letting out a breath I turned to my father one last time – the final time I would ever see him. 'Stay away from us, and stay away from Nicholas. Now get the fuck off my car.'

Shoving him aside I helped Stella into the passenger seat and then calmly strode to the driver's side, buckling myself in and driving away without so much as a glance in my rear view mirror. I didn't need to look back; all that was back there was my past, what was important was my present and my future, and hopefully the answer to both of them was sat in the passenger seat next to me.

As I drove I became aware that I was shaking all over from the whole encounter, but I drove long enough to get us away from my father and around the corner to a quieter suburban street which lined Primrose Hill before pulling over.

Stopping the car I switched off the ignition and turned to Stella. 'I can't drive at the moment, would you take a walk with me for a while?' I asked, indicating to the open parkland behind me. Showing her my shaking hands I attempted a weak, crooked smile which she returned before nodding and getting out of the car. To be honest I wasn't sure if I was shaking because of my father, or because of the insight that seeing him had given me into my own life – all I did know was that I needed to man up and share a few things with Stella.

What a fucking day this had been. If anything was more likely to get me collapsing from stress then it was today's sequence of events; meeting my ex, Stella's ex, and then finding my father at Nicholas's house – talk about utterly hellish, but Stella was still here, still with me, and that was all that mattered to me right now.

Taking her hand in mine I enjoyed the warmth I felt from Stella's touch as we strolled together into the park in companionable silence. Gradually, my trembling began to subside as she gently rubbed the back of my hand with her thumb, somehow seeming to transfer her strong calmness into me. This woman was good for me. Probably too damn good, but I wasn't letting her go, not now, not ever, and it was probably time I told her as much.

'All my life I thought my father loved me but just didn't know how to show it ... and I guess I thought I loved him too. But seeing him today so hell bent on bringing misery to his sons,' I shook my head and grimaced, 'that's not love, I see that now, I finally understand.'

Huffing out a long breath, I stopped beside a small lake and stood in front of Stella, tipping her face up so I could look straight in her eyes. 'I never thought I'd be capable of such feelings, but what I feel for you ...' I paused and shook my head unsure how to vocalise all the emotions inside me. 'Fuck, Stella it's crazy, the passion, the possessiveness I feel, I've never experienced anything like it before and I never ever thought that I'd say these words, but I ...' my throat went dry, just as before when I'd tried to tell her I loved her. Why the fuck couldn't I say it? It was three lousy little words, and I couldn't even man up enough to say them. Stella's eyes opened wide as she stared up at me in anticipation, I heard her swallow loudly but she didn't say anything and I panicked that I might lose her if I wasn't courageous enough to say how I felt.

'I ... I ... *fuck.*' Instead of saying words which had never meant a thing to me in my past I slid my hands into her hair and kissed her with everything that I had, hoping that my actions could convey what my words somehow couldn't. Finally pulling back from the kiss I saw Stella gazing up at me with wide, lust filled eyes and I smiled shyly. 'It'll always be you, Stella.' That I could say, but like a compete pussy my brain was still adamantly refusing to say the words I knew she would most want to hear.

A second later however, my fears were somewhat lifted as Stella raised a hand to my cheek and stroked her thumb across my stubble. 'It's OK, Nathan, I know what you mean, you don't have to say it ...' she murmured, then half sobbing, half laughing she flung herself at me, wrapping her arms around my neck and even jumping up and wrapping her legs around me too, where I caught her under her bum and held her to me tightly.

'Oh God, Nathan. I love you,' she mumbled as she sought my lips for a wet, tearstained kiss. She loved me? Even with my messed-up outlook on life Stella really loved me? Thank fuck for that. Now all I needed to do was say the words back to her, but I grudgingly admitted that might take some time. If I said them I needed her to know I meant them. I was fairly sure now that I loved Stella, these tumulus feelings inside me of protection, affection, and lust must surely equal love, but my parents had fucked up any views of love I'd ever had and I knew it was going to take some time for me to adjust to the fact that Stella really genuinely accepted me for who I was.

I had no idea where we'd go from here, or if a relationship could ever work out in the long run for someone like me with an angel like Stella, but I was finally ready to find out. What I wouldn't give to have a crystal ball and look into the future to see where I was a year from now. Would Stella still be with me? Or would I have reverted to type and scared her off? Grimacing, I knew that with my temperamental nature the latter was highly possible, and so I vowed to do everything within my power to treat this incredible woman how she deserved so that it wouldn't be the case. Who knows, perhaps in a year's time I'd even have managed to grow a set of balls and say the 'L' word to her.

Thank you for reading! If you enjoyed this book please consider leaving a quick review on Amazon to help spread the word!

Do you want to get your hands on that crystal ball that Nathan described? Then read the final gripping instalment of the Untwisted series, *Enlightened*, to see how the Jackson brothers are doing one year on from the heart wrenching day when their father walked back into their lives.

I write for my readers, so I'd love to hear your thoughts, feel free get in touch with me:

E-mail: aliceraineauthor@gmail.com
Twitter: @AliceRaine1
Facebook: www.facebook.com/alice.raineauthor
Website: www.aliceraineauthor.com
When I write about my characters and scenes, I have certain images in my head. I've created a Pinterest page with these images in case you are curious. I hope you enjoy this little glimpse into Nicholas and Nathan's world. You can find it at http://www.pinterest.com/alice3083/

You will also find some teaser pics for upcoming books to whet your appetite!

Alice x

The Untwisted Series

CARIAD

For more information about **Alice Raine**

and other **Accent Press** titles

please visit

www.accentpress.co.uk

For news on Accent Press authors and
upcoming titles please visit

http://accenthub.com/